The Viking Prince

A Gareth and Gwen Medieval Mystery

THE
VIKING
PRINCE

by

SARAH WOODBURY

To Taran
who thinks it's his turn

A Note about Godfrid the Dane

Godfrid the Dane makes his first appearance in the *Gareth & Gwen Medieval Mysteries* in the first book, *The Good Knight.* He comes to Anglesey at the behest of Prince Cadwaladr, but quickly realizes that the deal he's made is not quite what he thought, and Cadwaladr is not worthy of his allegiance. He takes it upon himself to keep Gwen safe and gives her up to Gareth when he comes to Ireland in search of her.

He and Gareth grow to respect each other, and Godfrid returns to Gwynedd in *The Fallen Princess,* on a quest to find the Book of Kells, which has been stolen, and again in *The Lost Brother,* in search of allies in his conflict with Ottar of Dublin. In both instances, he ends up aiding Gareth and Gwen in their investigations.

It is the dispute with Ottar that, in the late 1140s, drives Godfrid and his brother, Brodar. They seek to overthrow Ottar, whom they believe usurped their father's, and now Brodar's, throne.

With the approach of the summer solstice and the coming *thing*, the great meeting of the Danes in Dublin, Godfrid is faced with a mystery of his own, which he must solve if his brother's victory is ever to come to pass ...

The Viking Prince is his story.

Wind we, wind we such a web of darts
as the young soldier waged aforetime!
Forth shall we go where the fray is thickest,
where friends and fellows against strong foes battle!

Wind we, wind we a web of darts
where float the banners of unflinching men!
Let not our liege lord's life be taken
Valkyries reward the uncanny in battle.

Will seafaring men forsake their boats
and their dwellings on the outer reaches?
Now the web is woven; weapons are reddened—
in all lands will be heard the heroes' fall.

Awful is it to be without,
as the blood-red rack races overhead;
The welkin is gory with warriors' blood
as we Valkyries chant our war songs.

Charge we swiftly with steeds unsaddled—
hence to battle with brandished swords!

Song of the Valkyries

1

Dublin, Ireland
May 1148

Day One
Godfrid

"**I** want every street, every house, every boat searched for the culprit. Question everyone! We must find out what happened here. With a wound this grave, Rikard can't have gone far. I want him found! And if he went not of his own free will, someone will have seen something. Find that person!" Sturla, King Ottar's steward, scribe, and skald, stood in the center of the floor near a broken loom, giving instructions and emphasizing every point with a stabbing finger.

Godfrid wasn't exactly happy to see Sturla either, but he was even more displeased by the condition of the warehouse: trading items had been pulled from their shelves and scattered across the floor. Almost worse, two of the three looms, at which the weaver women should have been working, were upended, the racks, battens, and treadles broken into pieces. It was very much what he imagined a village would have looked like after his ancestors had sacked it.

Godfrid had included Rikard in the dangerous game he was playing against King Ottar, and now Rikard had been murdered and his possessions destroyed. Godfrid couldn't help but think this was all his fault.

"My lord. What brings you here?" Sturla's lips twisted, as if it irked him to have to use the honorific, and he very belatedly sketched a bow. His gray curly hair stuck up all over his head, adding height to his already lanky body, which appeared thinner than usual this morning. Sturla's face also had a pallor that implied he was unwell.

In reply, Godfrid chose to call Sturla by his first name rather than use his title. "Hello, Sturla. King Ottar sent me." It was a petty battle to fight, and Godfrid immediately modified his expression to something more accommodating. He could throw Ottar's name around when it suited him to do so, and he knew better than to reveal in word or deed how much he despised the king. He'd been hiding his animosity for five long years—for so long, in fact, that his polite exterior had become something of a second nature to him.

In this instance, though, his words were actually the truth: he'd been woken by a messenger from the king, telling him of a pool of blood and a missing merchant—and giving him the commission to assist in the investigation.

It might even be that his obsequiousness was finally paying off, and Ottar was beginning to trust him.

"Of course. I give way to the king's greater wisdom." Sturla nodded sharply, and then turned to the man next to him. "I'm sure you and Holm can sort out an appropriate division of labor."

Holm was the newly appointed Sheriff of Dublin and, at twenty-five, far too young for his exalted position. "Of course, my lord." He bowed, but his eyes were on Godfrid, and they weren't happy. "What did he hope for from you? Why exactly did he send *you*?"

That was the question of the hour, and Godfrid couldn't blame Holm for asking it. "The messenger did not say other than to suggest that my presence would bring another pair of eyes to a difficult scene. It is the king's understanding that you have a large amount of blood and no body. Nobody mentioned the rest." He gestured to the destruction around him. "What can you tell me?"

Holm sniffed. "We are just beginning our investigation."

In other words, *nothing*.

Godfrid let out a breath, striving for patience, knowing full well that Holm's attitude was to be expected. So he said, in as mild a tone as he could manage, "Where's the pool of blood?"

Holm sighed a little too elaborately. "This way."

Sturla, meanwhile, headed for the exterior door behind Godfrid. As he passed Godfrid's position, his shoulder came within a hair's breadth of banging into Godfrid's own, prompting Godfrid to swallow down laughter at the absurdity of the steward's posturing, even as he understood it too. Godfrid was the son of a deceased co-ruler of Dublin, one who'd held a lesser station than his supposed partner. Such a son would find little respect among Ottar's men.

Secretly, Godfrid believed they feared him, but they hated themselves for that fear, and so they disrespected him instead. Most of the time, Godfrid paid no heed to any of them, following a course set by his father long ago that he should at all times float above the petty sneers and opinions of others. He and Brodar, Godfrid's elder brother, needed to keep their eyes on the main chance. Nothing was to interfere with their quest for the throne of Dublin.

In the early years of his father's rivalry with Ottar, the division of loyalty had been more even, but with his father's decline and then death, Dublin had confirmed Ottar as sole king. The decision had been disappointing to say the least, but understandable as well. These days, Dublin sat in a precarious—and subordinate—position in relationship to the Gaelic Kingdom of Leinster, which was their only real buffer against the other kingdoms of Ireland. Their backs were to the sea, as they always had been. But the days of Danish dominance were past, and the sea was no longer the haven it had once been. Godfrid couldn't blame the leading men of Dublin for their fear of what the future held and their desperate attempts to hold on to what they had.

Godfrid left two members of his personal guard at the front door and followed Holm, who managed to swallow his disdain sufficiently not to delegate to one of his underlings the task of showing Godfrid the blood. As they walked past the three looms, their feet thudded on the highly polished boards that formed the floor of the warehouse, an example of the pride Rikard had taken in all of his holdings. The northern wall of the warehouse abutted the city's defenses, and the River Liffey, which flowed to the north of the city, was close enough that Godfrid could hear the calls of dock men at their work and the lap of water against the ships.

The missing man, Rikard, had been a merchant of some wealth and repute, with a fleet of boats, this warehouse, and a large hall in the southwestern quadrant of the city. He had many servants too, one of whom, a woman in her later twenties with a slave collar around her neck, had been attempting to clean up some of the mess. As Godfrid and Holm passed by, she turned to face the wall, as was expected of her in the presence of a nobleman who was not her master.

Godfrid himself had never held slaves, following the tenets of the Church, which, once the Normans arrived in Britain, had seriously curtailed the Dublin slavers' trade. While slave-taking in war still happened, most recently two years ago when one Irish clan had raided another, Godfrid found himself frowning to see that Rikard still supported the practice.

Holm halted at the back of the room in front of the rear door. A nearby flight of stairs led to a loft that ran all the way around the inside walls of the warehouse. The design was identical to that of Rikard's home—and Godfrid's own—except for the larger size of the building and the presence of an enclosed room in the southwestern corner of the loft. The door to that room was off its hinges, marking it as yet another casualty of the ransacking of the warehouse.

Like a steward introducing an entertainer for the evening, Holm gestured expansively to the floor and the pool of blood. "As you can see, robbery turned to murder."

As far as Godfrid knew, Holm had investigated exactly one murder since he'd taken office, if a tavern brawl where one of the participants ended up dead counted as murder. He'd seen a handful of other similar incidents as undersheriff before that.

Were Godfrid in Holm's shoes, he would have welcomed the help, but it was hard to blame the man for being offended at what appeared to be a lack of trust on the part of his king, and Godfrid could appreciate not wanting anyone looking over his shoulder, telling him what to do or what he was doing wrong. Holm might even be beginning to realize that his elevation to sheriff had more to do with his family's wealth and personal loyalty to Ottar than his skill.

None of that explained why Ottar had asked *Godfrid* specifically to assist Holm, but now that he was here, he was interested enough to stay.

The blood had pooled across three floorboards and been smeared across several more, as if a large object—possibly a body—had been dragged across the scene. The smears didn't go all the way to the door, implying that the body had been picked up eventually.

"What makes you think this blood is Rikard's?"

"He's missing." Holm appeared to just catch himself before he rolled his eyes. "He never came home last night, and nobody has seen him."

Godfrid snorted under his breath, wanting to protest that they shouldn't assume Rikard was dead until they saw the body. When it came to murder, Godfrid had learned from his friend Gareth not to assume anything, particularly not this early in the investigation. But he saw the wisdom in not antagonizing Holm further. If he was going to continue to please Ottar, he had to work with Holm—and there really was a disconcerting amount of blood on the floor. There was so much, in fact, that Godfrid couldn't see how its owner could be still alive.

Holm motioned jerkily with his head towards an overturned chair two feet from the pool. A length of finely woven rope—silk not hemp—was coiled on the floor underneath it, and the bottoms of the chair legs were stained with blood. Living in Dublin among seamen, Godfrid was used to seeing coarse hemp rope everywhere. This rope, however, appeared to be designed to be decorative, perhaps to hold back a curtain in a rich man's house.

"I'd wager next month's wages that Rikard was bound to that chair and tortured for the location of his silver and gold. When he wouldn't give up his wealth, they killed him rather than allow him to identify them to me. Then they ransacked the warehouse to find the wealth themselves." Holm declared this as if his conclusions should be obvious, even to a spoiled princeling such as Godfrid. "I'd say we are looking for rogue seamen, perhaps even Rikard's own men." Then his eyes widened. "They could have sailed on the morning tide, perhaps with Rikard in the hold!"

Godfrid put out a calming hand to him. "Why do you think a seaman is responsible?"

Holm gestured to the chair. "Those are seaman's knots in that rope."

"But not a seaman's rope, Holm." Godfrid was trying to speak gently. "If someone tied Rikard to that chair, he found the rope in the warehouse. He didn't come prepared."

Holm's expression showed grudging acceptance, and he didn't refute Godfrid's logic. "Rikard was an old man and a merchant. Who knew he had it in him to resist an intruder?"

Godfrid again found himself objecting to Holm's assumptions, and again had to say something. "You may be right, Holm, but I'm left wondering why whoever did this didn't take more? There is wealth all around us. Why leave it behind?"

"As you say, the intruder didn't come prepared. Perhaps Rikard interrupted him."

Feeling that he was better off not continuing this back and forth with Holm, Godfrid didn't answer. Instead, he returned his attention to the pool of blood, eyeing it with some trepidation. The fluid had covered several papers, as well as a polished-stone rosary, and he was glad he wouldn't be assisting the slave girl in the cleaning of it.

On impulse, abandoning in an instant his resolve not to irk Holm, Godfrid crouched to the pool, reached out a finger to the puddle, and dabbed at it, pulling some of the blood onto his forefinger.

Inevitably, Holm sputtered a protest. "I already did that."

Since he couldn't take back what he'd done, Godfrid sniffed the blood and put it to his lips—and his surprise at the smell and taste had him jerking upright and stepping backwards away from the pool. "You can't have, Holm, else you wouldn't have told the king that Rikard had been murdered."

"He *was* murdered, my lord. Nobody can lose that much blood and live."

"That would be true, Holm, if this were blood. But what we have here is wine."

2

Day One

Godfrid

"It can't be," Holm said, even as he crouched beside the puddle with his face a foot from the pool. Then, flushing red to his hairline, he moved towards the fallen chair, swooped his fingers through a smear on the floor near one of the legs, and held his fingers up to Godfrid's face. "Blood."

Godfrid grasped Holm's wrist and sniffed, at first tentatively, and then with a burgeoning frown. "You're right."

They looked at each other through several heartbeats. "So ..." Holm drew out the word.

Godfrid finished his thought. "So someone poured wine on the floor to make us think there was more blood here than there was? Why would anyone do that?"

"I don't know, but he had the foresight to use sweet wine, which is thick like blood."

Godfrid then ventured a genuine question, hoping Holm would understand it to be a peace offering of a sort: "Why was your instinct when you first arrived to test the blood from the smear rather than from the pool?"

Holm gave a jittering shake of his head, such that the braids that held back his blond hair from his face flopped around his shoulders. "The smears were already drying. I thought to test them because I would gain a better estimate as to how long ago they'd been made."

Godfrid was genuinely impressed and said so.

"Not that the knowledge is of enormous help." Holm shrugged, the few moments of respect making him more accommodating than he'd ever been in Godfrid's presence. "Whatever happened here happened hours ago. Sturla sent my men to search the nearby houses for answers, for Rikard, and for the culprit. But if he has any sense, the latter should be long gone by now."

"Maybe not," Godfrid said. "The city gates are guarded, and while the guards don't stop everyone who goes in and out during the day, they do look at everyone who comes and goes at night. The northern gate that guards the crossing of the Liffey is closed to all comers, no matter their urgency. If whoever did this is native to Dublin, he knows the routine and could be hiding until he can leave with fewer questions. Whether or not it's too late already, we need to close all the city gates immediately and stop letting people enter and leave freely."

Holm shot Godfrid a piercing look, and Godfrid had the sense that Holm thought the idea was a good one but disliked admitting it. Fortunately, possibly thanks to their most recent exchange, his disregard for Godfrid wasn't so great that he refused to listen. He spun on a heel and snapped his fingers at one of his men, who hustled forward.

While Holm was busy ordering his people about, Godfrid walked all the way around the pool. It appeared smaller than it had a moment ago, seemingly drying rapidly now that it was day.

Once Holm dismissed his man and turned back, Godfrid shook his head. "Maybe we have it wrong and the blood and wine have nothing to do with one another. Maybe the wine was spilled by accident, and the culprit would be shocked to learn we confused it with blood."

"Then where is Rikard in all this?"

"I don't know."

"I don't know either." Holm's tone was nearly friendly.

Godfrid was glad now that he'd admitted uncertainty, as uncomfortable as it made him, since it had allowed Holm to admit it too.

Because he had always viewed Holm as Ottar's man through and through, Godfrid had never attempted to lure him to his side. He was seeing him now through new eyes, wondering if the sheriff's attitude was merely bluster, rather than genuine personal animosity. It wasn't unusual for a man promoted beyond his capacity to take out his insecurities on those around him.

"What of Rikard's wife and child?" Godfrid asked.

Rikard's wife, Sanne, was thirty years younger than her husband, closer to Godfrid's age than Rikard's, and the daughter of Thorfin Ragnarson, another prominent Dublin merchant. It wasn't impossible that she'd grown tired of the marriage and wanted to hurry along the day when she became a widow.

"They are with Arno, Rikard's business partner. When he went looking for Rikard at his home this morning, Arno learned that he'd never returned last night, so he came here and discovered the blood and the destruction." Holm lifted one shoulder. "At least Rikard died with his boots on."

Among the Danes, dying of old age wasn't the ideal way to end one's life. Godfrid had feared such a fate would be his father's, but fortune had intervened in the form of an attack on Dublin by the men of Brega, a lesser kingdom within Meath, upon whom, in recent years, the Danish settlements to the north and west of Dublin had been encroaching more and more.

Knowing that death was near, Godfrid's father had insisted on taking part in the battle and was among the two hundred Danes killed. Godfrid missed his father, but the fortitude he'd shown in rising from his bed to take his place in the fight had inspired all of Dublin—and was one of the reasons Brodar had growing support among his countrymen for the throne, now that Ottar's leadership hadn't produced the prosperity and expansion they craved. Brodar and Godfrid had made it clear to all and sundry that the only reason they hadn't raised an army to attack Brega and avenge their father's death was because both Ottar and King Diarmait of Leinster had absolutely forbidden it.

"We don't yet know if he's dead, Holm. Please keep that in mind."

Holm snorted his disbelief, before adding, "Why do you keep staring at the puddle?"

Godfrid crouched again and flicked out his hand. "Is there less wine here than before?"

As befitting a building owned by a man with a fleet of boats, the wooden floorboards were tightly-fitted and well varnished. The wood wasn't porous enough to absorb wine—at least not at the speed the puddle appeared to be shrinking.

But before Holm could answer, a fine leather boot appeared within Godfrid's line of sight, albeit not in the wine itself, and Godfrid looked up to find the freckled face of Conall, the king of Leinster's man in Dublin, glaring at him, his hands on his hips.

"What have you done now?" In the last year, Conall's Danish had become nearly fluent.

Godfrid straightened, giving himself the full advantage of every inch of height he had on Conall, who was a good six inches shorter than he was, and putting every ounce of offended pride that he could muster into his voice. "You speak as if I make a habit of murdering merchants in their warehouses."

"Do you? Do you want to confess now so as to save your king the trouble of further investigation?"

Holm ducked his head in obeisance to Conall and then said in an undertone to Godfrid, "I'm sorry. Good luck." He headed towards the front of the hall where the last of Holm's men and Godfrid's own guards were already edging out the door.

Godfrid pressed his lips together to hide his smile. Holm might have been interested enough in Godfrid's thoughts about the pool of wine to stay, but at Conall's arrival, he was beating an immediate and hasty retreat. No matter how much they disliked Godfrid themselves, no Dane wanted to witness Godfrid's humiliation at the hands of Conall. And such had been the power of Leinster over Dublin in recent years that all were forbidden to offend King Diarmait's ambassador in any way.

Though fleeing with the rest, Holm, at least, had the decency to comment over his shoulder. "Godfrid had nothing to do with Rikard's death, my lord. We have learned what we can here. We'll leave you to it."

Then the door slammed shut behind him, leaving Godfrid and Conall alone to face off against each other.

"Cowards." Godfrid laughed and spread his arms wide to embrace the Irishman. "How is it with you? I've missed seeing you these last few weeks."

Conall allowed himself to be enveloped, though after a moment he patted Godfrid on the shoulder, indicating he wanted to be released. Then the two men stepped back, both beaming.

"I am well," Conall said. "It's good to see you, even if under unfortunate circumstances."

They'd met for the first time a year ago when Conall had arrived in Dublin at the behest of King Diarmait, who also happened to be Conall's uncle. At the time, Godfrid had been distrusting of any Irishman, especially one who was so clearly an accomplished spy. That was the face Godfrid still put on whenever anyone was watching. But he and Conall had quickly come to an accord. At the start, they had their mutual friendship with Gareth in common and then discovered almost immediately that their perspectives on the world weren't so different either. The outward disdain for one another they showed to the world had become a game they played, to the great amusement of both.

"What do we have here?" Conall indicated the wine. "Besides the obvious, that is."

"Not so obvious, as it turns out. The pool contains wine." Godfrid pointed to the overturned chair. "The actual blood is over there."

Conall took in the oddity of the situation with a sweeping glance. "Rikard's?"

Godfrid lifted a shoulder. "We don't know, but Rikard *is* missing."

"It sounds like Holm is assuming he's dead."

"It may be a fair assumption." Godfrid shrugged again. "If so, I would be sorry. He was a good friend."

"Don't let Ottar hear you say that."

"I would never." Godfrid had known Rikard a long time, and until a few years ago the merchant had been outwardly supportive of Godfrid's father. But Torcall's death had put pressure on more citizens of Dublin than just Godfrid and his brother. Ottar demanded loyalty, and if a man wasn't prepared to give it wholeheartedly, or feign it convincingly, he found himself unwelcome at the palace. That would be of particular relevance to a merchant who relied on safe harbor in Dublin's port and looked to keep his taxes low.

Godfrid took a step closer and lowered his voice. "I've been looking for your return in hopes that we might speak. Brodar and I believe we have assurances from the majority of the leading men of Dublin that they will support Brodar when he calls for a vote at the summer *thing*."

Every year on the summer solstice, the free men and women of Dublin assembled for a great meeting to address grievances before they festered and, in certain cases, to elect their king. Ottar had earned barely enough votes to defeat Brodar after Godfrid's father died. This year, Brodar hoped to overthrow him. The Dublin *thingmote* was a forty-foot-high mound in the southeastern part of the city near Ottar's palace.

Conall nodded. "It seems to me that it really is now or never. Ottar will never be weaker than he is today."

"What does your king say?"

"He would like to know what benefit to him a change in leadership will mean. He feels he can control Ottar, and Leinster's power in Dublin has only increased under Ottar's rule. Your brother promises to be a different beast. My king isn't sure he's going to like the change."

"He will once he realizes how much bolder my brother is than Ottar. Ottar has grown tentative. Dublin's merchants won't sail as far and wide as they used to. We are no longer opening new trade routes. My brother promises to restore our power on the seas and in the marketplace."

Then Godfrid paused, thinking about how to phrase his next thought. It had been Godfrid's ancestors who'd first raided the Irish monastery on the shores of the River Liffey and later built the city in its place. To Godfrid's mind, Ottar had not only bowed to Leinster but groveled, and as much as Godfrid enjoyed the company of Conall—and respected him as a man—accepting the increased overlordship of Leinster had left Dublin much diminished. Bad enough to be a client kingdom at all, but to be so much weaker in just a few years was unconscionable after centuries of conquest. Inside, Godfrid was embarrassed that money had become of greater interest to the Danes than their pride.

Once Brodar overthrew Ottar, as King of Dublin he would swear loyalty to King Diarmait, as Ottar had done. He would also swear that he had no intention of rebelling against Leinster. But the truth was, if things continued the way they were going under Ottar, soon Dublin would not just be a client state, it would cease to exist as an independent entity at all.

"And he will pay a tax to Leinster on that wealth, of course."

"Of course," Conall said, though he was unable to keep the wry tone from his voice.

Godfrid grimaced. "For now, King Diarmait keeps the rest of Ireland at bay. Though I hate to admit it, we are not as strong as we once were. We cannot trade freely if we are worried about defending our borders from attacks by Connaught or Ulster—or Brega."

Conall bent slightly at the waist. "I will tell my king to be prepared for your move, though I must tell you that he agrees to nothing. At the same time, he will not personally intervene in Dublin's internal affairs."

"Does Ottar know that?"

"I have told King Ottar that he has Diarmait's full support as long as he can maintain power. Ottar might interpret that to mean that Leinster will come to his aid if his throne is threatened, but that was only an impression I left him, not a promise."

Godfrid had been hoping for at least that much and allowed himself a small sigh. "Thank you. I will tell my brother."

Conall shot him a quick grin. "King Diarmait has also said nothing at all about *me* aiding and abetting. Believe you me, I did not press him on the matter."

Godfrid laughed outright and clapped his friend on the shoulder. "I have missed you while you've been away. What have you been doing?"

"I will tell you later. Not here." He gestured to the upheaval in the warehouse. "Meanwhile, Ottar has tasked you with investigating Rikard's disappearance. Or death, if that's what has happened. Why would he do that?"

Godfrid shrugged. "I have been puzzled about it since his messenger appeared on my doorstep. I fear he is testing my loyalty in some fashion. I'm just not sure how."

Conall's expression turned thoughtful. "Perhaps Ottar asked for you because he knows something of what happened here—and wants to stay as far away as possible from what might be discovered. He can't help that Holm takes the lead in the investigation, but if things go badly, much better to blame you for it."

Then, as if Conall's words hadn't caused enough dismay in Godfrid's heart, the slave girl appeared in the corner of his vision, on her knees collecting polished stones that had fallen to the floor. He spun towards her, cursing. He and Conall hadn't been speaking quietly, and she couldn't have helped but overhear their conversation. He'd fallen into the trap of dismissing from his mind the presence of a slave, which, if he wanted to keep his conspiracy with his brother and his friendship with Conall a secret, was a stupid thing to do. "You there!"

Conall reached for Godfrid's arm. "You don't have to mind her."

Godfrid turned to his friend, too angry at himself to moderate his tone. "Why not?"

"She's an ally." Conall gestured in the woman's direction. "I brought her to Dublin as my spy."

3

Day One
Godfrid

G odfrid laughed, taken completely by surprise.

While Conall looked rueful, the woman herself appeared indifferent to Godfrid's astonishment. More than ten years younger than Conall, making her roughly thirty, she approached and curtseyed. "My lord, it is a pleasure to finally meet the man Lord Conall has told me so much about. My name is Caitriona, but please call me Cait."

She had a Gaelic lilt to her Danish, but was otherwise fluent, and was outspoken in a way Godfrid understood Irish women to be. She was also well-spoken and apparently educated, as Godfrid supposed any close associate of Conall would have to be.

More out of habit than thought, he put his heels together and took Cait's hand. "Godfrid, Prince of Dublin." Then, he looked at Conall. "What is going on?"

Still looking rueful, Conall spread his hands wide. "As you well know, Rikard's warehouse has become a crossroads of a sort between King Ottar and allies he doesn't want the rest of Dublin to know about. We installed Cait here as the intermediary between Rikard and me, so I wouldn't have to meet with Rikard directly." He grimaced. "We also have begun to fear that one of Rikard's servants is a traitor, spying for Ottar. Installing Cait in the slave quarters seemed the best way to root him out."

Godfrid's eyes narrowed as he looked from Conall to Cait. A headscarf held back her hair, but a few strands framed her face and sleek black ends showed down her back. Her eyes were gray-green, similar in color to Conall's, and she had a smattering of freckles across her nose and cheeks. "That was taking quite a risk, installing a woman as a slave, wasn't it? The danger from men that put her in—"

A snort from Caitriona dismissed the argument. "I can handle wandering hands, my lord."

"You can't, actually." Conall shot a quelling look at the woman, who appeared remarkably complacent about her employer's unhappiness, and then he looked back to Godfrid. "Rikard knew who she was and that he had to protect her. He put out that she was his, and nobody was to touch her."

For Rikard to have accepted a beautiful woman into his household was entirely in character for the merchant, since each of his three successive wives had been younger and lovelier than the previous. Some men refused to admit they were getting old.

"Even that was unnecessary," Cait said flatly. "I was one of Rikard's weaver women. A slave, yes, but of a higher station. I was in no danger from him, his men, or anyone else."

Godfrid studied Caitriona. "It's a credit to you that you could so successfully hide your light under that headscarf."

Cait seemed to prefer answering questions by showing rather than telling. Between one breath and the next, her shoulders hunched, her mouth turned down, and her forehead wrinkled into a mask of sadness, making her look like nothing more or less than the drudge she had been pretending to be.

Then she blinked, straightened, and transformed back into her true self again. Godfrid could only admire the skill and her willingness to diminish her beauty. Few women had the confidence. In his case, even cultivating the art of deception daily, he was too large a man to be very good at hiding. He stood out in a crowd when shrouded by a cloak on a dark night.

"Wait a moment. If she was a spy for the King of Leinster—" Godfrid's brow furrowed, "—and if Rikard knew of it, that means Rikard was working *with* King Diarmait outright. Since when?" What he left unsaid, because he felt a little hurt at the slight, was that Conall hadn't bothered to mention any of this to him.

"It has been only since you last saw me. She's been here three weeks."

"I could have watched over her."

But then, when Conall replied by canting his head, Godfrid gave a low grunt. "Which might have given the game away, since why would a prince of Dublin be paying attention to one of

Rikard's weaver women, even if she is beautiful? You leave, and she arrives, with the intent to lull us into a false sense of security, to make us think we aren't being watched."

"Us?" Conall gave a sharp shake of his head. "Not you. Ottar."

Godfrid drew in a breath. "Didn't you just tell me that King Diarmait isn't going to openly support Brodar?"

Conall expression turned regretful. "For now, he sees no need to do so. However, he wanted to know the full story of what was going on in Dublin under the surface before making a decision. It was Cait's job to give him that insight."

That appeared to be all the apology Godfrid was going to get. And it was possible that none of this was Conall's idea, not just Cait's role in the deception. Conall and Godfrid knew enough of each other by now that he deserved the benefit of the doubt. "Rikard owed Diarmait that much?"

Conall's expression turned wry. "Who do you think Rikard's biggest trading partner is? Rikard's ships travel the seas, but far better and less risky to trade closer to home. Rikard needs Diarmait's good graces and, in recent months, my king has been deeply concerned about the decline of his revenue from Dublin."

Godfrid's eyes widened, finally understanding what this was about. "King Diarmait thought Ottar was skimming." And at a curt nod from Conall, he continued, "And that's also why he is willing to look the other way when my brother overthrows him. Even if King Diarmait won't say, he is interested in the wealth my brother might bring in."

"Enough to give him a chance," Conall said.

Godfrid let out a sigh. "Why didn't Rikard tell me any of this? Why didn't you?"

Conall shrugged. "My king insisted on absolute secrecy. Spy rings are most effective when the spies involved don't know each other and don't necessarily share with one another the information they discover."

Godfrid ground his teeth at that, but again, he couldn't argue. As his mother once told him when his father was being particularly stubborn, *A king does what a king does, and lesser men have no right to complain.* "To tell you the truth, I had wondered in recent weeks if I had lost Rikard's support."

Conall shook his head. "I assure you the opposite was true. Rikard needed to keep you at arm's length to make Ottar trust him. Besides, if that had been the case, Rikard would have sold you to Ottar, and you would be in chains today rather than Ottar's errand boy."

Godfrid chewed on his lower lip. "And perhaps Diarmait was willing to consider the possibility that *I* was the traitor— maybe not to Ottar but to another kingdom within Ireland? One that might support my brother outright in exchange for transfer of authority over Dublin from Leinster to them?"

The silence from Cait and Conall gave him all the confirmation he needed.

Conall lifted a hand apologetically. "I tried to tell him otherwise, but—"

"You must do his bidding. I understand." Godfrid made a dismissive motion of his own. "But does Rikard's death mean that Ottar discovered Rikard was working for you?"

Cait gasped. "Oh no! Could it be?"

Godfrid put out a hand to her. "Rikard was a grown man. Whatever is going on here cannot be *your* fault."

Her face was pale, reflecting the horror within her. "You can't know that, my lord. I could have done something to give him away."

Conall cleared his throat from Godfrid's other side. "From the quality of the messages that have come through Rikard's hands on behalf of Ottar in the last week, I would say that he knew nothing of either your friendship with Rikard or ours. The messages are too inflammatory."

"You sound very certain," Godfrid said. "You've seen them?"

Conall gestured to Cait. "She has seen them. I would have found a way to alert you soon enough if there was anything that needed your immediate attention. In fact, Rikard demanded it and was upset that he couldn't share what he knew with you personally."

Mollified, Godfrid gave Cait a slight bow. "You must tell me."

Cait's expression turned grim, transforming her face yet again. He could imagine her as a Valkyrie, beautiful yet deadly. "I will, but not here."

Godfrid studied her. "Did Holm question you before I arrived?"

She laughed, which gave him his answer before she spoke. "Me? A woman and a slave? He didn't even see me." She paused. "Just as you didn't."

"I noted you, but you turned away before I could see your face, and then the blood distracted me." Godfrid was uncertain as to why he was justifying his behavior to the Irish woman but felt compelled to do so anyway.

And then he mocked himself because he knew the reason. Caitriona was a beautiful, intelligent, foreign woman. Why he couldn't settle down with a good Danish girl, he didn't know. But he hadn't, and he was long past believing that he would find one who suited him.

"You would tell me if you saw anything last night or this morning that would help us, though, wouldn't you?" he asked Cait.

"Of course, I would, but I was blessedly asleep all night in the slave barracks." As was customary in Dublin, Rikard housed his slaves near the warehouse rather than among the residents of the city. "I heard nothing until Arno stormed into our quarters this morning, demanding to know what had become of Rikard."

Because most people were killed by loved ones or friends, if Rikard was, in fact, dead, Arno would be the next most likely suspect after Sanne. And even if Rikard's disappearance wasn't down to Arno, Godfrid couldn't help but wonder if Arno had done a little destruction of his own before waking the slaves.

As far as Godfrid knew, the two men had been close companions the whole of their lives, but Arno was only the business partner, not the wife or child. With Rikard's death, there could be some question as to ownership of the contents of the warehouse, and he could be concerned about having to split the wealth with Sanne—or the king, who would be most interested in whatever wealth he could gain in taxes from the death.

Conall pursed his lips. "This is the center of Rikard's operations. How could nobody have noticed a culprit entering? And why did nobody arrive sooner than at dawn this morning? Surely Rikard had guards to protect against theft?"

Cait put up both hands, warding off her lord's implied accusations. "Certainly he did. I think he was more concerned about theft than any threat to himself or even one of his slaves escaping. The fact that no guards were on duty last night was Rikard's own doing, not ours. He sent everyone away because he had a private meeting and wanted no one to witness to it."

Finally they were getting somewhere. "All night long?" Godfrid asked.

Cait shrugged. "Apparently. We were told not to go anywhere near the warehouse last night lest we interfere, and Rikard specifically commanded us not to enter the warehouse this morning until summoned. I was looking forward to a rare chance to sleep late. It seems obvious to me that whoever he was meeting with in secret was the one who killed him."

Conall met Godfrid's eyes. "So he knew the man who came. I think that's good news, actually." Then Conall looked at Cait.

"What isn't good news is the reason he didn't tell *you* what he was doing. That was the entire point of you being here."

"I don't know why he didn't." She shook her head.

"I'd like to know if he told Arno." Godfrid's eyes narrowed at the thought. "Speaking to him will be my first order of business."

"If Holm hasn't already poisoned that well," Cait said.

Both men looked questioningly at her, and again, she raised her hands. "Neither Arno nor Rikard respected Holm. I believe they had a different candidate in mind for sheriff."

"I certainly did," Godfrid said, "but my brother and I had no say in the matter, and Ottar chose loyalty to him over experience."

Conall barked a laugh. "Ironic, isn't it? Because of that inexperience, when he has an actual murder in need of investigation, Ottar has to bring in you."

Godfrid rubbed his forehead, wishing for a large mug of mead to stave off the headache he felt coming on. "And look at you two! Your presence here today, Conall, is rather ironic, don't you think, given what you were doing in Shrewsbury? Chasing slave girls then too, weren't you, though none were spies, that I recall. And from what you told me, that adventure also began with a puddle of blood and no body."

"For Gareth it began that way. I was already in captivity." Conall bent forward to study the floorboards. "Thankfully, the blood wasn't mine. The girl who died was later found in the River Severn."

"We may never find Rikard if he's in the River Liffey," Cait said.

She had a mischievous glint in her eyes and a healthy sheen to her skin that should have told anyone who looked at her that she hadn't been a slave long. But as she'd pointed out, slaves were ignored until they were needed. For Godfrid's part, he could have looked at her quite a while longer. But then—while mocking himself for being distracted by a woman—he remembered what he was here for and returned his attention to the pool, which appeared yet again definitively smaller.

"As I said to Holm, it would have been difficult to get out of the city last night unnoticed. Dead or alive, Rikard should still be within the city walls."

Straightening, he looked around for a likely tool and latched upon a flat piece of metal that was lying on the floor a few feet away, amidst the fallen papers and spools of thread. Approximately two feet long and an inch wide, it curved upwards on one end. He hefted it, studying its carvings.

"What is that?" Conall asked.

Godfrid shrugged. "I've never seen anything like it before. It isn't Danish."

"It's a prize Rikard's men brought back from the Isle of Man," Cait said. "I have no idea what it's for."

"I believe I do." Godfrid stuck one end of the tool into a narrow slit between two floorboards—through which he'd finally realized the wine had been draining one drop at a time while they'd been talking—and pushed down. Expending less effort than he'd anticipated, he raised up a square of floor, revealing a trapdoor with recessed hinges and stairs leading downwards into darkness. The first three treads were stained with wine.

Cait peered into the vault below and said somewhat breathily, "Is that—is that Rikard lying at the bottom of the stairs?"

4

Day One

Conall

Conall grabbed a lantern off a nearby table and held it high as he and Godfrid descended the steps in a hurry. Cait didn't follow immediately, showing an uncharacteristic squeamishness, which Conall wasn't going to argue with. Conall himself stopped abruptly on the bottom step, but Godfrid was already hovering over Rikard's body, which lay a few feet from the stairs.

Rikard was turned on his left side with his left arm stretched above his head, his upper arm pillowing his cheek, and his right hand near his face. In death, his expression was peaceful, and his eyes were closed. From this distance, Conall could see no obvious wounds on the body.

"Is there any way he's alive?" Cait said from the top of the stairs.

"No. He's dead." Conall said.

Godfrid had put his fingers first to Rikard's neck and then to his lips, shaking his head all the while. "The body is still warm, so he can't have died very long ago at all, maybe even within the last few hours."

"While we were standing around talking, he was dying down there in the dark?" There was horror in Cait's voice, and Conall's glance upwards revealed that her hand was to her throat.

Having made one last check for a beat at Rikard's wrist, Godfrid looked towards the top of the stairs too. "I don't believe that to be the case, Cait. He's been dead longer than we've been here."

"He doesn't appear to have a mark on him." Conall came down the last step, his lantern light illuminating the body.

"The blood and overturned chair upstairs indicate torture, but—" Godfrid frowned, "The only damage on him I can see are a few broken fingernails from scrabbling in the dirt. The blood under the chair remains unexplained."

Conall pursed his lips to study the body. Reflecting their warlike antecedents, most Danes wore tunics with tight pants tucked into their boots, but Rikard had been dressed formally, in a merchant's robe with a heavy gold chain around his neck. "He is fully clothed. Perhaps his abdomen is bruised."

Godfrid sat back on his heels. "Could someone have dumped the body here to hide it?"

"Why not leave him on the floor of the warehouse? It isn't as if we weren't going to notice the wine." Conall stretched out a hand to the chain, lifting the emblem on the end to feel its weight.

"Whatever the man who came after him wanted, it wasn't his wealth, or at least not easy wealth," Godfrid said, watching him.

Conall dropped the pendant. "And then there's something odd here." He crouched by Rikard's right hand. The floor of the vault was simple dirt, and Rikard's fingers had become claw-like as they clenched the ground in death. "He's etched letters into the earth. G O D." He named each letter separately. "It's Danish, yes?"

"Yes, of course. It means, 'good'. But why would Rikard write such a thing on the ground?"

"I can't begin to guess, unless he meant to write your name, Godfrid."

Godfrid blanched, straightening from his crouch and watching as Conall carefully lifted up Rikard's right wrist so they both could read the letters beneath it more clearly. The man's wrist was warm enough that Conall felt he should be able to feel a beat, but none was forthcoming.

Godfrid glared down at the writing, his hands on his hips. "I don't understand."

Cait finally came down the stairs, stopping one step up from the ground where Conall had stood earlier. "Likely he knew he was dying. You should be honored, my lord, that his last thoughts were of you. He clearly wanted to tell you something."

"In death, all ruses tend to fade away," Conall admitted. "It was more important to get a message to you than to keep Ottar convinced he was loyal to him."

Godfrid shook his head. "If only I knew what he was trying to say." He looked up, encompassing both Cait and Conall in his gaze. "This last hour has been a revelation to me, and I find myself wondering what else I missed or know too little about. I am not cut out for intrigue."

"You've done well enough these last five years on your own," Conall said bracingly and went to lay Rikard's hand back on the ground.

Before he dropped Rikard's wrist, however, Cait stopped him and, with a sweep of her foot, wiped away the writing. "I think it would be best if we kept this piece of evidence between the three of us."

Conall didn't argue and backed away from Rikard, trying to look at the scene with fresh eyes, wanting it to look natural to Holm when he arrived.

Godfrid swallowed, but then he nodded, accepting, as Conall silently had, what needed to be done, even if his sense of rightness was affronted.

Conall would have been surprised to learn that Gareth had ever destroyed evidence in this way. Though, on second thought, Gareth generally investigated murder at the behest of his own lord, not for a rival one, and Conall knew for certain that if Hywel needed evidence to disappear, Gareth would be the one to make sure it never saw the light of day. He might walk away from his service to Hywel afterwards, but Gareth would never betray his prince. Hywel was not King Owain Gwynedd's traitorous brother, Cadwaladr.

Cait also took a step back. Whatever fear or shock had held her at the top of the stairs during the initial discovery of Rikard's body was gone, replaced by a calm practicality that was a hallmark of the way she lived. Cait had never been one for drama or hysterics.

"Am I blind, or is Rikard indicating that chest?" She pointed to one of many set against the northern wall of the cellar.

Godfrid moved Rikard's other hand, the one pillowing his head. A line with an arrowhead on the end had been sketched in the dirt underneath it. "You could be right."

This time, it was Conall who bent to smooth the surface of the floor, as Cait had done earlier, and adjust the position of Rikard's left hand. "Another thing nobody need wonder about."

Cait took in a breath. "I'm thinking that if we spend any more time alone in the warehouse, it will begin to look suspicious, even to someone as inexperienced as Holm. He might even begin to wonder if you two are getting along. Perhaps I should climb back up the stairs and scream."

Godfrid guffawed, the sound echoing around the small space. "I can't wait to see what Holm makes of you."

"He won't even mark me. Just you watch." She shot him a grin, hiked her skirts, and trotted up the stairs.

"You want to cover your ears for this," Conall said.

Eyebrows raised, Godfrid did as Conall bid, and then Cait opened her mouth to release the most agonizing, grief-laden scream Conall had ever heard, and he'd heard her scream before. To add to the authenticity, she fell to her knees on the edge of the trapdoor—careful to avoid the residue of wine that remained on the floor—and bent over, her arms wrapped around her waist, sobbing.

Conall left Godfrid going through Rikard's pockets, in a quest for more information, and himself headed up the stairs. One of them should greet whoever came first through the front door and prepare him for what they'd found. A moment later, he was glad he had thought to do so because he was twenty feet from the vault when the big double doors were pulled wide, and Holm charged into the warehouse.

Conall waved a hand to catch Holm's attention and then again in an impatient gesture at Cait, telling her to move out of the way and stop sobbing. She shot him a smirking glance, which thankfully Holm was too distracted to notice, before doing his bidding, fading towards the far wall of the warehouse where the lantern light shone less brightly.

Because managing Holm's understanding of the situation was the first priority, Conall put his hand on Holm's upper arm and guided him towards the trapdoor. "We found Rikard. Let me warn you that he's dead."

"How did he get down there?" Holm came to a horrified halt at the edge of the hole. Now that the trapdoor had been opened, the pool of wine had drained fully down the steps and was more of a smear everywhere than a puddle.

"We have no idea." Conall had no trouble affecting a concerned and yet unhelpful attitude.

Holm shook his head, as if the vagaries of men's failings never ceased to disappoint him. For an enforcer of the law, he might be disappointed a great deal too often. He edged his way down the steps, careful to avoid marring his boots in the sticky wine. Conall followed, hoping he really had taken care of everything they'd rather Holm didn't see. Conall also thought it unwise to have Holm and Godfrid in close proximity for any length of time, though they appeared to be getting along better today than Conall had ever witnessed.

"How did he die?" Holm's skin was normally pale, but as he gazed down at Rikard's body, it was a sickly yellow in the lantern light.

"That we don't know either." Conall sniffed. "Godfrid has found no ligature marks or evident blood. You clearly need someone with more experience to assist you."

The dig was directed at Holm himself as well as at Godfrid, but Godfrid's reply came gently, almost as a whisper, indicating sympathy rather than scorn. "If you're going to vomit, please don't do it down here."

Holm swallowed hard. "Don't worry. I won't. I have seen dead men before many times."

"I'm sure you have." Implying that Holm was lying, Conall edged the sheriff off to one side. On more practical terms, if Holm really was lying, it would be better that he didn't vomit close to Rikard's body.

But Holm's color was already better. He had wisely turned away for the time being and, instead of bending over Rikard, he'd started moving around the vault, eyeing the trunks and crates that filled the small space. Then he turned to Godfrid with surprise on his face and in his voice. "I didn't know this place was here. Did you?"

"No," Godfrid said. "Rikard was very good at keeping secrets."

"So it seems! This may have been the best-kept secret in Dublin, next to the name of Queen Helga's lover."

Godfrid drew in a surprised breath of air, and Conall found himself holding his breath too. Queen Helga was Ottar's wife. Holm was almost humming now as he bent over a crate containing carved wooden boxes and didn't appear to notice his companions' shock.

"Queen Helga has a lover?" Godfrid finally managed to say with apparent casualness, though Conall wasn't fooled.

Holm looked back at them and blinked. "No, of course not. I was jesting. That's the point. She doesn't have a lover. That's why it's a well-kept secret."

Conall looked at the sheriff a bit sideways. "It's just that Rikard had this vault, so you see our confusion."

"Never mind. Forget I said anything. Since when were you Irish so humorless?" Holm made a dismissive motion. "Pardon me for speaking out of turn, my lord. I meant nothing by it. It doesn't look like anything has been disturbed." Then, perhaps to cover his discomfort, he continued poking through Rikard's things. "Sanne is going to be the most eligible woman in Dublin."

Godfrid's expression darkened, but he didn't rebuke the sheriff, and Conall finally realized that Holm was running at the mouth not because he was uncomfortable with being in the same room with a dead body but because he was excited. He was surrounded by wealth the likes of which few men had ever seen and was actually rubbing his hands together as if he could already feel the gold running through them. The man appeared to have all but forgotten about Rikard's body at his feet. Of course, as a Dane, a love of gold and plunder was bred into his bones.

Conall cleared his throat. "Perhaps, for now, we could get back to Rikard's death?"

"Of course. Of course, my lord," Holm said. "But just because it's too soon to say out loud doesn't mean every eligible male won't be thinking it."

Godfrid nodded. "He's right, my lord. Best to acknowledge the truth when spoken."

Holm shot the prince a grateful look, but Conall shook his finger at Godfrid. "What could you possibly know about it? Best speak only of what you yourself understand."

It was a weak chastisement at best, but what with one thing and another, Conall didn't feel on top of his game at present. The comment did have the desired effect of hunching Holm's shoulders and distracting him from his search of the vault's contents.

Conall had spent the last year in Dublin, but he couldn't yet say with confidence that he understood how Danish people thought. Diarmait had warned Conall from the very first day that if he was going to survive, he needed to be prepared for intrigue. While the Irish nobility were perfectly willing to stab a brother in the back to gain a throne, the threats that preceded such action generally were made openly. Dublin, however, was a very different society from Leinster. Brodar and Godfrid had spent the last *five years* pretending that they didn't hate Ottar. Their patience and willingness to wait for their revenge defied all comprehension.

"So, tell me." Conall's words came out clipped. "I gather Rikard doesn't have another heir, a son perhaps? That would make things easier."

"He doesn't." Holm sent him a furtive look, possibly trying to evaluate the extent of Conall's poor temper. "He *had* several sons. One was killed in battle, and two were lost at sea two years ago. Finn, the younger of them, was a good friend of mine."

Conall grunted. His ignorance irked him more than a little. But then, the Danes were far less demonstrative than the Irish and didn't like to talk about themselves or their emotions in a meaningful way. He wondered if Cait had known about these lost sons.

Among the Danes, the number of wives made widows by the death of their seafaring husband rivaled the number of husbands made widowers by the loss of wives in childbirth. Within the Danish community, Rikard's three marriages were hardly unusual. While it was true that the Irish could be seafarers too, they voyaged with less conviction and liked the feeling of land beneath their feet more than these Danish invaders. Conall had to admit, however, from what he'd heard about Denmark, Ireland was a far more appealing and hospitable land than the stony earth from which the Danes hailed. The Danes had gone *a Viking* for good reason.

Following Conall, though he didn't know it, Holm lifted Rikard's right wrist and dropped it. "He hasn't been dead very long, has he?"

"You know something about measuring time of death?" Conall asked.

"Enough to know that a man hasn't been dead long if the body is still warm." Holm didn't seem to want to look at Conall anymore, because his next question was directed at Godfrid. "My prince, can you pinpoint the time more specifically?"

If he'd decided that Godfrid was the lesser of two evils, so much the better. Conall was perfectly happy to absorb whatever animosity Holm wanted to direct at him if it spared Godfrid the same and bolstered the illusion that both Godfrid and Holm served King Ottar above all else.

Godfrid canted his head. "I'm hardly Gareth the Welshman, but I am with you in thinking that Rikard's death couldn't have taken place before midnight and likely occurred close to dawn. I lifted his other limbs before you arrived, and they are stiffening now, but it will be several more hours before the process is complete."

Conall, delighting in being insufferable, sneered. "We knew that timing before we found the body."

Holm glanced up. "Why do you say that, my lord?"

"Rikard sent his servants away last night. If you speak to the men who should have been guarding the warehouse, they will confirm that they were told not to return until Rikard summoned them."

Holm frowned. "My men questioned Rikard's servants already, and they reported exactly this. But how did you know of it?"

"I have my sources."

To Conall's satisfaction, his words had the effect of putting up the sheriff's hackles. The role of official ambassador was a new one for Conall. As a spy, it was almost always best to melt into the background, as Cait had done for the last three weeks and was continuing to do now. But it was Conall who was used to being the one who didn't ruffle anyone's feathers and remained polite at all times. He couldn't say that the haughty superiority he was currently affecting came naturally to him, but he was finding that, if he put his mind to it, he could manipulate people as an outspoken critic just as easily as when he spoke in whispers.

Godfrid too was glaring at Conall with evident distrust. In truth, Godfrid had a right to be perturbed by what Conall hadn't told him and might become even more so once they had a chance to talk further. Up until Shrewsbury, Conall had always worked alone and prized his ability to live without companions. Now he found himself with good friends in Gwynedd and Dublin, friends about whose opinions he cared. It was a little unsettling.

But for now, the two Danes were unified in their grinding teeth, clenched jaws, and hatred of all things Irish, of which Conall was the spokesman, for lack of a better example.

Godfrid looked away and spoke softly to Holm, "Perhaps it's time we took him out of here?"

Holm gave a jerky nod. "If you and I lift him up the stairs, I can get my men to take him to the church for his laying out. Bishop Gregory might want to oversee his funeral personally."

Gregory, the Bishop of Dublin, acted as shepherd to the people of the city from his seat at the Cathedral of the Holy Trinity. Unlike Irish bishops, Gregory had been ordained in England by the Archbishop of Canterbury, a deliberate snub to the Irish Church on the part of the Danes. The Church of Ireland oversaw its own bishops and didn't look to England for authority. Pleasure at the independence of their church was another way Godfrid and Holm could form a bond against Conall, and Conall was pleased to have provided them with the opportunity for it.

The two men maneuvered the body up the stairs and laid Rikard on the floor, not far from the trapdoor but outside the smears of wine, which by now were all but dry on most of the floorboards. One two-inch-wide puddle near a corner of the trapdoor remained and, as Conall watched, a single burgundy drop plunked onto the step below.

By now, Cait was truly in the shadows of the side wall so Holm wouldn't notice her. He had been so distracted by the finding of Rikard's body that he hadn't remembered, even now, that it had been she who'd screamed. Nor had he questioned why she was in attendance at all. As Cait had said, the Danes were taught from birth to take no notice of slaves, even one as beautiful as she.

Holm spoke again to Godfrid, still being polite. "I would like to know how you found him, my prince?"

Conall answered before Godfrid could, usurping his accomplishment and accompanying his words with a superior sniff. "The wine was disappearing, which made it obvious to me that there was a hole in the floor we didn't know about. Godfrid had been standing over the pool for a quarter of an hour already and hadn't noticed! Once I knew what to look for, I found the gap between two floorboards, and once the trapdoor was pried up, the hidden vault was revealed."

It was a good thing that Holm had turned to look at Conall, because it gave Godfrid time to swallow down his amusement.

Meanwhile, Holm tapped a finger to his chin, frowning as he thought. "Earlier, I believed Rikard had held out against the torture, which now we know was intended to coerce him to reveal his vault. Obviously, he gave up its location. But if he gave up the location, why was his vault not ransacked, like in the rest of the warehouse, and his wealth taken? In fact, if the intruder or intruders were after his secret vault, why ransack the warehouse at all? And why leave Rikard's most valuable possessions untouched?"

"Those are good questions. It doesn't make sense, does it?" Godfrid was back to agreeing with Holm.

Conall risked a query of his own. "And who does the blood belong to? We assumed that it was Rikard's, but from the state of the body, that is clearly not the case."

Holm clapped a palm to his forehead. "That means someone else must be dead or wounded and near to death! While we've been talking, he's been dying, just as Rikard died. We must find him before it's too late!"

"Good idea. Where should we start that we are not already looking?" Conall put his nose in the air.

Holm's shoulders sagged. "I don't know. My men are searching the houses and structures around the warehouse, but it will take days to search all of Dublin."

"An impossible task." Conall gestured to the raised trapdoor. "That's why we spent so much time in the vault, hoping for an indication of where the culprit might have gone. Furthermore, things are not entirely what we thought at first. Am I the only one who thinks it's strange that Rikard ended up in the vault *before* the wine was poured on the floor?"

Holm had been turning away, ready to set off to find men to do his bidding, but now he turned back. "How do you figure?"

Conall made a broad gesture. "Two things: first, the warehouse was ransacked before the wine was spilled, since what fell to the floor is covered in it. Second, the wine pooled near the trapdoor but, as you can see, when we opened the trapdoor, the wine spilled down the steps. If Rikard had been put down there *after* it was spilled, it would have disappeared before we arrived."

Holm blinked twice at Conall, but he was forced to nod and admit that Conall's reasoning made sense. "How did you open the trapdoor?"

"With a metal tool I found nearby, as if it had been tossed aside after use because someone was in a hurry." He directed a snort at Godfrid. "Another thing you didn't notice, my friend."

He said *my friend* in such a way as to imply superiority, and by way of a reply, Godfrid gave an obviously artificial grin. "My lord Conall is correct. I didn't notice the bar when I came in, and Lord Conall found it when he was looking for something like it to pry open the trapdoor."

Conall sniffed again. "I imagine you and your men added to the destruction of the warehouse during your quest to find Rikard."

Holm was offended, as well he should be. "Of course we didn't. We hardly touched anything." He gestured to Godfrid. "The prince can attest that we were still organizing the men when he arrived."

Conall scoffed his disbelief. "It seems clear to me that neither of you knows anything about investigating death. I will have to take a significant hand in the pursuit of justice for Rikard."

Holm didn't appear to know what to make of that, and to cover up his discomfort he looked away—and finally noticed Cait standing against the wall. "What about you?"

She blinked and curtseyed. "My lord?"

"You shouldn't have been cleaning up. Did you touch anything near the blood or the pool of wine?"

Cait looked demurely down at her feet. "No, my lord. I was attending to broken glass. I didn't want anyone to cut themselves."

"The slave knows nothing." Godfrid took a slight step to the right, blocking Holm's line of vision to Cait, who remained against the wall. "We should focus on why Rikard is dead and who it was that was tied to that chair."

"For once, I agree with the prince." Conall began to make a slow circuit of the room, taking in all aspects of the current scene: the body, the blood, the wine, the smashed trading goods. More than just the culprit was missing from their understanding. "What if we have two villains working at cross-purposes? It wouldn't be the first time."

Holm let out an involuntary guffaw, possibly imagining that his task had just doubled. "Surely not, my lord!"

"A merchant of Rikard's station would have made many enemies over the years," Conall said. "Leinster has increased the taxes on Danish merchants recently. What if he had something valuable to sell that he didn't want taxed?"

Godfrid cleared his throat. "If he had multiple bidders, who were competing against each other, and enough money at stake, one of them could have killed him rather than pay the asking price."

Holm accepted Godfrid's idea in a way he hadn't Conall's. "I am no merchant, but avoiding a tax would be a good reason to meet privately with a buyer in the middle of the night." He chewed on his lip, his brow furrowed.

"You may have the right of it." Godfrid stepped closer and put his hand companionably on Holm's shoulder. "Rikard may have unintentionally set himself up to be killed."

5

Day One

Caitriona

"Explain your plan going forward, Holm," Conall said abruptly, in that insulting way he'd developed.

Caitriona had never seen Conall provoke other men the way he'd been doing since Holm had arrived. She almost didn't recognize him.

"We have many things to see to, most of which should be accomplished quickly." Holm cleared this throat, his eyes on Godfrid rather than Conall. "I would be grateful for your further assistance, my prince. Your experience in these matters could be very helpful." The two Danes had come a long way over the last hour.

"What matters are these?" Conall stepped closer.

Holm looked embarrassed, though Cait wasn't sure why. "Investigating death."

"Regretfully, I do have some experience, thanks to Gareth the Welshman," Godfrid said.

The sheriff nodded. "You mentioned him earlier. I understand you know him well."

Conall laughed mockingly before Godfrid could reply. "I do too, since Gareth saved my life last year." He punched Godfrid in the shoulder hard enough to rock him backwards, which couldn't have been easy. When Godfrid had taken her hand earlier, she had felt the strength in him. He was twice the size of Conall too. "Godfrid and I should examine the body as soon as possible. Rikard may have wounds that aren't immediately visible."

Holm sent a look in Godfrid's direction that was both furtive and apologetic. "I will tell the priest to expect you. Meanwhile, my men and I will redouble our search for the culprit, as well as a possible second victim. The city gates are being monitored such that everybody who goes in and out of the city will be examined personally by me or by one of my men." Fortified with new purpose, he turned smartly on his heel and strode towards the main door. Once he was outside, Cait could hear him calling to his men.

With Holm gone again, Cait stepped out the shadows. "I would never say so to Holm, but trading goods aren't the only valuable items Rikard might not have wanted anyone to know about. The same could be said for secrets."

"You don't have to tell me that. We are all living proof." Godfrid grimaced. "I am most concerned that the traitor you mentioned killed him for those very secrets."

Cait nodded. "And the reason Rikard wrote your name in the dirt, my lord, was to warn you that your secrets were no longer yours alone."

Before today, Cait had seen Godfrid only once, the day after she arrived in Dublin. He clearly had no memory of it, but she'd been working her loom when he'd come to the warehouse looking for Rikard. After he left, she'd asked one of her fellow weaver women, Deirdre, about him and been regaled with all manner of stories of his life. Since then, Godfrid's name had tripped off Deirdre's tongue a time or two, always with respect and a morsel of lust. Cait had admired Godfrid's figure as he'd passed her loom, and having herself finally spoken today to the man, Cait was looking forward to telling Deirdre about him.

Initially, Cait had resolved to maintain a certain detachment from everyone in Rikard's household, the same detachment with which she had conducted her life since she'd left her father's house, having found it unwise to become emotionally invested in anyone outside her own family. While she wouldn't have wished death on Rikard, he'd treated her well only because he knew who she was. It was the other slaves who'd embraced her and taken her into their hearts as a friend and companion.

In Deirdre's case, raiders had taken her as a little girl from her home in northern Scotland. Now nearing sixty, she'd been a slave in Dublin virtually her entire life. She was of an age with Rikard, who had inherited her from his father. Because of her difficult life, she could have been despairing, but she maintained a quiet acceptance of her fate and entertained herself with gossip, her grasp of which was more extensive than anyone Cait had ever met.

The thought of her friend made her frown. Though an inveterate gossip, Deirdre hadn't been in evidence today, which was unusual to say the least. At a minimum, she should have been bobbing around the front steps of the warehouse, gathering whatever information she could from whomever she could. If there was news to learn, normally Deirdre couldn't be kept away. And if Cait hadn't been so distracted by Rikard's death and everything that had come with it, she would have thought of her friend sooner.

"Holm is doing what he can, but I can't talk to him about any of this, and thus, I need to keep significant amounts of information from him. If I am to discover how and why Rikard died, I am going to need help." Godfrid looked from Cait to Conall and back again. "Your help."

"You have mine, as you know," Conall said immediately. "But Cait is done." And as Cait opened her mouth to protest, he moved closer to her. "You must go now. Run straight to my house and stay put until I get there. With Rikard dead or missing, you can't stay here. It's time for you to come home." And then he said under his breath, though Cait overheard, "—long past time."

"What? What are you saying?" she replied in a fierce whisper. Rather than obedience, his command had produced the opposite effect to what he'd intended, something he couldn't have been surprised about.

Still, Conall tried again, taking her by the upper arms and looking into her eyes. "It's over, Cait."

"It isn't, Conall. I can be of help here. What is the point of any of this if I leave just at the moment when my knowledge can be of real use? I can help you discover who ransacked the warehouse and why Rikard is dead."

"No, Cait." Conall shook his head vigorously. "You can't precisely *because* Rikard is dead. I will not risk you as a slave of his household even another hour longer."

Godfrid put out a hand to Conall. "I don't mean to intrude on your business, Conall, but surely we can use her. She knows far more about the workings of Rikard's business than either you or I. If there's a traitor among his servants, now isn't the time to have Cait go missing."

Cait felt a frisson of satisfaction at Godfrid's support and that he was willing to listen to her with actual interest. For the last few weeks she'd been cultivating the submissive posture of an enslaved woman, and it felt good to throw it off, if only in the presence of Conall and Godfrid, and stand upright again. In the three weeks she'd been a weaver woman for Rikard, she'd grown tired of being continually ignored or dismissed—though no amount of torture would drag that admission out of her in front of Conall. Spying was all very well and good if one was a man, an ambassador—and nephew to a king—who could live and do as he pleased. It was quite another thing to become a slave girl.

At the same time, throughout her stay in Dublin, she had felt a certain degree of satisfaction in the way she had managed to be barely seen and never heard, and she'd been right when she'd argued to Conall that a slave girl was the perfect cover for a spy. The others with whom she'd been housed had not known her identity, and that meant, in front of them, she had to be treated as they were, and their lot had been hers. While she hadn't witnessed any beatings, and for the most part all of Rikard's slaves had known their jobs and done them well, it had been a strain to be continually viewed by everyone in the community as something *less*: unfree and of the lowest social class imaginable.

That false face was harder still to maintain because it was the exact opposite of her true station. While her people kept slaves, and she'd known slaves all her life, until she'd become one of them, she'd had no idea what it might be like to walk a while in their shoes. And yet, as a beautiful woman, she'd been underestimated all her life, and to some degree, she couldn't decide if she was more invisible when she wore her head covering or when she didn't.

Conall jerked his head at Godfrid. "You don't understand."

In reply, Godfrid turned his hands palm up. "Evidently not."

As the two men turned on each other, this time in a real argument, Cait backed away. "We should close the vault, don't you think? And we should leave a guard on the warehouse to protect everything inside."

Godfrid glanced over at her, momentarily distracted, as she'd intended, from his dispute with Conall. "My men will stay. If anything were to be stolen, we would be answerable to Sanne and Arno."

Her eyes still on Godfrid, Cait reached for the edge of the trapdoor. But before she could lower it to the floor, the rear door of the warehouse banged open, and she jerked around to see a man she didn't know entering. He was about her age, with the blond hair and sunburned skin of someone who'd spent his life on the sea. "You there! What are you doing?"

Instinctively, Cait recoiled at the anger in his voice and released the trapdoor, which closed with a bang. "I thought it best—"

"You thought?" The man bore down on her. "Slaves aren't here to think!"

Instantly, Godfrid bounded forward, one arm coming around her waist and the other extended, palm out to hold the newcomer at bay. "I suggest you reconsider your tone."

Conall, meanwhile, moving nearly as quickly, intercepted the man before he could reach Godfrid or Cait and grasped his jacket by the lapels. Conall wasn't a large man, but he could be menacing when he chose to be. "How dare you speak to my sister in such a fashion!"

Beside her, Godfrid let out an audible gasp.

Meanwhile, the newcomer's face flushed right up to the hairline. "Your-your—" At first he appeared prepared to defend his rights to his last breath, but then his eyes strayed to Godfrid and widened. He swallowed down whatever retort he'd been about to make. "My lord Godfrid? Please, I didn't know you were acquainted with this woman, or I would not have spoken thus to her!"

Now it was Godfrid's jaw that dropped, though not over Caitriona's true identity. "Finn? Is that you?"

"My lord, it is!"

Cait would have demanded that Godfrid let her go, but whatever was happening here went beyond her momentary awkwardness.

At the mention of the newcomer's name, Conall released Finn, shoving him back slightly so he staggered. "This is Rikard's son? I thought he was lost at sea."

"As you can see, I am found." Finn spread his arms wide, regaining his confidence now that he'd been recognized and it appeared that nobody was going to harm him. Then he put his heels together and bowed to her. "I apologize, madam. I thought you were a slave and that you were interfering in my father's affairs." His glance went to Godfrid. "My lord, she *is* wearing a slave collar."

"A fact I will remedy right now." Godfrid pulled a ring of keys from an inner pocket of his clothing and, his arm still around Cait's waist, guided her away from Finn and Conall.

"Conall's sister, eh?" he said, in an undertone as he went through several of the keys until he found the one that fit into the lock of Cait's collar. "You couldn't have told me sooner?"

"I'm sorry." And she was. "The farther down the road of not telling you we got, the harder it was to figure out the best way to explain, and I knew how shocked you would be when we told you the truth."

"I am shocked." Godfrid slipped the collar off her neck.

"Don't blame Conall. I was the one who talked him into letting me become his spy." She rubbed her throat, feeling where the collar had cut in all these weeks. "In truth, I am not sorry to be rid of it."

"How are you siblings anyway?" Godfrid said. "I thought his father died when he was an infant."

"He did. We share a mother, King Diarmait's sister." Then she tugged at her head covering and shook out her hair, letting it spread out over her back and shoulders. She could do nothing about her rough clothing, but she hoped the fall of hair would distract anyone who wondered why Conall's sister was so poorly dressed. "Where did you get the key?"

"I took the ring from Rikard's pocket while your brother was greeting Holm. I had a feeling that I might need them, and I didn't want to risk them being appropriated by somebody else. Before too much time passes, or anyone asks where his keys have disappeared to, we must determine what these others unlock."

Conall, meanwhile, was still glaring at Finn, his hands clenched into fists. "How is it that you are here?"

Finn wet his lips, his eyes skating from Conall to Cait to Godfrid, who had his arm around Cait's waist again as he guided her back towards the center of the floor. He had returned the keys to his pocket, and he held the slave collar behind his back. "You have the advantage of me, I'm afraid. You know who I am, but while I recognize Prince Godfrid, I don't know who you are. Please forgive my terrible manners, but I have returned after two years' absence to learn that my father, who I have so longed to see, is dead."

Conall subsided at the apology. "I am Lord Conall, Leinster's ambassador to the throne of Dublin. This is my sister, Caitriona."

"Their mother is King Diarmait's sister," Godfrid added helpfully.

Finn made a sweeping gesture to encompass the warehouse. "It is true, then, what they are saying? My father really is dead? I heard them speaking of it on the docks and again when I was examined at the gate just now."

"Yes," Godfrid said. "I am very sorry."

"He was murdered?"

Godfrid tipped his head to imply uncertainty. "We can't be sure of anything yet. We found him dead in his vault."

Finn looked away, blinking his eyes rapidly, seemingly trying to regain control of himself. When he next looked back to Godfrid, however, his eyes were clear. "Am I to understand that this blood everywhere is his?"

Cait saw no reason to remain silent and spoke freely. "That, at least, was mistakenly reported. What you see is predominantly wine."

Finn's head swung her way, and he appeared to really see her for the first time. She ran a hand through her hair, trying to freshen it and make herself look like she belonged in Godfrid and Conall's company.

Godfrid squeezed her waist, and though she didn't look up at him, she was pretty certain he was glowering at Finn. Ever since she was fifteen years old, Cait's appearance had affected virtually every man she encountered. Conall had once accused her of being a hypocrite, first to complain that her looks made it difficult for anyone to take her seriously, but then to use her appearance to dazzle when it suited her. He wasn't wrong, but in this case, she felt no guilt whatsoever.

Finn bowed one more time. "Again, please accept my humblest apologies for my misunderstanding."

Then the front door to the warehouse slammed open, and men's boots thudded on the floor. They all turned to see Holm reentering the warehouse, several of his men in tow. He didn't look happy.

Godfrid spoke low in her ear. "Time to look like you belong here."

If Godfrid hadn't still had his arm around her waist, Cait would have responded by fading towards the back wall. Her collar had come off so suddenly, they hadn't concocted a plan for dealing with Holm—or King Ottar, for that matter, were he to discover that King Diarmait had inserted her into his midst as a spy.

"The king has asked for a full report—" Holm broke off from what he'd been about to say—not because he'd caught sight of Cait, but rather because Finn had started towards him.

The two men stared at each other, both open-mouthed, and then they laughed and met in the center of the hall for an enormous hug.

Finn pounded Holm on the back. "My brother. It is so good to see you." Then he stepped back to look Holm up and down, admiring his chain of office. "You have done well for yourself."

Holm attempted a look of modesty and deflected the comment. "One of my men reported the arrival of a ship belonging to Rikard this morning but not who captained it!" He turned to the others, joy on his face. It made it hard for Cait to despise either of them. "It's a miracle!" Then Holm caught sight of Cait. He blinked, and then glanced questioningly at Godfrid.

Godfrid obliged with an introduction. "May I introduce Lord Conall's sister, Caitriona."

Holm had no choice but to bow over her hand. "It is my pleasure, madam. I am only sorry that our meeting is taking place under such unfortunate circumstances."

She smiled sweetly. "I came looking for my brother this morning and heard he was here. I didn't know about the dead man, or of course I wouldn't have entered the warehouse."

Conall smiled benignly. "I will escort her home shortly."

With her hair down, Holm appeared genuinely not to recognize her as the slave who'd been wailing the last time he'd come into the warehouse. And in the face of the utter certainty of Godfrid and Conall, Holm didn't have the wherewithal to object to her presence and seemed relieved to turn back to Finn. "My friend, how is it that you are here?"

Finn's joyful expression dimmed. "It is a long story, which I will tell you in due course. Suffice to say, we arrived this morning after a lengthy journey."

She could feel a sudden intensity in Godfrid, who asked, "Is Dublin your first port of call in Ireland?"

Finn glanced at him. "I went first to my father's house in Wexford. When I left two years ago, he was spending most of his time there." He gestured to the warehouse. "Obviously in my absence he moved the base of his operations to Dublin. Without my brother to oversee things here, perhaps he didn't have a choice. I spent the night at our house in Wexford and returned to the boat the next morning. Sad to say, the wind wasn't in our favor, so it took longer to get here than I'd hoped." He looked down at his feet. "So much for my grand entrance."

His tone was mournful, and Cait didn't take his comment as selfish so much as lamenting. Her heart softened towards him even more at the genuine grief she heard in his voice. Though she'd never been separated from her mother for more than a few months at a time, she knew well the excitement and anticipation of seeing her again after an absence, especially if she hadn't sent word that she was coming.

Conall now looked at Holm. "Have you discovered anything about the men with whom Rikard met last night?"

Even though Conall's tone was relatively mild, Holm bristled.

Cait had little or no patience with the way Danish men continually sized up every other man in the room, comparing intelligence and strength and telling themselves that they were worthy. Rikard, even though he was past sixty, a merchant, and no warrior, had been as bad as any other. Holm appeared to be equally so, his insecurities brought to the fore by his promotion to a position he was unable to properly execute. Even if Holm had tamped down his hostility towards Godfrid, any acknowledgement of another man's abilities brought his own shortcomings into sharp relief.

Sadly for him, between Godfrid and Conall, Holm didn't stand a chance. Conall was always the smartest man in any room he entered. And Godfrid, for all that he was larger physically than any man had a right to be, wasn't far behind.

As Conall raised his eyebrows at him, some part of Holm seemed to know it, since he subsided quickly, his shoulders fell, and his expression became more conciliatory. "Nobody saw anything." Then Holm shook his head. "Slaves and dock men aren't the most reliable witnesses. They like their mead and their sleep."

"And you found no evidence of another victim?" Godfrid asked.

"Regretfully no." Holm indicated the door with a tip of his head. "I have returned because the king has asked for an update. In this matter, as in any matter, I'd rather not keep him waiting."

6

Day One

Godfrid

Godfrid resisted the temptation to refuse the summons. Before his father's death, refusal would have been his right, not that he would necessarily have done it then either, since refusal would have made him look petty. These days, with Godfrid's father dead and Ottar confirmed as the sole King of Dublin, he was Godfrid's king too. It was annoying to say the least.

So he nodded. "Of course we will come. Our only goal is to be of service."

Behind him, Conall snorted derisively, as he would.

Whether because he sensed the tension in the room or merely because he was anxious to meet the king, Finn immediately set off for the door, side-by-side with Holm. Seeing the king was necessary for Finn if he wanted to claim his inheritance, and Godfrid didn't know if the issue would be complicated by a prior agreement Sanne and Arno might have come to as to how the business would be divided once Rikard died. After Finn's mother had died at his birth, Rikard had married again, but this second wife had died within five years of the marriage. Then Rikard had married Sanne when Finn was ten years old. Among Danes, by the time a son is ten, he spends most of his time in male company, so Godfrid didn't know how close Finn and Sanne had ever become, or if Finn had resented Sanne's influence over his father.

Godfrid allowed Holm and Finn to get ahead of him and then turned to Cait, who stood hesitating in the center of the floor. "You should come as well. I know you didn't intend to take this course just yet, but you should be introduced to the king as soon as possible."

"Not wearing this." Cait gestured to herself.

Godfrid thought that even in her plain dress, Cait looked like nothing more or less than a princess, but Conall nodded in agreement. "I can't help but think we've made a mess of things. For now, maybe it's best if you stay here with Godfrid's guards."

Cait's eyes lit. "After three weeks of being surrounded by them every day, I have a pretty good idea about the warehouse's contents. We have been assuming that the warehouse was sacked because someone was looking for something specific. Who's to say that it isn't still hiding here? I will go through what I can while you're gone."

Godfrid jerked his head to Jon, his captain, who stood in relationship to Godfrid as Gareth did to Prince Hywel. While Jon didn't know about murder, he saw everything though jaundiced eyes, had no trouble keeping Godfrid's secrets, and was one of the few people who knew that Godfrid and Conall were friends. His nod told Godfrid that he would protect Cait with his life, if it proved necessary.

Thus, Godfrid and Conall set off for Ottar's hall in the wake of Finn and Holm, wending their way through the narrow streets of Dublin. The city had grown in size from the muddy spot on the banks of the Liffey that Godfrid's ancestors had founded hundreds of years earlier. These days, the palisade encompassed over one thousand houses, most crammed so closely together that a man could walk from one end of the city to the other in hardly more than a quarter-hour.

Holm and Finn had started out a good dozen yards ahead, and they appeared to be walking fast in order to maintain their lead. There was some risk in Godfrid and Conall being seen talking to one another without fighting, but Godfrid had a serious issue he could no longer put off discussing with Conall, so he furrowed his brow as if he were intensely angry. "There is still one thing I don't understand."

"Only one thing?" Conall jested back, a snide expression on his face. Anyone watching would think they were in the middle of their usual bickering.

But for once, Godfrid found himself genuinely angry, and he spit out his question. "How could you leave your sister alone as a slave in Dublin, even to respond to a summons from your king? I don't have a sister, but I would never willingly risk her the way you did."

Conall walked a few more steps before replying, and then he glanced at Godfrid with that far-seeing stare of his.

Truthfully, that was all the answer Godfrid needed. "Ah. You mean you didn't? Where have you been hiding all this time?"

"I shouldn't have been offended that you asked, because I would have needed an answer too, no matter how well I knew you. I've spent these last weeks as part of a stranded crew from Ulster." He laughed, making sure that the sound was loud enough to reach Holm and Finn, who walked a little faster in response. "Fergus mac Cormac at your service. Our ship hobbled into port needing extensive repairs. I've been fifty yards from Cait at most the entire time."

Godfrid let out a relieved sigh. "I am very glad to hear it. So ... what happened last night?"

Conall growled under his breath. "It was time to discard Fergus in favor of Conall, but I couldn't just reappear at my house without having come through the western gate. With our ship repaired, we sailed away with the tide yesterday afternoon. We went only as far south of Dublin as the mouth of the River Dargle, in order to meet with my ambassadorial entourage. I bathed, since that hadn't happened nearly often enough these last weeks; shaved off quite a becoming beard, if I do say so myself; and donned my chain of office, in order to ride back to Dublin as myself this morning. I believed Cait could come to no harm in a single night."

"Cait herself was fine, so you were right on that score."

"But not Rikard." Conall hummed low in his throat. "And yet, I am grateful her sojourn as a spy is over. She spoke the truth when she told you I fought her on it, even if she did learn more about the workings of Dublin in three weeks than I'd learned in a year." He shook his head. "Since her husband died, she has been responsible only to herself and the king."

"She's a widow?"

"For more than a year now."

"What about her father?"

"He died." Conall gave him a piercing look. "I *am* sorry that I wasn't honest with you."

Godfrid still felt slightly affronted by the entire scenario, but he tried to put his hurt feelings aside. Conall was loyal to his king and his people, and his friendship with Godfrid, while beneficial—and enjoyable—for both of them, could not take precedence over duty. "Is there something more I should know before we meet with Ottar?"

"We will talk tonight, just the three of us. There is a great deal to tell you." Then Conall lifted a hand and sharply clapped Godfrid on the shoulder, in a show of camaraderie that anyone watching would know was false. Godfrid made sure to look disgruntled.

Then he quickened his pace, hastening to catch up with Holm and Finn, who by now were within a few streets of Ottar's palace. He fetched up beside Holm and made a show of sighing with relief, as if he couldn't wait to be rid of Conall. "Thanks for nothing," he said out of the corner of his mouth.

Holm actually grinned. "I don't know. I think he's starting to like you."

Rikard's wealth had been made on the dock of the Liffey in the northeastern quadrant of the city, but he'd built his house near the western gate, essentially as far from the dock as he could manage while still being inside the city walls. In turn, Ottar's palace lay in the southeastern quadrant, set apart from the rest of the city by its own ten-foot-high palisade, in the area between the Liffey and the Poddle that had once been the entire settlement.

Ottar claimed that the walls, which had been built since he'd become king, were there as a last line of defense in case the outer walls of the city were breached. The Normans built that way all the time, and it made good sense to do so in Dublin, a city perpetually surrounded by enemies, but Godfrid still found the division irksome and pretentious. In the absence of an actual assault, they served daily as a reminder to the people of Dublin— and to Godfrid—that Ottar ruled them.

Though Gwen had insisted that Dublin was entirely flat, her perspective on the landscape came through the eyes of someone born and raised in Wales, a land of mountains that drew the eye in every cantref. Ottar's palace had been built on an escarpment on the high point above the River Poddle, overlooking the tidal pool created by the intersection of the Rivers Poddle and Liffey. But it was still hardly higher than the houses around it, and certainly not higher than the adjacent *thingmote*.

The palace had once been the home of Godfrid's family, and he couldn't enter it without a deep pang at the loss of his father. Once Ottar had been confirmed as co-ruler, he'd moved into the palace, and Godfrid's father had removed his household rather than share the space with a usurper. Godfrid ground his teeth a dozen times a day at how far his family had fallen.

With Holm in the lead, Godfrid, Finn, and Conall were welcomed through the palace gate into an extensive compound. Because of the need to house soldiers, servants, and visiting dignitaries close by, many other buildings had been constructed within the walls. As they passed a series of craft halls, the pungent smell of candle-making wafted towards them. Space in Dublin was at a premium, but Ottar's walled compound had slightly more room between buildings than the rest of the city.

The need for space and the freedom to expand was one reason the Danes had made their peace with Leinster a hundred years earlier. For centuries, in the forefront of every Danish mind had been the constant fear of attack and the knowledge that they needed at all times to be prepared for it. But if they were to expand their empire—and to survive—their options had been two-fold: tear down the southern and western walls and rebuild them in a wider circuit or forge such a certain peace with the Irish who surrounded them that Dublin's citizens felt comfortable taking up permanent residence outside the city.

In the end, they'd done both. These days, farms and fields surrounded the city for miles around, even venturing, as in the case with the city's leather-workings, north across the Liffey.

Since it was early morning, the compound was bustling. With single-minded purpose, Holm forged his way across the courtyard with Conall, Finn, and Godfrid in his wake, to find King Ottar standing in the middle of his hall, berating one of his underlings. It was an oddly familiar scene, hardly dissimilar from Godfrid's entrance into Rikard's warehouse earlier that morning, except with Ottar as the central figure instead of Sturla. The hall itself was magnificent. Though essentially the same size as Rikard's warehouse, the walls were lined with trophies of conquest—weapons and tapestries—rather than trading goods.

The skald, meanwhile, stood a few feet away, his expression impassive. But, as usual, Godfrid could feel Sturla's eyes taking in everything and everyone in an assessing manner. In retrospect, he thought it just as well that they'd left Cait at the warehouse. Sturla was one of the few who might not be seduced by her beauty and would not overlook the poor weave of her dress.

At their appearance, Ottar flicked his fingers at the servant, who bowed and scurried away. Before disdain rose to the front of his mind, Godfrid reminded himself that there but for the grace of God went he, and that pride could not feed a man's family. He'd swallowed down his pride and shame every day for the last five years, so he could hardly blame the men who surrounded Ottar from doing the king's bidding. Godfrid himself was doing exactly the same, evidenced by the fact that he was here. The Danes had fallen far, it was true, but it was Ottar who was riding them all the way down, and Godfrid would be wise to remember it.

The only alternative for Godfrid would have been for him to leave Dublin, forsaking his brother and his inheritance, and forge a new life somewhere else. It wasn't impossible. He could think of several foreign courts that would welcome him and his men. Danes had been leaving home in search of a new life for centuries. But he wasn't that desperate. At least not yet. Brodar was committed to moving against Ottar at the summer solstice. Godfrid could swallow down his hatred a little longer.

At the sight of Conall, Ottar's expression transformed from a mask of superiority to apparent delight. "Lord Conall! We've missed you these last weeks! When did you return?"

"Just now, my lord." Conall accorded Ottar a polite bow. One of the consequences of Godfrid and Conall's apparent animosity was that Ottar was more inclined to treat Conall as an ally. "I heard about Rikard's death and thought I would look in before coming to greet you."

"What can you tell me?" Ottar said, still focused on Conall. "Rikard is, in fact, dead?"

"He is, my lord. His warehouse was ransacked, implying that an intruder was looking for something." Conall made no mention of the vault.

Ottar's eyes snapped with anger, though not directed at the men before him. "The intruder stole his wealth?"

"Not in the main, not as far as we know, though we have yet to do a true accounting."

"Then what did he want?"

"We don't know. Given that the warehouse was sacked, it may be that he didn't find whatever it was he was looking for."

"How did Rikard die? My men tell me there was much blood on the floor."

"That was an error, my lord. Much of what we thought initially was blood was actually wine, possibly spilled to cover up the blood the intruder couldn't wipe away."

Ottar had been pleased to speak to Conall, but now he directed his attention to Holm, who quailed slightly under the king's gaze. "Do we have any clue as to the identity of the villain?"

"No, my lord. I have sent my men to question everyone who lives or works within a stone's throw of the warehouse. They have found nothing so far, and I will likely have to expand the search. In addition, I ordered the main gates of the city closed to free traffic."

Ottar's nostrils flared at that, as unhappy about this news as he had been about Conall's. "Why?"

"The culprit may still be in the city. It seemed a sensible precaution," Holm said, without mentioning the fact that it had been Godfrid's idea.

So far Godfrid had said nothing, and he was happy to be ignored, but he felt compelled to come to Holm's rescue. "My lord, the servants report that Rikard sent everyone away so he could meet with his visitor in private."

Ottar wet his lips. "In the middle of the night?"

"So it appears, my lord."

Such a meeting was by definition illicit, and Ottar's eyes became thin slits at the thought, angry and just barely controlling his agitation. Godfrid could almost feel undercurrents boiling around him, but he didn't know what they carried. Ottar glanced at Sturla, who gazed back at his king, still expressionless. If Godfrid hadn't been watching closely, he might have missed the hint of a nod Sturla directed at his lord.

Holm coughed. "To be honest, my lord, the scene is confused. There is blood, but perhaps not Rikard's, since a brief examination of the body revealed no overt wounds on him. And yet, Rikard is dead and his warehouse ransacked."

"It would be unwise to assume anything yet," Conall said in a tone of authority. "Men are posted at the warehouse to prevent anyone from entering until its contents have been gone through to determine what, if anything, was taken."

Godfrid could only admire the way Conall touched upon Cait's task without actually mentioning her name or who she was. So far, in fact, he had almost entirely refrained from saying *we* or *I* and had kept all identification of the participants as vague as possible.

"What of Rikard's silver and gold?" Ottar asked.

Godfrid put out a hand, palm up. It was a gesture that implied supplication, one Godfrid often deliberately used in Ottar's presence. "I apologize, my lord, but we can be certain of nothing at this time. Given the destruction, we find it possible that what the intruder was looking for is still there. We think it would be wise to find it, whatever it is, before it becomes a matter the heirs must sort out among themselves."

Ottar looked somewhat sideways at him. "Heirs? Are you speaking of Sanne and Arno?"

"And me." Finn had remained a few paces behind the rest, waiting with admirable patience for them to tell their story, but now he stepped forward. "My lord." He went down on one knee before Ottar. "I am at your service."

Ottar blinked. "Do I know you?"

"I arrived this morning to find my father dead and his murderer walking free. I am Finn, Rikard's youngest son."

Finn should have named himself when he went down on one knee, but Godfrid couldn't fault him for his dramatic timing. The only off-note to the entire scene was that he had arrived the same day his father may have been murdered. It was a little too soon in Godfrid's mind for pleasure in the spectacle.

Godfrid regretted now that he hadn't taken Holm aside and warned him against giving Finn a rundown of the investigation during the walk to the palace. Whether or not Holm wanted to admit it, after a two-year absence, he didn't know Finn anymore, and his friend was now at the top of the list of suspects to be questioned about Rikard's death. Just because he said he arrived after Rikard was dead didn't mean that was what had actually happened.

Ottar reached down and grasped Finn's upper arms to raise him up. "You're Finn? We thought you were lost at sea!"

"My brother remains lost, my lord. But as you can see, I am found."

The young man had a way with words, Godfrid could give him that. Ottar's eyes went to Holm's, and the sheriff nodded. "I recognized him immediately, my lord. Growing up, we were like brothers."

Ottar actually looked pleased, an expression rarely seen on his face. His own eldest son had died a few years before in yet another misguided foray into Wales. All he had left were three daughters and a six-year-old son, upon whom all of his hopes and dreams now rested. "You must share a meal with me and speak of your adventures."

"Of course I will, my lord. Just say the word, and I will be there."

Godfrid settled a hand on the young man's shoulder. "I am very sorry for your loss, Finn. It is tragic that your father died on the very day of your return."

Finn bobbed his head. "Thank you, my lord. I just hope we can discover how and why it happened."

"We will." Godfrid growled the promise, though he hadn't actually intended to say anything at all. It had come out all on its own.

Then Sturla approached the king with an intent expression on his face. "If I may have a moment of your time, my lord."

"Of course." Ottar turned away, though not quickly enough that Godfrid couldn't see the flash of relief that crossed his face. Sturla, as always, had read his lord's mind and rescued him.

But Holm put out a hand. "Before we go, my lord, I would ask for the continued assistance of Prince Godfrid. We have a great deal of ground to cover, and I feel that time is of the essence."

Ottar turned back. "That is acceptable to me if it is acceptable to him." He raised his eyebrows at Godfrid.

Godfrid canted his head graciously. "I am pleased to continue if the sheriff thinks I can be helpful."

Then Ottar looked at Conall. "Does Leinster have an interest in Rikard's death, my lord?"

Conall dipped his head. "It does. Rikard had many trading interests in Leinster. My king will be concerned that the man responsible for his death be brought to justice."

A smile quirked at Ottar's lips. "I am not unaware that you and Prince Godfrid have not always been on the most cordial of terms, but I'm sure you can put aside your differences for the good of discovering what happened this morning." Ottar looked directly at Godfrid.

He didn't flinch, but he did protest, "My lord, I really think—"

Ottar cut him off. "Couldn't you?"

Godfrid smoothed his expression to one of grim acceptance. "Of course, my lord." He stuck out his arm to Conall, who gripped it a little too hard. "I seek only to be of service."

"As do I." Conall released him and stepped back. "It has been suggested that Godfrid and I inspect Rikard's body, but as a more urgent first step, we will speak to the widow. I believe Holm intends to pursue his inquiries in the area around the warehouse."

"This is what you wish, as well, Holm?" Ottar asked the sheriff.

Holm bowed deeply. "Yes, my lord."

Ottar's eyes narrowed as he took in all of their faces. "So be it. Keep me informed."

7

Day One

Godfrid

Feigning a stiff cordiality, Godfrid and Conall left the palace for Rikard's house. Told that Sanne was still at Arno's home, they then inquired for her there, at which point they were directed back to the warehouse. Finn accompanied them to both initial stops, and now he forged ahead, anxious to speak to his stepmother.

By now it was past noon and, for Godfrid, the shine was beginning to wear off the day. "I'm remembering some of the more tedious aspects of investigating."

"And admiring Gareth and Gwen more and more for what they do." Conall's boots scuffed in the dirt of the road. "They saved my life."

Godfrid himself had never been a captive, but he could well imagine the fear, anger, and frustration that Conall still felt at his near-death experience.

"I'd heard good things about Shrewsbury's sheriff, but he was mustered to fight for King Stephen. Gareth and Gwen just happened to be in the town. If they had arrived a few days later, or had been less able investigators ..." Conall's voice trailed off as he shook his head.

"But they did come, and they were able."

"I have never been one to spend overmuch time on my knees, but I prayed for deliverance, for me and for the women I was captive with, and—" Again, Conall was unable to finish his sentence, this time swallowing around a closing throat.

"And He sent *them*." Godfrid put a hand on Conall's shoulder and squeezed. In all the time they'd spent together this year, they'd never talked about Shrewsbury except lightly, even jestingly, in passing. It was the way men usually dealt with hardship, except perhaps late at night when they were deep in their cups of mead.

A pig burst from a nearby yard, nearly running Conall and Godfrid over, followed by two boys whose job it was to corral it. The whole lot of them had passed before either man could assist, but it ended the moment of intimacy. With lighter hearts and higher heads, they hastened to catch up to Finn, if, for no other reason, than to protect Cait from him—or perhaps vice versa.

They still had a few blocks to go, however, so Godfrid ventured to ask, "Was this your plan all along, by the way?"

Conall shot him a wicked grin, understanding immediately what Godfrid was asking. "It came to me on the walk to Ottar's palace that if I could arrange things so our partnership would look like someone else's idea, it would be best for everyone. I knew you'd play along without giving the game away." He smiled more broadly. "Ottar paired you with me to annoy you. It is always gratifying when other people behave exactly as you think they might."

Then they were at the warehouse. With a nod to the guard, Godfrid entered to find the widow and her daughter a few feet away, pale-faced and weepy, with Finn's arms wrapped around them both. Looking past them, Godfrid noted that the trapdoor remained closed, and Cait was standing twenty feet from it with her hands clasped in front of her. Their eyes met, and she nodded. He knew without her telling him outright that all continued to be well down in the vault. Cait's hair remained around her shoulders, and she was wearing a deep green overdress that distracted the eye from the original brown dress with which she'd started the day.

"Oh my poor Rikard!" At the sight of Godfrid, Sanne abandoned Finn and ran to him, and he had no choice but to put his arms around her and hold her as she sobbed. She was tall enough that the top of her head came right up to his chin. She clutched at his cloak, and as he patted her back, he couldn't help but remember Holm's comment about her eligibility as a wife.

The others looked on, and while Conall's expression showed sympathy, it was soon replaced by impatience. Godfrid was feeling impatient too, not so much with Sanne, who had the right to her grief, but with the circumstances that required him to question a widow about the death of her husband within hours of its discovery.

But then again, she was a suspect, and what better way to disguise her guilt than to drown him in tears?

His face ashen, Finn still held his eight-year-old sister, whose name Godfrid suddenly couldn't remember, despite having attended her christening and seen her dozens of times since then. The girl had her arms around Finn's waist and her face buried in his stomach.

Nearby on the floor was a cloth doll, and Conall bent to pick it up before going down on one knee before her. With as gentle a voice as Godfrid had ever heard him use, he got her to look at him. "Shall someone take you home, little one? You shouldn't be here."

The little girl shook her head emphatically. "My father is dead. It is my duty to mourn him."

She wasn't wrong, and at the sound of her daughter's voice, Sanne finally pulled away from Godfrid, as if realizing only now the impact that bringing her daughter to the scene of her father's death would have on the child. And as she turned away from him, Godfrid was genuinely surprised to see that her eyes held no evident tears, nor were they red from weeping.

His eyes narrowed at the widow's back before he glanced again towards Cait, who gave him a sardonic smile. She appeared to have known already that some element of Sanne's grief was feigned, whereas Godfrid had been totally fooled. In retrospect, that Sanne didn't love her husband shouldn't have been a surprise to him: Rikard was thirty years older than she, and their difference in age meant they would not have been natural cohorts.

While Godfrid himself had avoided marriage until it could be for love, few women had that luxury. When Rikard had offered for Sanne, she'd had a duty to her family to accept. The marriage had united two wealthy merchant families, and merchants could be as clear-eyed about the necessity of alliances as noblemen.

Sanne had been born into wealth and shouldn't have been desperate for a husband, but she might have desired status on her own terms, out from underneath her parents' wings. A loveless marriage to a wealthy older man had given her that, as well as a child, albeit not a son. Rikard had already been fifty when they'd married, so the odds had been better than good that he would die long before she did, and at thirty Sanne could find herself a wealthy widow with an enviable degree of independence and a real say over her future, much like Cait.

And how could Godfrid argue with her decisions and her deception when he himself had lived a lie for the last five years? Who was he to judge another for deciding that her best course of action was to get along?

Grunting to himself at these revelations, he caught Sanne's elbow—perhaps more gently than he might have done a moment ago when he had been judging her harshly—and guided her towards a seat at a long table set near the southern side wall, one of several tables in the hall but the only one currently not turned on its side.

He dragged a chair out from underneath a fallen cabinet. "Please, sit."

Then he turned to Cait, eyebrows raised, and mimed drinking from a cup. Mostly Danes drank ale or mead, which were the most common drinks in Ireland, not just in Dublin. But Rikard's contacts allowed him full access to the best wines from Europe, and as one of Rikard's slaves, Cait would know where to find some.

From where Godfrid stood, he could see three metal goblets and two pitchers underneath a stack of shelves, but Cait immediately set off towards the back of the warehouse, returning a moment later with a carafe and three different goblets on a tray. He fleetingly hoped that she wasn't bringing the same kind of wine that had been poured onto the floor, but then dismissed the thought as pointless to worry about. Sanne was unlikely to know or care.

Godfrid poured the wine into a goblet for Sanne and then into a second one for Cait. With a tip of his head, he indicated that she should take it and the chair set next to Sanne's. It was a not-so-subtle reminder that, although he'd asked her out of necessity to fetch the wine for him, she was no longer a servant.

After a moment of hesitation, Cait accepted the chair. "Thank you, my lord."

Sanne took a sip, and then a longer one. When she put it down, her eyes were slightly unfocused, and he wondered if this was perhaps not the first portion of wine she'd drunk today.

Godfrid found a stool to sit on that put his head approximately even with hers. His aim was to appear as unthreatening as possible. But before he could ask a question,

Sanne said, "I can't think of anything I know that could be of help to you. Finn told me about the meeting with the king. I have nothing to add."

"Please understand that I need to ask anyway."

Sanne dabbed at the corners of each eye with a handkerchief. "I don't know why. My husband didn't talk to me about his business."

"I can attest to the truth of that." Even as he spoke, Finn prowled around the warehouse, touching items here and there but otherwise not disturbing them. The young man had an intensity which Godfrid hadn't seen in him two years earlier. It boded well for the future of Rikard's business. Then again, his inability to stay still could be the result of nervousness.

To include him in the conversation, Godfrid poured wine into the third goblet, and while Finn accepted it, he didn't drink. Conall, meanwhile, produced a sweet cake from a hidden pocket in his robe to give to Sanne's daughter. She bit into it, and her eyes went wide. "Thank you, my lord!"

"It was my favorite when I was a child." He straightened from his crouch, a little stiffly, Godfrid thought, and took the girl's free hand in his to guide her to the table.

Sanne herself was drinking again and didn't even look at her daughter, so Cait gestured the little girl closer and took her onto her lap. The ease with which the pair interacted told Godfrid that they knew each other well.

Neither Finn nor Sanne had yet remarked on Cait's transition from slave to noblewoman, but it could be that Cait's presence in his warehouse was a piece of business Rikard *had* discussed with his wife. Finn, of course, had seen Godfrid remove her collar. Given that he'd shouted at her a moment before that, and knowing now that she was Conall's sister, left him no room to question Cait's continued presence in the warehouse.

"Anything you can tell us would be helpful." Free of the little girl, Conall gently eased into a chair across from Sanne. Her chair was angled towards Godfrid, who remained on his stool, with his back to the front door of the warehouse. "Do you know of anyone who might have wanted to harm your husband?"

Sanne looked rueful. "No! Nobody! He had business rivals, of course. I would tell you if I knew anything at all."

"So you don't know with whom he was meeting last night?" Godfrid asked.

"No, my lord. He said nothing about it to me." As she spoke, her eyes briefly skated away from him before returning to his face.

"Did he seem normal to you?"

"In what way?"

Cait leaned forward, requiring Sanne to turn in her seat to look at her. "I think my lord Godfrid is asking if he was showing unusual emotion. Was he nervous? Excited? Worried?"

Sanne bobbed her chin, finally understanding what they were asking. "He was definitely worried, but he was excited too. He paced around the house for an hour, snapping at the servants, before escorting me to Arno's house. I made an attempt to inquire what was preoccupying him, but he told me that it was business, and I wasn't to concern myself with it."

"And you didn't?" Godfrid said.

She made a noncommittal motion with her head. "As I said, he never told me anything about his business. He didn't think it was something I should be concerned about. The warehouse was his domain, and the household was mine." She scoffed slightly under her breath. "He never talked to me about anything he thought was important." But then she canted her head towards Cait. "Except for you, my lady. With you, he actually came to me, asking for my advice."

Godfrid felt he was finally hearing from the real Sanne. "What did you tell him?"

"That he would be a fool to refuse to bring Lady Caitriona into his household. Leinster rules Dublin, whether or not we like to admit it." Again, Sanne looked at Cait. "I have not commented on the loss of your collar but, of course, I noted it. I hope you won't take offense when I say that I was confounded to learn what your king intended you to do. Please forgive any behavior on my part since your arrival in which you were not treated with the utmost respect."

Cait waved her hand dismissively. "You couldn't give away with word or deed who I was. I took no offense."

Still, Sanne wet her lips, by appearances a little nervous. "And to think Rikard made me ask you to teach Marta to weave!"

Godfrid was pleased to have learned Sanne's daughter's name without having to reveal his ignorance, and Cait smiled. "It was my pleasure, and Marta is a quick learner. You should be very proud." Then she leaned closer and took Sanne's hand. "I realize that this is a painful time, but I would ask that you continue to keep my secret. From now on, I must be only Lord Conall's sister with no connection to your former slave."

Sanne gave a tsk. "You have no need to worry on that score, my lady. What you did is simply too shocking to be believed. It is still astounding to me that your king and your brother allowed it." Then she paused and lowered her voice. "I am not a gossip. Your secret is safe with me."

"Thank you," Cait said. "Please know that while my husband was not murdered, I am also a widow and have sat where you sit now. I am sorry for your loss."

Sanne nodded, appearing to blink back tears, but then she swallowed hard and seemed to regain her equilibrium. "Rikard was gleeful about pulling the wool over Ottar's eyes. I think he hated Ottar almost as much as you do, my lord." She bobbed her head in Godfrid's direction.

Godfrid wasn't pleased to have her speaking of his feelings out loud, even if in safe company, so he changed the subject. "Did he often have meetings late at night at his warehouse?"

"Not to my knowledge, but I often retire before he does. If he went out after I went to sleep, I wouldn't know about it." She gazed away from him again, and her eyes were less focused than before.

"You sleep soundly enough that you don't notice when he comes to bed?" They were skating towards territory that Godfrid found uncomfortable, but with neither Conall nor Cait jumping in, he felt he had no choice but to be the one to continue to ask the questions.

"I sleep with Marta."

Godfrid's parents had always shared a bed, but separate pallets were not an uncommon arrangement for a married couple, especially during the years when a child needed her mother at all hours of the night.

While she'd been speaking to Cait, Sanne appeared to have her attention drawn by something in the back of the warehouse. Godfrid was sitting on her other side, so he couldn't see her face, though he wondered if she knew about the trap door. And then Conall drew her attention to him again. "Rikard must have entertained his business associates in your home with you at his side."

"Of course he did, but I would always retire to my quarters before the serious discussions began."

"Was that also true when you met with Arno and his family?" Godfrid asked.

Sanne nodded. "Arno's wife is older than I am." She was invested enough in the conversation by now that her grief, feigned or otherwise, was put aside. "And he tells her more than my husband told me. Rikard insisted that I had nothing to do with money or trade. Why do you think he took such pains to build his manor where he did? He wanted to keep his family as far away from the docks as possible."

"You said that Rikard escorted you to Arno's house before leaving for the warehouse. Did you not miss him when you returned home later?"

"We never went home. Marta and I were at the coming of age celebration of Arno's thirteen-year-old daughter. You know how those go on all night." She looked at Godfrid for confirmation, and then to Finn, as the other Danes present, since they would understand.

But it was Cait who nodded. "We celebrate for our daughters too. Is it usual for men to attend?"

Sanne shook her head. "Not for the ceremony itself, but very often husbands, fathers, and brothers are part of the event. Arno welcomed Marta and me to his house and then oversaw the roasting of the pig in the yard. I saw him later holding court with the other men at tables set up outside for them."

"And yet, Rikard didn't attend," Godfrid said, not really as a question.

"No." Sanne dabbed at her cheeks with her handkerchief. "After he said goodbye to us at Arno's front door, I never saw him again."

Cait leaned forward and squeezed her shoulder. "Had they a falling out?"

"Not as far as I know. You'll have to ask Arno, of course, but their behavior with each other was the same as always." Then Sanne's expression turned thoughtful. "Still, I'd be surprised if he doesn't tell you that something was different about Rikard these last few weeks."

"Different how?" For the first time, Finn appeared to be paying close attention.

Sanne turned in her seat to look up at him. "He was more tense and snappish with me and Marta. Because he was so determined not to bring his business home, he always put on a serene face when he walked in the door. Of late, that mask had started to slip. But again, I couldn't tell you why or what was bothering him. *Don't worry your pretty head over business matters, my dear.* That's what he said." She snorted. "As if telling me not to worry could somehow stop me from worrying. Knowing what was wrong, no matter how terrible, would have been better."

"Did he give an explanation as to why he wasn't at the celebration?" Godfrid said.

"Business," Sanne said. "Always business."

"What did he tell you about when he would return?" Cait asked. "And what did you do when he didn't?"

"He said the meeting would run late, so I shouldn't plan on seeing him until today. He keeps an office on the upper floor," she gestured towards the back of the warehouse, "where he has a bed. It has a door he can lock, and of course the warehouse is always guarded by his men."

Godfrid nodded. "I noted the room earlier." Perhaps twelve feet in length on a side, the room in question took up the full width of the loft. While a railing ran around the rest of the loft to prevent anyone from falling from the height, the room itself was fully enclosed by walls. "I haven't yet had a moment to enter it."

"He keeps his account books there," Sanne said.

Immediately Finn stopped his prowling and strode off in that direction. Godfrid watched him go with narrowing eyes, and without waiting to be asked, Conall rose to his feet and went after him.

At his departure, Sanne turned to look at Cait. Marta had fallen asleep with her head resting on Cait's shoulder. "I would hope you would speak to your uncle on our behalf. Rikard is dead, but that doesn't mean we don't intend to honor our contracts."

"Is that going to be up to you?" Cait asked.

"I am confident that Finn and I can come to an agreement. My husband did not share his interests with me, but I am a merchant's daughter. I know more about how to manage a warehouse than Finn does." The weeping widow was all but gone, replaced by the confident daughter of Thorfin Ragnarson, Rikard's long-time rival.

But then Sanne spun back to Godfrid. "Unless something has happened with the business? Do you know something I don't?"

Godfrid put a calming hand out to her. "I have heard nothing untoward about Rikard's business. Certainly, the wealth that surrounds you now is still here."

"What about Rikard's gold and silver?" Cait said. "Do you know where he kept it?"

"That I do know. We kept the most valuable items in the treasure chest at home." Again, her eyes strayed towards the back of the warehouse.

It was time to find out why. "Do you know about the vault?"

Sanne's mouth fell open. "You-you know about the vault?"

"We do," Godfrid said. "Rikard showed it to you?"

"I thought he never spoke to you about business?" Cait said.

Sanne sniffed. "Business was one thing, wealth another. With Marta and me as his only heirs, Rikard made sure I knew where his valuables were hidden."

Cait nodded in a somewhat more conciliatory fashion. "Rikard was found dead at the bottom of the stairs."

Sanne's hands clenched into fists. "Was everything taken?"

"Not that we can tell. It was not ransacked like the warehouse," Godfrid said, interested that Sanne seemed far more concerned about Rikard's wealth than the fact that he'd died alone in the dark. "We will need you to come with us and tell us if anything is missing."

"Of course. Now?"

"We might as well." He rose and put out a hand to Sanne to help her to her feet.

Cait had been holding the still sleeping Marta all this time, and now she stood too and carried the girl across the floor, heading towards the stairs to the corner room where Sanne had said Rikard kept a bed.

Sanne watched her go. "Rikard loved his wealth more than anything." She sighed, her expression turning rueful. "Certainly more than he loved Marta and me."

8

Day One

Caitriona

Cait had been walking away from Sanne when she'd overheard her tell Godfrid that her husband hadn't loved her or his daughter as much as he'd loved his wealth. It wasn't Cait's place to reply, since Sanne had been talking to Godfrid, but, to Cait's mind, Sanne's assessment was exactly right. Rikard had been perfectly content to have been no more than mildly fond of his wife, but he had naturally assumed that his wife loved him. In fact, Rikard had taken her entirely for granted.

And after three weeks spent observing the relationship, Cait didn't think she was projecting her own marriage issues onto Sanne either. Like Sanne, Cait had been married to a much older man, one who enjoyed having a young wife on his arm, so she knew both what to look for and what it felt like. Sanne's role had been to appear beautiful at all times, with perfect skin and the softest hands Cait had ever seen on a woman, without even a needle pinprick or calluses from handling the tight threads of the loom or the shuttle.

Unusually, she did no chores, not even teaching her daughter to weave. That task had been delegated most recently to Cait. And while Sanne claimed to have slept on a separate pallet from her husband so she could take care of her daughter, Cait knew for a fact that it was Marta's nanny, a young slave named Tilda, who slept with the girl and attended to her needs most nights. There was a reason Marta had come willingly to Cait: she was used to being ignored by her mother.

Cait hadn't given her husband a child, but outside of that fact, her marriage hadn't been so different from Sanne's. It had been arranged by her uncle in an attempt to forge ties with the neighboring kingdom of Munster. She and Niall been married for eight years, which was approximately seven years and eleven months longer than Cait would have preferred. His death had freed her to be her own woman—or at least given her the courage to fight for her right to be one.

At the time of the betrothal, Cait had not protested her marriage. As the daughter of a sister to the king, she had known her duty, and Niall had been a handsome man, noble, respected, and wealthy. Unfortunately, Niall had not turned out to be the man of her dreams, and she couldn't blame her uncle and father for not knowing about Niall's gambling and womanizing ways. As far as Cait was aware, no whisper of his vices had come to her family before the wedding. Conall had made inquiries too, but it may be that Niall's people were so pleased to learn of her coming to his lands that they'd outright lied about his proclivities.

Regardless, her marriage hadn't been a success, made worse by the fact that she hadn't conceived a child within the first year—or ever. Like Rikard with Sanne, over time, Niall became indifferent to her. She had become akin to an item on display for sale more than a lifelong companion, and as awful a person as it made her, she couldn't deny that his death in a riding accident hadn't come too soon.

Before her sojourn in Dublin, her uncle had suggested a new marriage for her—to Donnell, one of the princes of Connaught. Cait had objected strongly, never mind that Donnell was the heir to the throne of not only Connaught but of the High King of Ireland. As a widow, refusal was her prerogative under Brehon law, though it was rarely invoked within a royal family, where every daughter *and* son was raised to understand the importance of alliance. Cait didn't want to marry Donnell. She didn't want to marry *anyone*.

Conall had supported her decision, in part, she suspected, out of guilt for making such a terrible mistake with Niall the first time around. She was aware, however, that her uncle hadn't given up on the idea, and she suspected he'd agreed to her becoming a spy to humor her on the way to softening her defenses. The irony was that she'd felt less like a slave in Dublin than she had in Imokilly.

Cait laid Marta down on the bed in the office. Before today, she had only ever stood in the doorway to speak to Rikard. It had been the first place she'd gone after the alarm had been raised by the pool of blood, now known to be wine. She'd been worried about what might have been taken by the intruder, who'd pulled everything off the shelves and cleared the table of documents, but she didn't know enough about what the office had contained in the first place to tell if anything was missing. The account books were still there, now stacked in a pile by Conall and Finn, who were leaving the room as she arrived with Marta.

She returned to the main floor to find the others gathered around the open trapdoor. In one of Cait's last acts as a slave, while the men had been conferencing with Ottar, she had wiped up the last of the wine, so they were able to stand at the top of the stairs without marring their shoes. Still, she hadn't chosen to do anything about the wine on the stairs, since that would have necessitated pulling open the trapdoor and entering the vault again. While she was very curious about what Rikard had stored down there, the existence of the vault was still not common knowledge, and she hadn't wanted to explain to anyone what she was doing.

When Cait approached, Sanne was staring down at the smeared wine. Evidently impatient with her hesitation, Finn went down the steps ahead of her.

"It's only wine," Cait whispered in her ear. "In death, your husband showed no sign of injury." It still remained to be seen whether or not that was entirely true, but it was close enough for Cait's purposes. Whatever had been done to him, his death hadn't been a result of stabbing.

Godfrid also noticed Sanne's reluctance—and guessed the reason for it—because he began rummaging through a pile of scattered goods near the stairs. He came up with an armful of hemp sacking, which he proceeded to lay on the steps over the wine spots. "Perhaps this will help."

Cait watched him work, acknowledging how rare it was for a man of Godfrid's station to be so casual about service to others. He'd had an idea, and he'd implemented it. While that might not be remarkable in and of itself, he'd solved the problem himself rather than asking a servant to fetch the sacking and do it for him. He was so sure of himself—so sure that he was worthy—that he didn't need to prove anything to anyone. She honestly had never seen that before from any nobleman—maybe even any man—except her brother.

Brushing away further noises of concern on Cait's part, Sanne descended the steps and stood on the floor of Rikard's vault—*her* vault—shivering.

Cait followed and moved off the steps to stand where Rikard had written Godfrid's name, in case some sign of the lettering remained. She didn't mention that Sanne herself was standing where Rikard had died. The vault was so small that there was no way to avoid the spot.

Finn stood a few feet away. "Until today, I'd forgotten this was here. After we built it, my father never let me enter it again."

"Why not?" Godfrid lifted the lantern he held to more fully light the room.

"He was grooming my older brother to take over the business after him, not me. I didn't mind, since a trader was the last thing I wanted to be."

Godfrid laughed under his breath. "You wanted to go *a Viking.*"

"I did." Finn laughed back. "It's in our blood, is it not?" Then his face fell, and his voice turned sad. "Our intent was to sail as far west as Iceland. While the seas can be very dangerous between here and there, the Icelanders are always short on supplies and profits are great." Finn lifted one shoulder in an apologetic shrug. "Once in Iceland, I decided to strike out on my own. I have no excuse for it except I was young and criminally foolish. I left my brother in charge of the ship and our men and joined another crew sailing west."

"To Vinland?" Godfrid actually gasped the words.

At first Cait thought he was horrified, but then she realized it was excitement, not fear, she was hearing in his voice. Three weeks in Dublin was long enough to realize that what she'd heard growing up about Danes was true: it was every Dane's dream to sail west to the horizon. If there be dragons, so be it. Better to have seen a dragon and died in the attempt to defeat it than not to have sailed west at all. As Finn had said, going *a Viking* was in their blood.

She herself had no desire to leave Ireland. No land could be more beautiful—and that wasn't just her opinion. Travelers from Europe and beyond to her uncle's court claimed the same.

But Godfrid's expression had turned rueful. "I gather things did not go well after that?"

"We made it as far as Greenland, but the weather was very bad, and the seas froze solid. We spent a terrible winter on that lonely shore and almost died." He looked at Sanne and Cait. "Greenland isn't green, you see. And although the sea ice melted eventually, our boat had been damaged in one of the winter storms. We tried three times to sail back to Iceland, but each time we were forced to turn back because our ship wasn't seaworthy. There are no trees in Greenland with which to repair it.

"Finally, a ship arrived from Vinland on its way home, and those of us who still lived were able to barter our way on board. We arrived in Iceland to find my brother had fallen ill and died within weeks of my initial departure. I can't help but think that, had I stayed, he might have turned for home and been spared the sickness that swept through Reykjavik."

"Whether a man lives or dies is in the hands of God. You know that." Though as Godfrid spoke, he retained the faraway look in his eyes from his visions of Vinland.

Sanne appeared disinterested in her stepson's account and asked no questions of him nor professed her sympathy for the loss of his brother, who was also her elder stepson. While he'd been speaking, she'd been slowly spinning on one heel, inspecting the contents of the room.

Cait put a hand on her arm to get her attention. "Is anything missing?"

Sanne shook her head. "I haven't been down here in several months, but nothing looks disturbed to me. What about you, Finn?"

Finn shook himself. "As I said, I was never allowed down here. Treasure chests could be missing, and I wouldn't know it."

"If chests were missing, there would be an outline of where they'd stood in the dirt." Godfrid pursed his lips as he studied the young man. "You do realize that everything that was your father's is yours by right now, providing you make dispensation for Sanne and Marta and pay the proper tithe to Ottar."

"Which of course I will do." Finn bowed in Sanne's direction. "My father's house is your home for as long as you choose to live in it. Tell me what you need or what you would like, and I will provide it."

Sanne gazed at him, and Cait saw the moment she realized that she was truly a free woman. As when Cait had thrown off her mantle of slave girl, Sanne's shoulders straightened and her chin came up. "Thank you, Finn. After your father's funeral, I think I would like to return to the house in Wexford with Marta, but perhaps I could make a firm decision later."

"Of course," Finn said. "As I said, whatever you need."

Sanne nodded and then climbed the stairs to reenter the warehouse proper. Cait glanced upwards in time to see a last flash of Sanne's cloak as she disappeared, and then she heard the thump of her footsteps as she climbed the stairs to the office where Marta slept.

Conall waited until she was out of sight and then turned back to Finn. "What about Arno? Will you continue the partnership with him?"

"I left my desire for seafaring in Greenland. This business is my father's legacy, and I will not abandon it. I will do whatever I have to do." Finn made an impatient gesture with one hand. "If you don't mind, I will do an accounting of what is here later." He left the vault, taking the stairs two at a time as if he couldn't wait to leave it. Cait couldn't blame him, since for him the vault must have the smell of death about it. A moment later, Cait could hear him greeting Sanne and Marta, who had come down from the loft and were leaving too.

Conall waited until the main door slammed shut. "Does anyone else find it odd that he would leave us here unattended?"

"He appears to trust us," Godfrid said.

"Well, he shouldn't." Conall looked from one to the other. "You two stay here. This is our chance to search the vault. Maybe something here will tell us why Rikard died, and also what he hid. Leave Finn to me."

9

Day One

Conall

Even after living in Dublin for a year, Conall was still not entirely comfortable with the stares he garnered every time he walked the streets of Dublin alone. He was determined never to show vulnerability, however, and to that end, on the way out of the warehouse, he snagged an apple from a basket that was waiting to be taken to the market, and sauntered as casually as possible after Finn.

Learning Danish had helped in his comprehension of what made the people behave as they did, but until Conall had encompassed the importance Danish men placed on strength and bravado, the very attributes he himself was affecting today, true understanding had eluded him. The crowning of Ottar as ruler of Dublin was a perfect example.

Only six years ago, Ottar, as the son of the King of Man, had brought an army to Dublin in support of Torcall and to fight against, as usual, the men of Brega and their allies. Ottar had been instrumental in the victory, and with Torcall an old and ill man, the people of Dublin had invited Ottar to become co-ruler with him. What only a handful of people knew, Godfrid among them, was that, in order to gain the throne, Ottar had bribed a faction of Dublin's merchants. Six years on, he still had their loyalty, in large part because he'd threatened to expose them if they wavered. Rikard had been among the bribed, as had Arno and Thorfin, Sanne's father.

The former king Torcall hadn't realized how much support he'd lost and the precarious position he was in until it was too late. Brodar and Godfrid had been younger and less experienced then, unable to protect their father and salvage his throne. Both sons had learned to be less trusting and more underhanded since then. While Brodar would never possess Ottar's cunning, he had a practical mind and a genuine gift for strategy. While the Danish army had defeated the men of Brega under Ottar's leadership, the victory had been due more to greater overall numbers than any particular genius on Ottar's part. These days, Ottar's rule had degenerated to the point that the king appeared to have only sycophants.

Upon leaving the warehouse, Finn should have escorted Sanne and Marta to Rikard's house—his own house now—but instead, he turned in the opposite direction, towards the docks. That was a far more interesting place for him to be going, and Conall found himself more than a little curious as to what this prodigal son would do next.

First Finn had to pass through the gate that guarded the river entrance to the city. According to Holm, the gates had been closed, but either that order was being ignored or someone had decided that it was too much of a hindrance to commerce to actually have to open and close the gate whenever anyone wanted to pass through it. Regardless, the dock gate was open, and people were moving in and out of it, most with no more than a wave of a hand in acknowledgement to the guard.

While Rikard's warehouse was inside the city walls that ran along the course of the Liffey, the docks, by necessity, were outside the palisade. Finn strode through the gatehouse at a fairly rapid clip, raising a hand, as others had done, to the guard, who merely nodded and waved him through.

Conall's eyes narrowed to realize that, despite Finn's two-year absence, already the guard at the gate knew him. Then again, his resurrection, along with Rikard's death, would be all over Dublin by now, moving from house to house like a fire from one thatched roof to another.

Still frowning, Conall paused a moment, not wanting to appear to be following Finn, and thus was forced to wait a few beats until several more men had gone in and out of the gate. Then he tossed his apple into a nearby pigpen, straightened his shoulders, and walked with high head under the archway.

The soldier on guard duty bowed at his approach. Conall was glad to be recognized as himself rather than Fergus the sailor, who'd been in and out of the gate a hundred times in the last three weeks. Danes had red hair often enough that Conall didn't stand out in a crowd, and he'd attempted to improve on his chances of not being recognized by growing a beard and cutting his hair short. He'd then hid his hair under a woolen cap, which he'd rarely taken off, even to sleep. Enough time had passed since then that his hair had grown a little. Coupled with being again clean-shaven, he was looking more like the ambassador from Leinster should.

Conall had surprised his uncle when he'd taken on the ambassadorship of Dublin. It was outside his former scope of activities. But after his sojourn in Wales, though Conall would never admit this to anyone, he had been skittish. Being captured, beaten, and imprisoned had shattered his confidence, and he had known within himself that he couldn't undertake another assignment like that one until he made himself whole again.

Disguising himself as a seafarer had been a promising first step, and he could honestly say that he'd enjoyed his time on Dublin's docks. If nothing else, the hard labor had been good for him. He was past forty now, a time when many men went into decline. He had almost died in Shrewsbury, and he had found the thought not to his liking. He wasn't ready to sit before the fire like an old man, to drink mead and argue.

Once through the gate, Conall paused, his eyes questing for Finn. He finally spied him walking west along the waterfront, wending his way among dockworkers and their goods.

Conall watched for a moment, and then he waved at the guard, whom he could still see underneath the gatehouse, beckoning him to come to him. When the man obeyed, Conall pointed ahead to the figure of Finn and, feigning ignorance, asked, "Who is that man who walks ahead of me?"

The guard answered immediately. "My lord, that is Finn, returned from Iceland after being thought dead these last two years. Have you not heard? He is the son of Rikard the Merchant, who died today."

"That's Finn? He is younger than I imagined. When did he arrive in Dublin?"

"Only this morning, my lord." The guard gestured towards a ship moored at the far end of the wharf. It appeared Finn was heading straight for it. "That is the ship he came on. There has been much joy among the sailing folk today. More than one husband was restored to his wife, though I'm sorry that Rikard died before he was able to see his son."

"Are you certain of the timing? It's such a tragedy if you're right."

The guard blinked at the question, and when he spoke next, he drew out his words, enunciating them carefully, as one does when trying to convey an idea to someone with a poor grasp of one's language. "I am sure."

Conall patted the man on the shoulder. "Thank you for the information."

The guard looked slightly mollified. "My pleasure, my lord."

The guard went back to his post, and Conall continued along the dockside after Finn. The first Danish adventurers to Ireland had simply pulled their boats up the bank to moor them, but with prosperity and growth, an actual wharf had been built, with pilings driven deep into the riverbed. Today, the dock stretched nearly the entire width of the city from west to east.

Unfortunately, a hundred years or more after the original construction, the dock was not being properly maintained. Conall had just spent three weeks in and around the dockside and had made an inventory of every snapped off piling and rotted support. Dublin needed a new wharf, and although Ottar had sworn to invest in its construction, the work had not started. Fortunately, that neglect hadn't extended to the palisade wall, which was rebuilt every few years because, if it wasn't, the supporting timbers that had been placed deep in the soil of the riverbank would rot away and the wall would fall.

All things being equal, as a man of Leinster, Conall was in favor of maintaining as weak a king in Dublin as possible, but instead he found himself irritated with Ottar's failure to keep his promises, which was only one of many objectionable qualities. He was also a blowhard and had an eye for other men's wives. His rule seemed to consist of outsized promises that never came to pass, and he promoted men beyond their capacity, men such as Holm, caring more for their personal loyalty than their integrity or ability to do the job they'd been set. And if all that weren't bad enough, when things went wrong, it was never his fault, never because of his actions or his failure to act.

And yet, even with all that, he could have been forgiven if the prosperity and increased wealth he'd promised to bring to Dublin had ever come to pass. But it had not, despite his sacking

Kells several times and following Prince Cadwaladr to Anglesey. Ottar still didn't understand that wealth didn't come from a single raid or adventure anymore. It was made day by day, week by week, by men working towards a common goal.

It was because of Ottar's lack of vision that Conall had wished for some time, even before his appointment as Dublin's ambassador, that his king would support Brodar more openly. Though Diarmait had been angry for some time about his loss of revenue from Dublin, up until now, he had accepted Ottar's excuses. To Conall's mind, it was long past time Ottar was held accountable for his lack of stewardship.

Continuing along the dockside, Conall stopped within hailing distance of Finn's ship, observing Finn as he'd stopped to speak to the man in the bow. The conversation didn't last long, and Conall was able to hear only bits and pieces of Finn giving the man an outline of the events of the last hours. After the man bent his head to express his sorrow at Finn's loss, Finn moved on down the wharf, greeting numerous men along the way, with his ultimate destination the main door of the warehouse of Thorfin Ragnarson, Sanne's father.

The ground in Rikard's vault had been dry, even with all the rain they'd had this spring. But this warehouse was on the wharf, where the land was saturated with water much of the year. Thorfin had taken the danger into account and put the main floor of his warehouse on stilts. It was a recent construction too, built over the remains of what had once been a barracks to hold slaves before auction. These days, the auction house had fallen into disrepair as well, as not only Rikard but most other merchants in Dublin had ceased to buy and sell slaves in any kind of quantity.

Before pulling the door wide, Finn looked left and right, in a way that implied he was worried someone was watching him. Conall ducked behind a large crate, hoping that he'd hidden in time. Then, after a moment, he stood on his toes to look over the top of the crate, to find that Finn had disappeared.

"May I help you, my lord?"

Conall spun around at the thick Welsh accent and then smiled at the squat, bow-legged sailor standing before him. "You are of Gwynedd?"

"Born and bred." The man tugged his forelock. "Excuse me for speaking out of turn, my lord, but haven't I seen you in the company of our Prince Hywel?"

Conall laughed. "You have." He paused, hope rising in his chest. "Is he here?"

"No, my lord. When I left, he was occupying the palace at Llanfaes."

Conall gestured to Thorfin's warehouse. "The man who just entered. Have you seen him before?"

"Yes, my lord," the Welshman answered immediately. "That's Finn, heir to Rikard, who died today."

"Is that so? When did Finn arrive in Dublin?"

"Just this morning, just as his father was dying, it seems." He lifted his chin to point at Finn's ship. "I was asleep when he docked, but I heard them come in. Just before dawn, it was."

The information confirmed what Conall had already heard. It was a relief, really, to know that Finn could have had nothing to do with his father's death. The murder of a father by a son would have torn Dublin society apart.

After dismissing the sailor, with a request that when he returned to Llanfaes he give Prince Hywel his greetings, Conall stared at the door to Thorfin's warehouse. He very much wanted to know what was happening inside. Finn hadn't yet visited his father's body, nor even asked where it was. His comforting of Sanne had been perfunctory at best and, as far as Conall knew, he hadn't even been to his father's house. And despite assuring Godfrid that he would continue his alliance with Arno, he was currently visiting the warehouse of Sanne's father, who also happened to be his greatest business rival.

There could easily be a good explanation for everything Finn had done, but Conall didn't know what it was. Since he couldn't barge into Thorfin's warehouse and demand answers—at least not yet—he decided to return to Rikard's warehouse to discover what Godfrid and Cait had found in the vault.

Other than each other.

Conall grinned.

10

Day One
Godfrid

"Is this how it was for you after your husband died?"

Cait looked over at Godfrid, apparently startled by the question. They were the only two people left in the warehouse, other than Godfrid's own guards, who remained at their posts, one at each entrance. "Are you wondering if I am comparing my experience to Sanne's?"

He nodded. They'd known each other for only a few hours, so he had no right to a serious answer, but he was hoping for it anyway.

She frowned as she thought about what to say. "Even had I loved Niall, I think I would have felt freed at his death. Among my people, no woman can be forced to marry, but at the time, I was too young to understand what I might gain by refusing. I could only see what I'd lose. What was never explained to me, because my uncle didn't want me to understand, was that I had an obligation to myself and to my future husband to say no."

"You didn't want to displease your family. It would have felt like a betrayal." Godfrid canted his head. "We all feel that way when we are young." He paused. "So you never loved him?"

"He gave me no reason to love him. My sense is that Sanne felt the same about Rikard. He treated her with a kind of detached benevolence, but she was no more than an appendage to him. I found that a hard way to live, tied to a man who cared nothing for who I was inside." She gave a low laugh. "I have no idea why I'm telling you this. I haven't said this to anyone."

Godfrid didn't know why either, but he wasn't going to complain. "It is easier for men. If we want to avoid family entanglements, we go to sea, and it looks like adventure. Just ask Finn."

Cait smiled. "I see why my brother likes you. At first, I thought you were just another member of his collection."

"His collection?" Godfrid wondered if he should be offended.

She put out a hand to him in a gesture of appeasement. "He likes people who are different from him. Traveling to strange places and meeting new people—and making friends—that's what he does."

"I like that too."

"Apparently, so do I." She smiled before adding, "The fact that I feel a kinship with Sanne doesn't mean I'm certain she didn't sneak out of the party and kill her husband. Dublin isn't so large a city that the warehouse is too far from Arno's manor house for her to have made it there and back. Any absence could have been explained by a long trip to the latrine."

"You told me yourself that Rikard cleared everyone out of the warehouse. He was meeting someone not his wife." Godfrid took in a breath and let it out. "Speculation is fine, but we should keep it to a minimum. And we should work hard not to assume anything."

"Is that what Gareth the Welshman says?"

Godfrid laughed. "I suppose he does."

"Well, he's wrong."

Godfrid guffawed, but then looked hard at her. "Why do you say that?"

"We speculate all the time, as we should." Cait pursed her lips as Godfrid continued to gaze at her. "And we are certainly assuming a great number of things, all of which are very sensible."

"For example?" Godfrid's tone was amused and curious rather than offended, which encouraged Cait to go on.

"For example, we are assuming Rikard was killed for a reason, not by chance. We are assuming his death has something to do with his business or his spying. We are assuming that the little girl whose family lives down the street from the warehouse is not the murderer."

Godfrid laughed again. "You are absolutely right, and by way of our assumptions, I am beginning to wonder if Rikard's death itself was unintended. He could have been in the vault of his own accord and merely died. He was an old man. Perhaps his heart gave out."

"So not murder." Cait nodded. "That doesn't mean there was no crime."

"Another assumption." Godfrid canted his head. "I grant your point."

Cait blushed. "I don't mean to offend. Conall speaks very highly of Gareth's abilities."

"For good reason. And I believe Gareth's point in telling us not to assume was to emphasize the danger in allowing one's assumptions to guide the investigation too soon, excluding possible paths of inquiry prematurely."

"And I grant that point."

With a new camaraderie, they began to move about the room, lifting lids and prying into the various crates and chests, particularly the one to which Rikard had been pointing. It was locked, and Godfrid pulled out the ring of keys to find the one that opened it. Then the main door banged, and they both jumped. Someone taking long strides crossed the floor, and then Conall appeared at the top of the stairs.

At the sight of them with their hands in Rikard's things, he grinned. "Good. That's the chest he was pointing to, Cait."

As usual, she bristled slightly at his tone. "That's why we opened it first, but all I can see are bolts of silk. They're lovely, but they don't convey treachery to me."

Conall came down the steps. "We need to think harder about why Rikard was found down here, but with nothing missing."

"As far as we know nothing was missing," Cait pointed out. "If the item was small, the men who put him here could have taken it, and nobody but Rikard would have been the wiser."

"And since he's dead, he can tell us nothing," Godfrid said.

"It all comes back to him writing your name." Cait looked up at Godfrid. "Let's focus on that. There has to be something here." She began to remove the bolts of fabric from the trunk, handing them to Godfrid one at a time to create a large stack in his arms, until she finally exposed the wooden bottom. She leaned forward. "That's not right."

Godfrid set the bolts on top of a nearby trunk and peered with her. The bottom plank of the trunk wasn't fitted correctly in the trunk's frame.

Meanwhile, Conall measured the depth of the trunk's interior and compared it to the exterior. "It's a false bottom."

"One that someone didn't take the time to seat properly." His heart beating a little faster, Godfrid got his fingers underneath the uneven edge. He wiggled it until the whole plank broke free, revealing a hidden compartment containing books and papers.

Cait waved a hand at her brother. "Close the trapdoor! We don't want anyone coming upon us unaware."

Conall bounded up the steps and pulled the trapdoor closed, plunging them into near darkness. Godfrid grabbed the lantern he'd brought and set it on a hook conveniently located on the wall above the trunk, likely for that very purpose. No light came through the ceiling to shine on them, making him think that their light in the vault could not be seen inside the warehouse proper, and they could truly continue in secret.

Cait bent forward with a frown. "I would have said that aged account books and papers aren't a very exciting find, but the very fact that they're hidden implies they're important."

Conall picked up one of the books and opened it to somewhere in the middle. "These aren't account books, Cait." His hand actually trembled as he set down the first book and picked up another. "They're ancient texts."

Cait looked over his shoulder and wrinkled her nose. "I knew I should have paid closer attention when you tried to teach me Latin."

Conall looked at Godfrid. "Could Rikard read it?"

"Yes. His uncle was a priest, and besides, he needed to be able to read it in order to communicate with traders and suppliers from other countries. Arno and Thorfin read Latin too." Godfrid poked his nose between them, scanning the writing. "It's the four gospels. Look at those illustrations!"

Some years ago, Godfrid had been pleased to restore the Book of Kells to the men of Brega as a peace offering. Had he known how quickly they would break the peace again—and kill his father—he might have kept it. Then again, he'd made a promise to Gareth's abbess friend, and that wasn't something he would ever violate.

"Could these have been what the thieves wanted?" Cait asked. "Books?"

"They are worth their weight in gold to the right buyer." Conall gently put the one he held back in the trunk and picked up a paper scroll. Once he unrolled it, he held it at arm's length before he could begin reading. Like most men Conall's age, it seemed his eyes were going. But then a moment later, his skin paled under his freckles.

"I may have found what we're looking for." Conall moved so Godfrid could look over his shoulder at what was written on the paper.

Godfrid scanned the Latin. "It can't—it can't mean what it says."

Conall looked up at him. "It's a contract for your brother's death."

Cait gasped. "Ordered by whom?"

"Ottar's seal is at the bottom," Godfrid said, "and I recognize the hand of his skald, Sturla."

Godfrid could sense the hatred Ottar felt for Brodar radiating from the document. It wasn't just that they were rivals for the throne. Brodar had an air about him, an authority, that couldn't be bought or traded for. For all that Ottar had grown up as the son of the King of Man, he didn't have that innate confidence, and he hated the feeling of inferiority.

Not that he was alone in that. Most men hated to feel inferior. More than that, they feared it, and to Godfrid's mind, it was fear more than anything else that made Ottar a bad king. Too afraid to move forward or back, he did nothing. Certainly he didn't have the *muinin*, the confidence, to confront either Brodar or Godfrid directly.

The secrecy surrounding the document, however, was self-evident. If Brodar died of unnatural causes, his followers would be very suspicious, and who was to say that the uneasy peace in Dublin wouldn't devolve into civil war. The same fear tied Brodar's hands as well, since outright hostilities—or outright murder, as the case might be—would bring down upon Dublin the wrath of King Diarmait, despite his assurances of neutrality. Godfrid believed his people could withstand any attack from Leinster, but once a battle was engaged, nobody could predict the outcome with certainty.

Conall began rolling up the paper with rapid movements. "Where is your brother now?"

"At his manor house five miles southwest of Dublin. His wife just gave birth to his first son after four daughters."

Conall tucked the scroll inside his jacket. "The fact that the scroll is here rather than out in the world gives me hope that we have a little time. I will ride immediately to warn him."

"No, Conall." Cait put out a hand to her brother. "Neither you nor Godfrid can leave Dublin. We can't give Ottar any indication in word or deed that we know about this. It should be me who goes."

"I am not sending you out into the countryside on your own, and you should know better than to ask," Conall shot back.

"Someone needs to watch Godfrid's back," Cait said. "If Ottar has called for Brodar's death, an order for Godfrid's might not be far behind."

Godfrid put a hand on her shoulder. "My men can protect me. Besides which, I am inclined to think that if I had a price on my head, I would know it."

Conall grunted. "Maybe. At the very least, this explains why Ottar assigned you to this investigation. He wanted to give you something to do, to distract you, so you wouldn't be paying attention to what he was up to. Perhaps that's why I'm here too. Maybe he manipulated me instead of the other way around."

"All the more reason to hurry before he begins to wonder what happened to the death warrant," Godfrid said. "What should I tell Ottar or Holm when they ask where you've gone?"

"Tell them I am pursuing a new lead, as Gareth might say. If pressed, say that you feel uncomfortable disclosing any information that might incriminate innocent parties. We have the upper hand now. We have to be smart about how to proceed."

Godfrid ground his teeth, frustrated with his inability to be in two places at once.

But Cait shook her head again. "If you must say something, tell Ottar we have reason to believe the culprit was Irish, and that we have tracked him out of the city. That should please him."

Godfrid felt a little better too. "We got lucky and caught a break—"

He broke off as footsteps sounded above them, followed by Jon's voice as he lied with admirable aplomb. "Pardon me, my lord, I must have been mistaken. I could have sworn they were here, but since they're not, I couldn't tell you where they've gone."

"Isn't it your job to watch over your master?"

Godfrid put a finger to his lips, recognizing the voice that replied. The Danes didn't have music in their blood like the Welsh, but when Sturla's deep voice bellowed out the sagas in the hall at night, he could make grown men weep.

"I am tasked with guarding the warehouse today, my lord. As always, Prince Godfrid does as he pleases."

Sturla scoffed, but he couldn't argue in the face of Jon's relentless politeness. "Young Finn came to see me earlier today and asked that I look over a trading agreement. Do you know where I might find it?"

"I apologize, my lord. I don't know anything about that."

Godfrid made a mental note to increase Jon's pay. This degree of loyalty and intelligence couldn't be replaced and needed to be rewarded.

Sturla's grumble of disapproval was audible. "Have you seen Finn about?"

"I'm sorry, my lord. I don't know where Finn is either. Perhaps Rikard's partner, Arno, could be of service? He would know far more about what you're asking than I."

Sturla grumbled something again, and then his boots paced away across the floor. The bang of the front door closing with more force than was strictly necessary reverberated all the way down into the vault.

A few moments after that, a knock came on the trapdoor. "He's gone, my lord. If you wish, you can come out."

Godfrid looked at his friends. "At this moment, we are one step ahead of Ottar, but if we are to stay that way, we need to behave as if everything is normal."

Cait sent him an admiring smile. "Turn Ottar's plan on its head, you mean?"

Godfrid looked at her, puzzled. "What do you mean?"

"We guessed that one reason Ottar assigned you to the investigation was to keep you occupied over here while he was busy conniving over there." She gave a saucy laugh. "Now we will do the same to him."

11

Day One

Caitriona

"You have insulted me for the last time!" Godfrid's face was red as he bellowed the words into Conall's face.

"They're only insults if they're not true." Conall laughed snidely before turning on his heel and stalking away up the street.

Godfrid watched Conall go, even making an obscene gesture at his retreating back, and then he reentered Rikard's warehouse. The argument had taken place on the front stoop and had been short but vicious. The two men had every expectation that news of it would spread rapidly around Dublin.

Now, Godfrid took a moment to rest the back of his head against the wall. "How did we do?"

"Well enough." Cait poked her head into the street and looked left and right before pulling back inside. "Plenty of people saw that. I confess that at times your hostility towards each other makes me uncomfortable, but I can also see why you two enjoy it so much."

"You're not alone. It makes everyone uncomfortable. That's why we do it." Godfrid straightened from his position against the wall and held out his arm to her. "After a year of it, nobody has any doubt that we hate each other."

"Thus, when you're seen in public, everyone leaves you alone, just like Holm and his men did." Cait took his arm. "It's very clever."

Godfrid made a face. "Maybe too clever."

"Why is that?"

They exited the building and started up the street. "I'm now escorting you in full view of all of Dublin. Everyone knows Conall isn't going to like that."

Cait laughed and tossed her hair, well aware of the furtive looks they were already garnering. "What he doesn't know won't hurt him."

Godfrid grinned. "And you have just assured that it will be the first thing someone tells him when he gets back."

Cait sniffed, still play-acting. "He believes he has the right to tell me what to do."

"Most brothers would say the same." Godfrid spoke lightly too, but another glance at his face showed a furrow of concern between his brows.

Cait let out a sigh. "Conall hasn't told you everything yet, by the way, and before this goes any further, I think I should."

She could sense a stiffening in his shoulders. "What do you mean?"

"These messages that passed through Ottar's hands included the latest word from Denmark."

She was right about the stiffening, which became more pronounced. "Denmark wouldn't interfere in Dublin on Ottar's behalf."

Cait raised her eyebrows. "You say that with certainty, but can you really be so sure? Everyone assumes the Danish king won't interfere because he never has. That isn't to say that one of the current pretenders to the throne wouldn't use Dublin as a base of power if Ottar convinced him of its advantages. The Welsh kings of Gwynedd have done it more than once. Why not Danish ones, whose blood ties, if anything, are stronger?"

Just as in Dublin, the throne of Denmark was currently under dispute by two men, Knut Magnussen and Sven Ericson. As in Ireland, among the Danes, while a king's son was a natural candidate for the throne, his right to rule was by no means a given. He had to be elected, chosen by his peers over other worthy rivals. That was why—more than victory in battle over Ottar, though, of course, a crown could be achieved that way too—the greatest concern for Godfrid's brother was to win the support of the leading men of Dublin.

"Which of the two claimants are we talking about?" Godfrid asked.

"Knut."

Godfrid scoffed. "Ottar is a fool if he thinks that idiot will save him from my brother and me. After Knut helps Ottar throw off the yoke of Leinster, what's to keep him from continuing as the King of Dublin, especially if there is wealth to be made here and Sven is in the ascendancy there?"

Cait made a noncommittal motion with her head. "Conall and I suspect that the bargain Ottar seeks ensures that he will keep control of Dublin once Knut achieves his goals in Denmark. Ottar is already a client king to Leinster, and I imagine he thinks it would be better to serve Denmark."

"It is farther away, I'll say that about it." Godfrid rubbed his chin. "Perhaps when King Diarmait learns what Ottar is plotting with Denmark, he might care a little more about which side gains the upper hand in Dublin?"

"You don't want that. Really you don't."

"Why not?"

"He, himself, might invade."

"He doesn't have the strength, and he knows it, not against our fighting men."

Cait stopped and put a hand on Godfrid's arm. It was more than a year since her husband died, making Cait well out of the mourning period, but it was still odd to find herself with a man who was not her husband or brother. "I don't want to argue with you, but the Irish perspective is different. You Danes have only ever had a foothold in Ireland. If we Irish had ever managed to unite against you, you wouldn't have lasted as long as you have. Our constant infighting is the reason you survive."

"The high king would not like to hear you say that," Godfrid said dryly, starting to walk again, more jauntily than before. "And I don't see the animosity and fighting among Irish clans stopping any time soon."

Before Cait had traveled to Dublin, Conall had laid out for her the current relationship between Brodar and Ottar and the stakes in their underlying tug of war. Becoming King of Dublin took wealth and men. Ottar and Torcall had initially shared the kingship because their factions had been evenly apportioned. With Torcall's death, some of Torcall's men had gone over to Ottar's side, preferring a man they knew to an untested one like Brodar, on top of being paid to defect, which is where Rikard came in.

Recently, Brodar had been working with Rikard to use his wealth and influence on his fellow merchants to encourage them to stand up to Ottar and come back to Brodar's side. While the simplest action Brodar could have taken would have been to assassinate Ottar, Brodar hadn't done it because he knew it would start his rule on shaky ground. To Cait's mind, to have done so would have been expedient and very Irish. Somehow, though they would deny it strenuously, the mighty Danes, who'd lived for seafaring and battle and confrontation, had become money-counters, fighting over coins.

Of course, her people had always thought with brawn instead of brain, which was why they remained constantly at each other's throats. It took only a few taunts and insults for an Irishman from Connaught to rip apart one from Leinster. As she'd said to Godfrid, that tendency to fight amongst themselves was what had allowed the Danes to gain a foothold in Ireland in the first place. It was why Ireland desperately needed a strong high king at all times.

For now, Dublin was back under Irish control, but that wasn't to say her people had learned their lesson. They were just as argumentative as they'd been hundreds of years earlier when the Danes had pitted one clan against another in order to carve out Dublin, Waterford, and Wexford for themselves. Cait didn't think her people were any better prepared for the next invasion, especially if the invader was more disciplined or numerous than the Danes.

While Cait was relieved Godfrid hadn't taken offense at anything she'd said, she couldn't explain his cheerful mood. "What is making you so happy all of a sudden?"

"It is a sunny day, I have a beautiful and intelligent woman at my side, and I have just learned that Ottar is conspiring with Knut of Denmark."

"And that makes you happy?" Cait had to do a skipping step to align her gait with Godfrid's. When she had been Niall's wife, she would spend two hours a day at most at her loom and the rest on her appearance, whereas in Dublin, she'd spent three solid weeks working in the darkness of Rikard's warehouse. She herself wasn't displeased to be outside, walking beside such a handsome and intelligent man, and she straightened her shoulders a little more.

He slowed his headlong motion to accommodate her shorter legs. "I can see now why Ottar needed to use Rikard as a go-between. If any of his allies knew of his plans, he might have fewer allies." He paused. "Do you have proof of what you've told me?"

Cait shook her head. "The messenger from Denmark refused to put anything in writing. That was a week ago, and Rikard and I were getting along well enough by then that I was hidden behind a curtain when he met with him."

"Which begs the question yet again why he didn't hide you behind a curtain last night."

Cait shook her head. "I don't know."

"Or even better, why didn't he come to me?" Godfrid's despair slowed his steps even more.

"As we told you earlier, Rikard was afraid he had a traitor in his midst, who would then discover your alliance and reveal it to Ottar."

"There's irony in that he could engineer a meeting between Ottar and an emissary from Denmark, but he couldn't figure out a way to communicate with me."

Cait made a rueful face. "And with Rikard dead, it's my word against Ottar's."

Godfrid tsked under his breath. "I'm sorry to say, the word of an Irish slave turned princess is unlikely to inspire confidence."

Cait wasn't offended by Godfrid's comment. It was the reason she hadn't done more about what she knew other than tell Conall. "I'm not a princess."

Godfrid drew in a breath as another thought occurred to him. "Could it be that Ottar was at the warehouse last night? Could he have ordered the warehouse ransacked?"

Cait shook her head. "Even if that were the case, why not let me witness the conversation as before?"

"We will find out." Godfrid patted her hand as it lay in the crook of his elbow and changed the subject. "Our walk together is not going unnoticed."

The streets of Dublin were busy with people, many on the way to the market or the fields, but others were simply loitering on their front stoops or talking casually with their neighbors. Cait felt their eyes on her as she walked by. "I'm getting the sense that you don't often walk with a woman."

"Not often, no."

"I'm still dressed as a slave."

Godfrid laughed. "Nobody is looking at your clothing, believe me." Then his eyes narrowed. "But we must correct that oversight immediately. Your overdress helps, but if I know the women of Dublin, every nuance of your existence is about to be examined in terrifying detail." He stopped then and there in the middle of the street, unhooked the cloak he wore around his shoulders, and swung it around her body.

The hem trailed in the dirt, of course, since he was a foot taller than she, but it was his summer cloak, so it was shorter and less heavy than what he would have worn a month or two ago. She hadn't been cold, but she accepted the added layer with appreciation. He was right that after the initial shock of seeing

Godfrid escorting a woman through the streets of Dublin, the quest to discover her identity would begin. It might already be underway.

"What are you going to say to Arno about me?"

"I will introduce you as Conall's sister, which you are."

"But why would I be assisting you?"

"Does it matter? There are a few advantages to being a prince. One of them is an ability to avoid questions if I want to." He canted his head. "Besides, it makes sense to have a woman involved in the investigation."

Cait still didn't understand. "I imagine most men wouldn't like to be questioned by a woman."

"True, but that's why it's good to have you with me. Your presence will be disarming and put men off their stride. In addition, you will have entry into the world of women that is entirely closed to me." He gave a slight smile. "Someday, I would very much like to have the honor of introducing you to Gwen."

Cait frowned. "With that name, she isn't Danish."

"Welsh."

Cait wet her lips. "The way you say her name makes me think she's a former lover." This was another reason to be thankful she was a widow, since it meant Godfrid wouldn't be embarrassed to be speaking of intimate things with her.

"Oh no!" Godfrid laughed. "I admit I wanted her to be, many years ago. But she had her sights on a better man than I."

"I find that hard to believe." Cait's hand felt warm in Godfrid's elbow. Truly, she would be wise to remove it. "I've always heard the Welsh have no fire in them. The Danes—and we before them—raided their shores many a time, and they never retaliated."

"They have a fire, but they didn't come to Ireland because they have no concern for any land other than their own. But that land? They'll fight to the ending of the world to keep it." Godfrid looked down at her. "That's something I think an Irish woman could understand."

"Certainly this one does." Cait paused, working to continue her query, but not wanting to appear overly concerned about it. "So … why did you forgo your interest in Gwen?"

"She married Gareth the Welshman."

"A man of infinite virtue, so it seems." Cait's words came out a little tart.

"Perhaps, but I think you'd like him, and I can see you and Gwen having much to talk about. She is less outspoken than you, but even when she says nothing, you can see her thinking things you'd probably prefer her to say."

Cait hummed under her breath. "I like my men a little rougher around the edges."

"Don't say that any louder, or every eligible man in Dublin will be knocking at your door." Godfrid laughed again and brought up his other hand to touch hers where it rested in the crook of his arm. He was telling her that he was glad she was with him. Cait was also not oblivious to the fact that walking this way with him proclaimed to the entire city that she was *with* him, and woe betide the man who attempted to get between them.

Cait herself may not have entirely decided what she thought of Godfrid, but she knew she definitely didn't want *that*.

12

Day One

Conall

Despite Cait and Godfrid's suggestions as to what they would tell Ottar, Conall thought it would be better if he wasn't seen leaving the city. On the way to collect his horse, it occurred to him that the best way to reach Brodar's house without causing any kind of comment was to disguise himself again as Fergus the sailor, the clothing for which he'd brought back to Dublin with him for just such an occasion.

To that end, he changed hastily in the kitchen, and then his steward sneaked him out the back of the yard when nobody was in the street. It was one of those times he was glad that all of his servants had come with him from Leinster, so he didn't fear that any of them would betray him.

The only hitch to his disguise was getting past the guard at the western gate. He'd given himself the worst horse in his stable, but it was still a fine animal. In the end, Conall decided Fergus needed the best credentials possible, which was a letter signed by

Conall himself. As he approached the gate, he waved it at the guard—knowing full well he couldn't read—and told him what it said.

The guard looked at it and then looked at Conall—and for a moment Conall feared the guard would demand to see Conall in person. That certainly would have been awkward.

But as always, nobody was going to argue with the ambassador from the King of Leinster, and the guard let him pass.

The subsequent ride to Brodar's manor took a little more than an hour, the contract for Brodar's death all the while burning a hole in Conall's pocket. He could feel the weight of it far more than the slight piece of paper warranted.

Located slightly southeast of Dublin at Tully, amidst rolling hills, which sloped gently downward from west to east, Brodar's house afforded views that would allow him to see an enemy coming long before he reached Tully. The farm consisted of a dozen fields, pastureland, a church, and a small village. Brodar hadn't inherited the throne of Dublin, but the land on the east coast of Ireland, land his family had spent centuries working, was still his.

At the entrance to the farm, Conall showed the paper he'd written for himself, the same one that had gotten him past the guard in Dublin. Likely the man who guarded the entrance to the manor couldn't read either, but he recognized the seal of Leinster and admitted Conall into the yard.

He'd been to Brodar's house only once before, having ridden from Dublin with Godfrid at the beginning of the year. It was then that Brodar and Godfrid had fully brought him into their conspiracy against Ottar. At the time, the palisade that had protected Brodar's manor had enclosed a smaller space that hadn't included the two towers Conall saw today.

As Conall dismounted, Brodar himself stepped out the front of his house, and the door was open long enough for the wailing of a child to echo into the yard. Though well into the afternoon by now, he appeared to have just finished his ablutions, since his hair was wet. Some Danes shaved elaborate designs into their hair to distinguish themselves from others, but Brodar had merely slicked his back from his face and bound it in a single tail at the base of his neck. His hair and beard were darker than Godfrid's, more brown than blond, and he was shorter too, though just as stocky.

Conall lifted a hand to him. "Congratulations on the birth of your child."

"Thank you. A son. God is good." Brodar's eyes narrowed for a moment as he took in Conall's appearance and then widened as he got closer. "My lord Conall? Is that really you under that hat?"

Conall laughed. "Yes, it is I, in the guise of my dear friend Fergus the sailor."

Brodar made a circuit around Conall, still laughing. "I like it. What girl could resist such a figure of a man?"

"You'd be surprised. Conall doesn't stand a chance by comparison." He had spread his arms wide as Brodar had inspected him, but now he dropped them. "We have to talk."

"So I guessed."

Conall tipped his head towards the newly constructed defenses. "I'm glad you're taking the threat of an attack seriously."

"I started the preparations for taking down the old wall and putting up the new one on the day after we talked. Are you saying that I'm going to be glad I did?"

Some might think Brodar foolish for leaving the city at all, but to Conall's mind, Dublin was no safer for him and his family. Conall knew for certain that Brodar had a boat moored on his land's tributary to the Shanganagh River, which would take him to the sea two miles away if he needed a quick escape.

"Definitely, and you'll know it too when I show you what we've found." He pulled the warrant from his coat and handed it to Brodar.

"We?"

"Your brother and I." Conall didn't think he needed to mention Cait's role in the investigation just yet.

Brodar unrolled the paper and began reading. He read the document through twice, his face nearly expressionless throughout, before he finally looked up at Conall. "Where did you get this?"

Conall explained how he and Godfrid had spent their morning, and at his conclusion, Brodar took in a deep breath. "I am sorry to hear about the loss of Rikard. He was a true friend if he died protecting me."

Conall didn't know if that was exactly what had happened, but he could see why it appeared so to Brodar. "So it seems."

"Odd that I'm still alive." He allowed the paper to roll back into a scroll and held it up. "Why?"

"The way I read it, Rikard was the go-between, not the intended recipient. This contract was on its way to someone else."

"Who never received it."

"Not unless this is merely a copy."

"Does Ottar know you have it?"

"Definitely not. Whether or not he thinks it has been delivered yet is also something I cannot say. Nor can I tell you if the person Rikard was meeting with last night in the warehouse has anything to do with this, or if that meeting was arranged for a different evening in the future. The fact that Ottar sent your brother to investigate Rikard's death, however, implies that he wasn't worried about what Godfrid would find.

Brodar looked rueful. "Godfrid and I got Rikard mixed up in our business, and it cost him his life."

"Godfrid said the same thing." Conall wasn't going to argue the point, as he too found it likely. He had no words of comfort either. When Brodar became king, he would be responsible for the lives of all his people. And when he sent men to war, which he would inevitably do, or to the sea to trade, some would never come home. A king had to accept his responsibility for that fact, and if he couldn't, he shouldn't be king.

When his father was alive, Brodar had been more reckless than he was now, as evidenced by his journey to Wales with Ottar at the request of Prince Cadwaladr, seeking wealth and status. Fortunately, he had not been among the Danes who'd actually ambushed and killed King Anarawd at Cadwaladr's behest. If he had been, he would be dead.

Brodar tapped the scroll against his thigh as he thought. "Sturla wrote in Latin, not Danish. Why?"

"I wondered at that too," Conall said. "Almost all court proceedings are done in Danish."

"As is most of our business. Our merchants correspond with one another in Danish to protect our trade routes and cargo."

Conall nodded. "You have a greater proportion of literate men among the leaders of Dublin than in any court I've ever been in, but most of these men read only Danish, not Latin, unless they are with the Church."

Brodar wrinkled his nose. "I would hope that, no matter their personal loyalties, my murder was not to be carried out by a priest!"

"Not a priest, perhaps, but what if the warrant wasn't meant to be read by Danes?" Conall's heart started beating a little faster. "Come to think on it, the Welsh are the same as you, preferring to correspond among themselves in Welsh, but when they have cause to communicate with another country, they switch to Latin." He paused. "Which potentially rules out collusion with Denmark, with whom I know Ottar has been corresponding."

Brodar took that news with hardly more than a narrowing of the eyes. "You are one of the few Irishmen who can read Danish."

"Thank you for not thinking your death warrant was meant for me."

But Brodar's head had come up, and his eyes were surveying his domain as if expecting any moment to be attacked. "Who do you suspect? Can I rule out Leinster?"

"My king can't have been the intended recipient, but he has rivals, as you know, any one of whom could be conspiring with Ottar to overthrow him." It was a direction Conall's thoughts had not taken him earlier. "I would tell you if I knew of a plan from any direction, not just from Leinster. I'm sorry to say that I don't."

Brodar continued to scan the horizon, the bags under his eyes plainly evident. The man was exhausted, to be expected of the father of a newborn. But even so, Conall read a knowledge and wariness within his expression that piqued his interest.

He took a step closer. "Why are you asking me for the identity of the intended recipient when you already know?"

Brodar pressed his lips together for a moment before answering. "I've seen the way you and Godfrid go at each other when anyone is watching. Godfrid didn't even tell *me* that it was a game until just before you came to visit. He trusts you."

"He does."

"And you trust him?"

"With my life, if it ever came to that." Conall had never put his feelings into words before, but now that he had, he knew he spoke the truth.

"I understand you have a mutual friend in Gareth the Welshman?"

"We do."

"He is a good man. Brave." He glanced at Conall. "I met him first, you know."

Conall canted his head, not wanting to digress, but curious about a story he perhaps hadn't heard in full. "I did not know that."

"We were leaving Aberystwyth, having taken the gold Cadwaladr owed us, when Gareth caught us on the beach. Instead of running me through, not that he could have, he joined our ship to sail to Ireland."

"To retrieve Gwen, his wife," Conall said, not as a question.

"She wasn't his wife then. I saw afterwards that perhaps I hadn't done my brother any favors, since he wanted her for himself. But he gave her up to Gareth."

Conall had guessed that there was more going on among Gareth, Gwen, and Godfrid than he'd heard so far. The trio hadn't been reticent about their friendship, but nobody had ever said that Godfrid had asked for Gwen. Then again, maybe it hadn't ever gone that far.

"Two men have developed a strong bond indeed when they can overcome that kind of disagreement," Conall said, pleased to have learned Brodar's side of the story.

Brodar canted his head. "You are not wrong, and you can learn much about a man on a journey across the sea. Despite what Godfrid may once have felt for Gwen, he no longer looks in that direction, and he and Gareth have had each other's backs."

Conall nodded. "So I understand, but I would hope that I have also earned Godfrid's trust this past year by my own actions."

"You have." Brodar breathed deeply. "Thus, I will tell you ... Your news only confirms the rumors I've been hearing coming out of the west. The men of Brega are rising again. Ottar has angered them many times over the years. It wasn't enough to kill my father. They want to push all the Danes into the sea and take the port of Dublin for themselves, never mind that they would have no idea what to do with it. They are not merchants like we are, nor explorers."

"Why, then, do you suspect they are involved with Ottar? He doesn't want Dublin pushed into the sea."

"Exactly."

Conall's eyes narrowed. "What are you saying? He is bribing them with your death in exchange for what? Peace? That's all the benefit to Ottar, and none to Brega. Why would they want you dead?"

Brodar frowned. "I don't know."

Conall scoffed. "It is Ottar who sacked Kells four times, not you."

Brodar managed a laugh. "War does make a man's blood flow in his veins."

"Sometimes a man thinks with the wrong part of his body," Conall said wryly. Then he put up a hand. "I wasn't judging. My people are no better, as you well know."

Brodar was very sober. "I find myself less in love with war these days. I would prefer not to foul my own nest."

"You see Ireland as your home." It wasn't a question.

"Of course." Brodar spoke as if it were obvious, which Conall supposed it should have been.

To the Irish, the Danes were interlopers, invaders. They always had been and always would be. But Danes like Brodar—and Godfrid—had never been to Denmark. To them Ireland *was* home, and they were no different from any other people, fighting like the devil to keep what they saw as theirs. Ottar was the exception, in that he had been born and raised on the Isle of Man. He clearly wanted to be *a* king, but he cared only about his own power. He would have been happy to be king of any country. He'd just seen opportunity in Ireland.

Brodar held out the scroll to Conall. "Has your king seen this?"

Conall didn't accept the document. "Not yet, but I agree that he should as soon as possible."

"He might be more inclined to support my cause if Ottar conspires not only against me but against Leinster." Brodar's tone was hopeful.

Conall nodded sharply. "I agree. May I suggest that you send a rider to him at once. I am constantly under watch—" he gestured to himself, "—thus the disguise, and I would rather not do it myself."

"Of course." Brodar dropped his arm and turned away, this time looking directly west. The ground sloped upward from his manor towards the hills in the distance. He was right to fear what might descend on him from those heights. "Godfrid told me once that you always think several moves ahead of everyone else. I confess, I wish I had that gift."

Conall was already in support of Brodar's claim to the throne, but his words were affirming. A man who could admit ignorance and fault was far more powerful than one, like Ottar, who could not. Bombast and bluster could fool people for a while, but when the promised prosperity didn't appear, they might start looking underneath the brash exterior for something more substantive. Too bad, in Ottar's case, they would find nothing there.

Then Brodar shook himself. "Where are my manners? Though my wife will wonder at entertaining an Irish sailor, may I offer you refreshment?"

"I must return to Dublin. Things are happening quickly now, and your brother may need me. The death warrant is real, but the rest is still guesswork. I fear for us all if we don't discover soon how and why Rikard died."

"Are you sure that it wouldn't be better to deflect and stall?"

Conall's brow furrowed. "Why would you say that? Don't you want to know what happened this morning?"

"We know what happened." Brodar held up the warrant. "As I see it, better that you fail. It will be one more black mark against Ottar's rule. This is a perfect opportunity to push my case with the merchants of Dublin."

Conall stepped closer, not happy to hear this suggestion. "Rikard didn't ransack his own warehouse."

"Ottar killed Rikard. Or Sturla did in Ottar's name, in which case you will only put yourself and Godfrid in danger by pursuing this investigation. No animal fights with greater ferocity than one that is cornered. Come the summer solstice, I don't want Ottar on the defensive."

"I grant you the point, but there's something you perhaps haven't thought of yet. Ottar never takes the blame for anything. If we fail to discover the truth about Rikard's death, he will blame Godfrid—and so will some of the leading men of Dublin, those still on Ottar's side. One of their own died under suspicious circumstances in his own warehouse. They will not like that the mystery of Rikard's death remains unsolved—and unavenged."

Brodar nodded thoughtfully. "You are correct, and I apologize for not seeing it sooner. I've changed my mind. You and my brother *should* pursue this matter, whomever it brings down. It will make my brother lauded throughout Dublin, and—" his eyes brightened, "—I am starting to see a way to turn this entire event to my advantage. I have been looking for a means to more closely align myself with a certain faction of Dublin's merchants. Sanne is not only Rikard's widow but the daughter of Thorfin, who owns twenty ships in his own right. *And* she is a beautiful woman."

Conall barely managed not to glower at him. "Brodar, your wife gave you a son today."

Brodar blinked at the rebuke, and then his face split into a wide smile. "I didn't mean for *me!* Godfrid needs a wife."

Conall wet his lips, hesitating to argue again, but he felt compelled to say, "I don't know that Godfrid would agree."

Brodar's expression hardened. "He knows how important it is for us to acquire allies among the men of Dublin. Once he realizes how perfect Sanne is for him and for our purposes, I have no doubt he will be pleased to do his duty."

13

Day One

Godfrid

As befitting one of the wealthiest merchants in Dublin, Arno's house rivaled Rikard's in size. Although Dublin continued to experience a genuine cramping inside the city walls, the population of Dublin had gradually been decreasing over the last few decades. Nobody liked to talk about it—or admit it openly—but these days, every fourth of fifth house was empty. Thus, by razing several empty homes to the ground, Arno had carved out a patch for himself that gave room not only for his house but also for pens to house animals, a stable for his horses, and workshops. Like Ottar at the palace, Arno had created a small kingdom for himself.

And like all wealthy men, Arno had many servants and retainers, one of whose entire job was to maintain a presence at the entrance to his compound. The man perked up at the approach of Godfrid and Cait, and while he didn't leave his post to escort them to the house, he did send one of the servant boys running to warn Arno of their arrival.

Once inside the courtyard, Godfrid could still smell the pig that had been roasted the evening before, and he sensed a certain somnambulance among the people, understandable since none of them had slept—possibly at all—the night before. With the discovery of Rikard's body, they would have been on call to Arno and his family all day too.

By the time Godfrid and Cait arrived at the front door, another servant was opening it. She curtsied politely and ushered them into a large hall, again very similar to Rikard's or Godfrid's own. Virtually every Dublin house, regardless of size, was constructed according to the same basic principles. Family life was centered on the main downstairs room, where there was a central fire, a table for eating, and fur-lined stools and benches to sit on in the evening. Most peasants could afford to build only a single room but, given opportunity and wealth, men endeavored to build up and out.

Like the warehouse, Arno's house had been augmented by a loft with stairs going up and curtains demarcating sleeping spaces for members of his family. In the rear of the house on the ground floor was a large loom surrounded by baskets of wool and sewing supplies. Back at the warehouse, Cait had spent her days weaving fabric to be sold at market and in foreign countries, but this loom was solely for the use of the women of the house. Weaving was the duty and responsibility of every Danish housewife. Thus, Sanne had been concerned that Marta learn the skill, and to that end, she had sent her to Cait for tutelage. Usually it was the privilege of a mother to teach her daughter, but perhaps Sanne wasn't as skilled in that regard as she would have liked and wanted Marta to learn from the best.

Godfrid took in the space with a sweeping glance before accepting the cup of mead another servant offered. She'd brought only one, so she intended for him and Cait to share. All homeowners were obligated to offer refreshments to guests, but there was a further subtlety about the sharing of a cup by a man and woman. The servant clearly thought that Cait was his.

Cait knew the subtlety too, but she didn't object and took a seat at the table. Thus, Godfrid chose to thank the servant as well and accept the chair set diagonally to Cait's at the head of the table. On another day, Godfrid wouldn't have sat in the seat that was clearly Arno's because a man was the ruler of his own house, and not even a prince should usurp that role. Today, Godfrid had a mind to put Arno at a disadvantage. Rikard was dead, and Arno was his business partner. Godfrid wasn't interested in making him comfortable.

After a few moments' wait, Arno himself appeared from his own private room in the back corner of the house near the loom. This room, like Rikard's office in his warehouse, had been closed off more definitively from the rest of the house by wooden partitions, forming a square room and using the mighty beams that held up the roof as corner posts. If Godfrid had to guess, Arno stored his business ledgers and wealth somewhere inside.

"You honor my house with your presence, my lord." Arno came to a halt a few feet away, brought his heels together, and bowed. He was a tall, thin man, what one might even call spare, with a full head of entirely gray hair. "How might I be of service to you?"

"We would like a moment of your time." Godfrid gestured to Cait. "This is Lady Caitriona, sister to Lord Conall of Leinster. She has agreed to assist me in my inquiries into Rikard's death."

"Of course. Anything I can do to help in this terrible time." Arno bowed separately to Cait and seated himself on the bench adjacent to Godfrid and opposite Cait.

By the sidelong looks being given Cait by the servant who brought Arno a cup of his own, she had overheard. In a moment, she would return to the kitchen to tell her fellow servants, and then Cait's identity would be all over Dublin.

Godfrid folded his hands on the table in front of him. He'd never led an inquiry before, but he'd participated in them, and he thought he knew what to do. He would ask questions and study the answers until something came along that sent him in a direction that would reveal the villain. That's how Gareth and Gwen appeared to do it, anyway.

But before Godfrid could ask anything, Arno leaned forward. "It is my understanding that Rikard died sometime after midnight last night. Please, my lord. I am desperate for news. Can you tell me what happened?"

"I can confirm that Rikard is dead. Otherwise, I'm sorry, but it is best not to comment on an ongoing investigation. Instead, I need to ask you some questions."

Arno sat back in his chair, clearly unhappy, but unable to deny a prince what he wanted. "Of course."

"I understand that you were the one to discover what you thought was a pool of blood and then roused Rikard's slaves and the authorities?"

"Yes."

"What were you doing at the warehouse?"

"Rikard didn't come home last night. Naturally, Sanne was upset, and I saw it as my duty to find him for her. I saw the state of the warehouse." Arno twitched. "Terrifying what happened to him. I found Holm at his house and told him what happened."

"I'm curious that you didn't stay," Godfrid said. "I would have thought you'd be concerned about the potential loss of trading goods and wealth."

"I am! Believe me, I am! But I had nothing to do with that aspect of the business. Rikard managed the ships and the warehouse. I dealt with our trading partners. I hardly ever went down there." He sniffed.

Raised a prince, Godfrid hadn't known there was a hierarchy within the hierarchy of merchants, beyond the amount of money they made. Rikard and Arno were at the very top, but Arno considered himself superior to Rikard. "You thought handling goods was beneath you?"

Arno replied smoothly, "Not at all. Rikard was simply much better at that sort of thing—" he gestured with one hand, "—dealing with sailors and workers and the like, than I was."

"Then what did you do?"

"I returned to my house to tell Sanne what had happened." He frowned. "I tried to stop her from going down there, but she wouldn't listen. All that blood!"

Cait glanced at Godfrid, eyebrows raised, and he gave a slight nod, letting her know she could tell Arno the truth.

"As it turns out, it was mostly wine on the floor, not blood," she said.

Arno blinked. "You tell me truly? But Rikard *is* dead."

During their conversation, Arno had hardly looked at Cait. Godfrid didn't think it was out of fear that she would seduce him, but because her beauty held little attraction for him—unlike Rikard, who'd had an eye for women. It was good to know what lured a man. Though Rikard had never said, he wondered now if the bribe Arno and Rikard had taken from Ottar had been at Arno's insistence.

"He is." Godfrid cleared his throat. "Are we the first to speak to you about the events of today?"

"I had a word with Holm earlier." Arno drained the contents of his cup and poured himself another from the carafe in front of him. "He hasn't returned to follow up, if that's what you're asking."

"What about Finn?"

Arno barked a laugh. "That fool of a boy? Sanne told me he was alive, but I haven't seen him." The merchant eyed him over the rim of his cup. "You're wondering if I'm concerned about his reappearance? Perhaps I murdered Rikard so that I might control the entire business, only to find his true heir brought back from the dead?"

"It had crossed my mind."

"I didn't kill Rikard. He was my friend and handled a portion of the business in which I have no interest. I travel a great deal, you see. Someone needs to stay at home. Rikard and I made a good team." With that statement, the merchant showed the first sign of grief, swallowing hard.

Before Godfrid could think of another question, Cait half-rose from her seat and leaned across the table to speak to both Godfrid and Arno, "If you'll excuse me a moment." She pushed away from the table and walked off towards the back of the house.

Arno looked after her, half-rising from his seat as if he might protest. Godfrid smiled benignly. "I'm sure it's just a woman's matter."

"No doubt." Arno continued to follow Cait's retreating back with his eyes, implying he was concerned about Cait roaming about his domain. But with Godfrid in front of him, and Cait as the sister to the ambassador from Leinster, he couldn't do anything to stop her.

Godfrid waited a beat and then prompted the merchant. "You were saying?"

Arno blinked and finally turned back to Godfrid. "Yes. Certainly. I am gone from Dublin most of the spring and summer, journeying through Britain, even to Normandy and France. It was only because yesterday was the coming-of-age ceremony for my daughter that I was here at all." He shook his head regretfully. "Lucky or unlucky, I can't yet tell which."

"What do you do in winter?"

Arno nodded, appearing to agree with Godfrid that it was good to be back to the main point. "The rest of the year I focus on the Irish trade. With peace, there is wealth to be made."

The way Arno said the word *wealth*, giving it weight, made Godfrid think he was right about what drove the merchant. It was no great insight, of course. The man was one of the wealthiest in Dublin. It didn't let him off the hook when it came to Rikard's murder, of course, but unless he was an excellent liar, he really didn't want to do Rikard's job.

"Why was Rikard not at the celebration?"

"It was no surprise," Arno said. "He was much happier working, believe me. I left him to it. His drive made us both money, and we have been partners for nearly forty years, as our fathers were before that. If he wanted to work, I wasn't going to question it."

"So the rumor that the two of you had a falling out isn't true?"

"Of course not! Who told you that?"

Godfrid waved a hand in a dismissive gesture, implying it was of no matter. Nobody had said any such thing, of course, but he was looking to penetrate Arno's relentless composure. "Did you know that he had sent all his servants away and ordered them not to return until he summoned them?"

Arno's jaw dropped. "No. I had no idea."

Do you know what he was doing or with whom he was meeting last night?"

"No. I wish I had. He didn't say anything about it to me."

"Do you know why?" Godfrid had already known that Rikard had not shared his spying activities for either Diarmait or Godfrid with Arno. He was the one who was secretive by nature, not Arno.

"Not at all."

"Perhaps he was hoping to do a profitable deal on the side."

Arno shook his head vehemently. "If you think that, you know nothing about Rikard. He would never be so underhanded. Besides, would he really be able to keep such a meeting secret? Nobody gossips like Dublin wives."

Godfrid gave him a half-smile, knowing that this afternoon his name was probably on the tongue of every one of them. "I take your point. Then why?"

Arno spread his hands wide. "That's your job to discover, surely?"

Godfrid made a motion with his head, not to quibble, but to clarify. "Obviously that is something we are working on. I still haven't had a chance to examine the body and determine *how* he died." The moment Godfrid spoke he wished he hadn't. He'd given

Arno a piece of information he didn't need. Gareth would be ashamed of him.

Arno folded his arms and rested his elbows on the table. "I wish I could be more help." He seemed to be breathing easier than he had a moment ago. Godfrid kicked himself again for somehow settling him.

Feigning relaxation, as if the interview was now over, he leaned back in his chair. "How is business, by the way?"

"Never better! I found a new producer of wine in the Moselle region of France." Arno rubbed his hands together gleefully, before remembering that he was supposed to be somber.

"What will you do about Finn?"

"I would hope that he is interested in taking his father's place. Have you spoken with him?"

"I saw him, of course, and while he is grieving, it does seem that he intends to step into his father's shoes."

Arno gave a sigh of relief that seemed genuine. "I was not looking forward to finding a new manager for the warehouse."

"Who might you have turned to?"

Arno frowned as he thought. "Thorfin, perhaps. He is Sanne's father, and if she had been the sole heir other than me, an alliance would have made sense, but now I don't know ..." his voice trailed off.

Godfrid raised his eyebrows, implying that he was waiting for more. Arno hemmed and hawed, but Godfrid hadn't dismissed him, so he couldn't leave, and eventually he had to fill the silence. "Thorfin and I have been rivals for many years. The wine contract

I spoke of? He was pursuing it as well. It would be awkward to suddenly become allies." And then he looked quizzically at Godfrid. "Speaking of allies and enemies, how is it that you are here to investigate Rikard's death?"

"King Ottar appointed me."

Arno let out a gasp that was partially a laugh. "Really?"

Godfrid leaned forward. "This surprises you? I have been nothing but loyal since my father died."

"Yes, you have." Arno shrugged. "Your brother lost the throne when we voted for Ottar. Nobody blamed him at the time for being angry, and since then, like you, his behavior has been impeccable. But none of you are close companions, are you?"

"We do well enough." Godfrid eyed Arno for a moment. "And you? Do you see Brodar in a different light? Is he now worthy of the throne?" Then he threw out a hand. "I'm referring, of course, to a time in the future when Ottar is no longer capable of serving."

Arno sat back in his chair, studying Godfrid, who reminded himself that this was a man who'd spent his life negotiating trade deals. Everything that he had said and done since they started talking could have been carefully calculated. "I am always open to a discussion."

Godfrid found himself swallowing, wondering if Arno was subtly asking for a bribe, as he'd been bribed by Ottar. "I will tell my brother."

"As you wish." Arno grunted and half-rose to his feet as Cait had done. "I must seek out Finn. I was hoping he would come to me, but now it seems I must force the issue." He paused still not standing fully. "That is, if you have no more questions."

"Not right now. If I haven't said already, please accept my condolences at the loss of your friend."

"Thank you." Arno strode away towards the back of the house.

Godfrid stayed where he was, going over his conversation with Arno in his mind. It hadn't been entirely unfruitful, but he found himself still with all the same questions. He hoped Cait had found more answers than he had.

14

Day One

Caitriona

Initially, Cait had risen from the table and made her way to the back of the house for no other reason than because she was bored by the conversation with Arno. She could tell from the first ten words he'd said that they were going to get only platitudes from him. And she knew from her time as a slave that the real workings of the house did not go on in the front room where the men lived, but in the servants' quarters and among the women at the back. If she wanted any real conversation about what had happened to Rikard she needed to start there.

It was obvious to Cait that Arno had cleared the hall in a hurry for his conversation with Godfrid, since whoever had been weaving had left the shuttle incorrectly aligned with the warp threads that were already in place. Cait's fingers itched to fix it, but she refrained, instead walking past the loom and pushing through the rear door. She found herself underneath a covered walkway that led to a large building. From the smells coming through the open doorway in front of her, it had to be the kitchen, and she followed her nose inside.

The bustle of servants indicated that preparations for a late-afternoon meal were well underway. For that reason alone, Cait hesitated in the doorway, not wanting to get underfoot. But just at the moment she decided to back out of the kitchen entirely, a woman spoke in her ear from behind her. "I know who you are, and you won't get away with it."

Startled, Cait turned to find a woman in her middle forties glaring at her. The fabric of the woman's dress was finely woven, and her head covering was embroidered at the edges, so Cait knew the woman was of a high rank. Thus, she made a not-so-wild guess: "You must be Arno's wife, Ragnhild. I am Lady Caitriona, sister to Lord Conall, the ambassador to Dublin from the court of Leinster."

The mouthful of names and titles tripped deliberately off Cait's tongue. Ragnhild was known for her sharp wit and intelligence, and rumor had it that Arno's success as a trader was due as much to his wife's insight as his own more affable personality and efforts.

Ragnhild blinked and stepped back, clearly having expected something else entirely to come out of Cait's mouth. "So it's true." She bobbed a curtsey, her complexion red to her hairline.

"Didn't your servant tell you who I was?"

"She did, but I confess I didn't believe her."

"You thought Prince Godfrid would lie?"

"No, of course not, but with Lord Conall away in Leinster, it seemed impossible that you could be who you said you were. Sanne felt for certain that her husband had a new mistress, and she described a woman she'd seen near the warehouse who looked very much like you. All of Dublin has seen you walking with Prince Godfrid, and I was going to chastise you for taking advantage of poor Rikard's death to deceive our prince."

The last comment was said with what sounded like hurt in her voice, and Cait's expression softened. She put a hand under Ragnhild's elbow and guided her out of the kitchen and back under the walkway. Anything they said to each other would likely follow the news of her identity all around Dublin, but she didn't want it to be her doing. She couldn't be angry at Sanne for telling people she was Rikard's new mistress because that was the story he had put out. Thankfully, Sanne hadn't told Ragnhild her name.

Cait made sure to keep her gaze steady and spoke the truth. "My brother returned to the city this morning, and I am astonished than anyone would confuse me for Rikard's mistress."

"M-my lady. I apologize. I-I—"

Cait waved a hand dismissively. "I forgive you. I heard the concern in your voice for both your husband and the prince. As it is, perhaps you can help me. Prince Godfrid is charged with discovering how and why Rikard died, along with Sheriff Holm, of course."

"Holm." Ragnhild scoffed, though this time not at Cait. "The man couldn't see a cat scratching his face." She gave a shake of her head and, in an instant, transformed into the intelligent businesswoman Cait had heard her to be. "If he is leading the investigation into Rikard's death, then it will go nowhere. No wonder the king asked Prince Godfrid to step in."

Cait found her brow furrowing. "Why did Ottar appoint Holm as sheriff if he didn't trust him with something as important as an unexplained death? That's a sheriff's job, isn't it?"

"Holm is Sturla's man, or at least he campaigned for his appointment." Ragnhild tsked. "What can I do to help?"

"Rikard was meeting someone alone last night at the warehouse. Do you have any idea who that could have been?"

"His mistress," Ragnhild said promptly.

"We have no evidence that he had one."

"You'll have to ask Sanne about that."

"Let's say it had something to do with his business. Have you heard anything about a rival or an enemy who might have wanted him dead?"

"There's always Thorfin Ragnarson. You've spoken to him, of course."

Cait didn't answer her question. "Why him specifically? He's Sanne's father."

"Arno acquired a contract recently." Ragnhild's eyes glinted. "We are all very pleased by it—all of us except Thorfin, of course, whose nose is quite out of joint. He wanted that contract in hopes that it would be lucrative enough to pay off his debts, which are substantial."

"Nobody has mentioned debts," Cait said. "Substantial how?"

"You'll have to ask him, but he lost three ships this spring alone. He had to borrow to replace them and the goods they were carrying. A month ago he accused Rikard of ordering his men to attack his ships. It's ridiculous, of course, but fear makes men do and think absurd things."

It was also a real motive for murder.

"I can guess why murdering Rikard would help. But why do you think so?"

"Obviously, with Rikard dead, the attacks would stop and, as Sanne's father, he would have a very good chance of taking over Rikard's business." She sneered. "Well, that was before Finn arrived." She paused. "It really is Finn?"

"Yes." But Cait thought back to her conversation with Godfrid about making assumptions and wondered if they were right to assume it.

Ragnhild looked Cait up and down in an appraising way. "May I ask, my lady, why your dress is so worn? You can understand why I mistook who you were."

Cait coughed into her fist to give herself time to improvise. "My trunk with all my clothing fell in a river that was running high as we forded it. This belonged to one of my servants. Making dresses takes time, and my brother was not prepared to redo my wardrobe on the day I arrived at his house."

"Oh that is so awful! All your beautiful dresses." Ragnhild put out a hand to her. "May I offer assistance, my lady?"

Bemused, Cait followed Ragnhild up a set of stairs on the outside of the house. They led to a doorway that allowed them to enter the loft without going into the main room. Below them, the men were still talking at the table, though as she peered down at them, Arno rose to his feet in something of a hurry and, after a few words to Godfrid, departed.

Godfrid looked up at her, eyebrows raised, and Cait held up one finger, hoping he'd understand that she meant for him to wait for her. Being in Ragnhild's company was akin to being swept up in a storm at sea. Cait could fight the way the current was taking her, but she'd probably survive much better if she followed it.

Ragnhild bustled around this section of the loft, laying out underclothing as well as a new dress. Cait wanted to ask more about Rikard, but she was uncertain how to frame a question in such a way that it would appear casual and not too prying.

In the end, she didn't have to ask anything at all, because Ragnhild was way ahead of her. "Sanne didn't kill Rikard, you know. Nor my Arno."

Cait drew in a breath. "Didn't she? How can you be certain?"

Ragnhild turned to look at her, an ornate veil for Cait's hair in her hand. "Did you speak with her?"

Cait nodded, and Ragnhild continued, "Sanne is an unhappy woman, not in love with her husband, but without the fortitude necessary for something like this." Then her eyes narrowed. "But you knew that."

"I noted immediately that she doesn't like to get her hands dirty."

Ragnhild laughed. "No, she does not. She even sent Marta to one of Rikard's slaves to learn to weave, Deirdre wasn't it?"

Cait didn't correct her, just smiled.

Ragnhild smiled back with satisfaction. "And my Arno could never hurt Rikard. He was not built for the day-to-day oversight of the warehouse. Who is he going to get to do it now? Finn?" She scoffed.

It was in Cait's head that Ragnhild would make an excellent warehouse overseer, and might be just the person for the job. "I'm surprised Finn hasn't come around to see you yet."

"He's afraid, for good reason." Ragnhild shot another amused look at Cait. "You don't know his story?"

Warily, Cait shook her head.

Ragnhild moved to undo the lacing at the back of Cait's dress and now spoke from behind her. "He wasn't supposed to go to sea on that journey." She paused, obviously enjoying the drawing out of the story.

Cait turned slightly to look over her shoulder at Ragnhild and obliged with the requisite question. "What? Why not?"

"That night would have been the signing ceremony for the betrothal papers of Finn to my Birgitta. He snuck aboard his brother's boat and sailed with the morning tide instead. We didn't realize this at first, of course, not until many hours after the ship had departed."

Cait looked down at her feet, smiling slightly. She might have done the same thing before her betrothal had she been a man. "He didn't love Birgitta?"

Ragnhild scoffed again. "Love? Of course he loved her. They'd known each other since infancy. It was marriage he didn't love. He wanted adventure first."

"He got it," Cait said as Ragnhild came around to the front to help Cait step into her new dress. "Where is Birgitta now?"

Ragnhild's eyes took on a faraway look. "Visiting her sister during her lying in."

"Not married yet?"

Instead of answering, Ragnhild tied the strings of the new dress and stepped back. "There."

Cait knew avoidance when she saw it, but since it didn't pertain to the investigation, she didn't pursue what was none of her business. "Thank you. I am overwhelmed by your generosity."

Ragnhild beamed. "It is my pleasure." Then she leaned in and said conspiratorially, "I had the dress made for my elder daughter, but she is far too fat to ever wear it again. As am I." She grinned as she patted her own belly. "And red is a terrible color for Birgitta. It looks much better on you."

A few moments later, Godfrid watched wordlessly as Cait descended the stairs, but his eyes told her that Ragnhild had been right about the dress. Ragnhild followed with Godfrid's own cloak over her arm, which she handed to him. "I don't think she needs this anymore."

Godfrid took it. "I would have to agree."

15

Day One

Godfrid

"It has been a very difficult day."

Godfrid's stomach growled at the mention of food. He'd had wine several times, but otherwise only bread and cheese, hastily eaten before he left his house that morning. Arno had neglected to feed him. "We should get something now, don't you think?"

But Cait and Godfrid had gone hardly more than three steps from Arno's house when Jon, Godfrid's captain, skidded to a halt in front of them. "We have found another body, my lord."

"Where?" Godfrid said.

"One street over from the warehouse. It belongs to a woman, and several of Rikard's slaves have identified her as Deirdre."

Cait's hands went to her mouth. "No!"

Godfrid looked down at her. "Who's Deirdre?"

"A fellow weaver and an incurable gossip. And my friend."

Godfrid's arm came around Cait's shoulders, even as he looked to Jon. "Take us to her." They set off at a rapid clip. "She slept in the barracks as you did?"

"She did." Tears were running down Cait's cheeks.

Godfrid tried to speak gently. "But not with you?"

"My pallet is closest to the stairs. She is the most senior slave, so she had her own small space with a curtain at the back."

"You didn't look for her this morning?"

"I would have had to step over the other women to reach her. That pool of wine put her whereabouts out of my mind."

Godfrid could feel Cait's anxiety, and he took her right hand while keeping his left arm around her shoulders. "I didn't mean to offend. It was a genuine question."

"I know." The words came out a wail. Tears she hadn't shed for Rikard were streaking down her cheeks. "I thought of her on and off all day, but with one thing and another, I never went to look for her."

The walk was distressingly short, though Cait gained control of herself in the last few blocks before the warehouse, to the point that she was no longer openly weeping. She agreed to stand back as Godfrid approached the alleyway to which Jon led them. A long bundle wrapped in hemp sacking had been pushed up against the warehouse wall. On another day, the bundle could have been anything, but it was body-shaped, and a hand had come loose from the wrappings and lay palm-up on the ground.

While Godfrid was not pleased to have another body on his hands, and he felt sorry for Cait, who remained by the corner of the street and the alleyway, white-faced and weepy, he couldn't help but think its appearance was clarifying to the investigation. Deirdre clearly had been murdered.

Holm crouched by the body and gingerly peeled back the hemp sacking. "Why on earth did you bring Lord Conall's sister to a crime scene?"

"Perhaps you haven't met very many Irish women, Holm, but when one sets her mind to something, it is impossible to change her course. She wanted to come, and her brother was not available to dissuade her."

Holm pointed with his chin to the other end of the alley, where several women clustered. "They tell me that this is Rikard's slave Deirdre."

"So Jon said."

The slaves were huddled with their arms around each other, sobbing openly. One was bent over with her arms wrapped around her waist. He found himself hating the sight of their collars, and his fingers itched to take the keys from his pocket and free each one, just as he'd done for Cait. One woman threw her apron over her face while another approached and fell to her knees beside Deirdre's head. A third, middle-aged and smelling strongly of roasting pig, possibly having acquired some of the leftovers from last night for today's dinner, stood over the body. She was the only one not openly crying, but her eyes were full of sadness and pity.

He glanced back to Cait. She was watching the slaves, but she didn't approach. She was caught in her own deception, since now wasn't the time to reveal to her friends that she was really Caitriona, niece of a king, and not a slave girl.

Godfrid unwrapped the hemp coverings to reveal a middle-aged woman dressed in plain clothing and also wearing a slave collar. Her face was badly bruised, along with her neck, though the slave collar itself didn't appear to have been the murder weapon. The red line around her neck was too thin, and as Godfrid bent to look, he saw strands in the wound where the rope that had killed her had broken the skin. His eyes narrowed to see them. To his eyes, they were of the same quality and color as the rope that had been coiled underneath the chair in Rikard's warehouse.

"Strangled?" Holm asked.

"So it seems."

Holm sighed and nodded. Then he straightened and began to shoo the gawking onlookers back down the alley, the weeping slaves among them. With Holm's back turned, Godfrid gave in to impulse and pulled Rikard's jumble of keys from his pocket. With a twist of the wrist, he unlocked Deirdre's collar.

By the time Holm returned, Godfrid was on his feet with the keys back in his pocket and the collar held behind his back. He waggled it and was unsurprised a moment later to have warm hands take it from him. The extra squeeze they gave him afterwards told him, as he'd assumed, that it had been Cait.

Holm lifted one arm. "She's barely warm. The arm resists me more than Rikard's did this morning."

"She's been dead some twelve hours, by my guess."

"That's not a guess. That's a certainty." Holm nodded. "Like Rikard, she died after midnight, maybe several hours earlier than her master, though we won't know for certain until we compare the bodies side by side."

"To that end, it's probably best that we don't do anything more with her here," Godfrid said.

Holm waved a hand, and four of Finn's workers sprang into action. One even found a section of an old door that was also cluttering the alley, and they loaded the body onto it. "Take her to the church, same as Rikard."

"I'll come with you this time." Godfrid stepped back towards Cait to allow the men more room in the narrow alley.

Meanwhile, Cait had mastered her tears. "Should I come too?" She kept her voice low so it wouldn't carry. "She was my friend."

Godfrid looked down at her. "I won't tell you no, though I'm not sure what your brother would say about it."

"He isn't here, and it isn't as if I haven't washed a body before and prepared it for burial. I did that service for my husband. I can do it for Deirdre."

He eyed her. "Are you sure this is what you want?"

"It's Deirdre," she said simply. "She needs a friend."

Godfrid rather thought that, if what the Church said was true, Deirdre was well beyond needing any of them, but he certainly wasn't going to say as much to Cait. The Dublin Danes had been Christian for two hundred years, but Godfrid still perceived heaven to be a place of feasting and levity rather than the more solemn land of piety of which the priests spoke. It was actually comforting to know that Deirdre now knew the truth, and he was about to say as much to Cait when she spoke again. "It was terrible not to be able to greet the other women."

"I noticed that you kept yourself well away."

"I'm going to have to speak to them. With Deirdre dead, they will be worried that something has happened to me too."

Godfrid pressed his lips together in a tight line, worried himself and knowing it would be best to choose his words carefully. He was perfectly happy to have her reverted to her normal state and would prefer that she never saw any of the other slave women again. He had been glad today, quite frankly, of the company. "It won't be easy."

They were walking ten paces behind Holm and the body, and he slowed his steps further to ensure that none would overhear them.

"I deceived them. It was only three weeks, but they treated me well and put a measure of trust in me. And all the while, I was living a lie." She gestured to herself. "They will hate me when they discover I was someone else entirely."

"I'm sorry." He canted his head. "Given how you feel now, is spying like you did here something you would choose to do again?"

The answer took a while to come, which pleased him because it told him she was really considering his question. "It's hard to say. I was thinking a moment ago that if I'd thought about the lying as having consequences, I would have been more guarded in my relations with the other women—and then I might not have achieved as much because they would have sensed that something was wrong and not have confided in me."

"We all make choices every day of our lives, and every choice has consequences. We're lucky if we are able to see beyond the immediate effects." He glanced at her again, sensing that she was back on a more even footing. "Your brother has the gift."

She laughed under her breath. "You don't have to remind me that I should listen to him more in the future."

He put up a hand. "That wasn't what I meant. I was simply pointing out that acknowledging another's strengths does not diminish one's own. I am not capable of doing what Conall does. That doesn't mean I'm not capable of other things."

Cait turned her head to look up at him, surprise on her face. "No man of my acquaintance has ever admitted such a thing before. But you're right, and I will keep it in mind the next time my instinct is to do the opposite of what my brother suggests simply because he suggests it."

"Worst case, you can see him as an asset, like a good hound," Godfrid said. "You might even find he can be useful."

That made her laugh, as he meant it to. "I'm going to tell him you said that."

Before he could protest that she absolutely must not, they reached the church, where they were greeted by Bishop Gregory himself, flanked by two assistant priests, who had just come through the door to the sacristy. Godfrid found it interesting that Holm had chosen to send Rikard's body to the seat of the bishop at

Christ's Church, located a stone's throw from Ottar's palace, when St. Audoen's, located in the heart of the city, was closer. At the same time, it wasn't a question Godfrid needed to ask with the bishop standing before him, and perhaps the decision said more about Holm and his perception of himself and Ottar than Rikard.

"This is a sad day for Dublin." Past fifty, though without a paunch or even much gray hair, Gregory was beloved throughout Dublin. He came across as kind and generous, but as a prince, Godfrid knew more. Gregory was the priest Godfrid most often went to for confession, and he was well aware of the strict sensibilities behind the genial manner.

Then, as they got closer, Gregory's eyes narrowed. "I thought ... I thought you already brought Rikard's body to the laying out room?"

According to Gareth, smaller churches often weren't prepared to deal with caring for the dead, since in villages those tasks usually took place in the dead person's home, managed by the dead person's family. In a city such as Dublin, however, special arrangements were sometimes necessary, often enough that the enclave around the church had a space built to accommodate the washing of bodies.

"We did." As the ranking man of the group, Godfrid was the one to whom Gregory had chosen to speak, not Holm, who stood respectfully to one side. "This is a second body that was just found, that of a slave woman named Deirdre. She was murdered."

Gregory's lips pinched, and his face grew a little paler than normal, but he nodded and gestured with his head that they should follow the path around the church. The two priests went ahead to show the way, and Godfrid gestured that everyone else should precede him. Christ's Church wasn't under the jurisdiction of a monastic order, but it was a large complex anyway, as it needed to be, with a dormitory for priests and the servants who looked after them, and the usual complement of kitchen, laundry, stables, and meeting rooms.

As they walked together, Bishop Gregory put a hand on Godfrid's arm, slowing him further. "This is a side of you I haven't seen before, my son."

"Which side is that, Father?" he asked, thinking of Cait, whom Godfrid had introduced but not explained.

"You are so serious and clearly on a quest for justice." His hand was still on Godfrid's arm, and he squeezed it. "Don't get me wrong. I have known you since you were a child, and you have always sought to do what's right. I know that, and I hope the penances I've given you over the years have reflected that understanding. But you seem different to me today."

Godfrid was almost afraid to look at him. Though Gregory had given him words of guidance over the years, he had never spoken so openly to him about Godfrid himself. Godfrid had often consulted with him, even when he felt his path to be clearly before his feet. The exception would be his maneuverings with Ottar, which Godfrid needed to keep between himself and Brodar. It would have been unfair to Gregory to expect him to take sides.

For that first expedition to Wales at the behest of Cadwaladr, over a carafe of wine, the two of them had hashed out whether or not Godfrid should go. Godfrid had decided he needed to do it, if only because it was a quick way to gain wealth, which it had been. The majority of the cattle now grazing on Godfrid's land were descendants of his share in the spoils, and the Church had benefitted as well, since every Dane had felt obligated to tithe in thanks for their good fortune.

But Gregory had made him see that whichever course of action he chose shouldn't be for Godfrid's own sake. It must also be in the service of his brother and as a representative of his father, and to show Ottar and his supporters that their family wasn't weak. Had he known that other Danes were being paid to assassinate King Anarawd, Gregory might have suggested an alternate strategy.

"I think I have been becoming different for a while," Godfrid finally said.

"We've both been too busy of late to share a cup." Then Gregory paused, looking ahead to where the body was just entering the laying out room. "Know that whatever the outcome, whatever lies in store for you, you have my respect and my blessing."

Godfrid was more than a little touched, and he put a hand to his heart and bowed slightly from the waist. "Thank you, Father."

The small laying out room contained two tables, which was fortunate since Rikard's body was already occupying one of them. Holm dismissed Finn's workers and turned to look at Godfrid with an expression of distaste. "I was supposed to report to King Ottar an hour ago—"

"Go." Godfrid gestured towards the door. "Do your duty."

Holm's stride wasn't unseemly in its haste, but his steps were quick as he returned to the threshold. Then he hesitated in the doorway and looked back. "Would Lord Conall care to join me?" He looked around, as if noticing for the first time that he wasn't there. "I haven't seen him since this morning."

Godfrid didn't know if he really had just noticed, or if it was a question intended to catch Godfrid in a lie.

Cait spoke up. "He had a few matters of state to see to. He should be along shortly."

"Good. Good." Holm didn't necessarily sound convinced, but he wasn't going to argue with Conall's sister. "I will take my leave."

With Holm gone, Cait moved to Deirdre's body. "Shall I unwrap her?"

"We both shall." Godfrid peeled back the sacking from the woman's face. Her eyes were closed, and she appeared peaceful in death, a truth belied by the red line around her throat and the bruising that accompanied it.

He didn't comment on it, since Cait was looking at the wound too. It was impossible not to notice it. In silence, they unwrapped the body, ultimately letting the wrappings drape off the table. When she died, Deirdre had been dressed for warmth, with a cloak around her shoulders. Her dress was finer than he would have expected for a slave, but then, she was a skilled weaver woman. She would have earned special status and special privileges.

Godfrid found it difficult to look away from the bruises on her face. She also had bruising on her arms, some that appeared in the distinct shape of a thumb or finger, and welts around her wrists.

Cait sighed. "The immediate implication is that she was beaten when she was alive."

He nodded. "I find it likely that it was she who was tied to that chair in the warehouse. Her broken nose could explain the blood on the front of her dress and on the floor of the warehouse. A bloody nose can produce a disconcerting amount of blood in a very short amount of time." He made a small gesture with one hand. "Do you feel up to going through her clothing? I don't know that I expect to find anything useful, but I know it's something that Gareth and Gwen do every time, just in case."

"I can do that."

Godfrid then turned to Rikard. Whether because Holm had told them to or on their own initiative, the priests had arranged for someone to undress and wash Rikard's body. He was now covered in a sheet, awaiting burial. Having him already undressed saved Godfrid time, but he knew Gareth would not have been pleased in case there had been something to discover in undressing Rikard himself. Godfrid couldn't do anything about it now, so he folded back the sheet to reveal Rikard's body to the waist. Twelve hours after his approximate time of death, the body was entirely stiff.

Cait glanced over from where she still stood by Deirdre. "Was Rikard unwell?"

Godfrid frowned as he looked down at the remains of his friend. "He is certainly thinner than I remember, but I don't know if that's just because he's dead." He bent forward to examine Rikard's wrists, which showed no bruising, implying he had not been the one tied to the chair. A quick look under the sheet showed no other wounds or bruising anywhere else.

Cait had her hand on Deirdre's belly and appeared to be praying, her lips moving silently. When she was done, she looked up. "A small blessing." She gave him a half-smile. "Deirdre was always one to poke her nose where it didn't belong."

"You said earlier that she was a gossip. In what way?"

"In every way. She was a slave her whole life, you know. She was never allowed a husband or family, so she took her amusement where she could." Cait shrugged one shoulder. "And bestowed her love where she could."

"On you, for example?"

"I was one of many."

"What about Rikard?" Godfrid's thoughtful expression became more focused. "Did she love him?"

Cait's mouth fell open, as if the idea had never occurred to her.

Godfrid looked rueful. "It has been known to happen. You and I were barely alive then, but Rikard may have been a very different person thirty years ago. Could she have gone to see him last night?"

"If he and Deirdre were lovers, they wouldn't have had to sneak around. He was her master. He could have had her any time he wanted."

"Did he? Ever have her, I mean."

Cait laughed mockingly. "She was his slave for forty years. Of course he took her to bed at one time or another."

"But recently?"

"In the three weeks I was Rikard's slave, I saw no sign of any relationship between them other than what was on the surface. If they were lovers, they gave no indication of it, and of course, Rikard had put out that I—" She stopped at the appalled look Godfrid couldn't prevent from appearing on his face. She swallowed before continuing. "I must point out that I couldn't watch all the time. I do need sleep."

"That the two of them were meeting could explain his desire for privacy."

Cait shook her head. "She was his slave. Who was there to protest or even care?"

"Sanne?"

Cait looked skeptical. "Sanne told Ragnhild that Rikard had a new mistress, namely me, and that she was upset about it, but is that the woman you know? Rikard wasn't twenty and Deirdre was no maid. She belonged to him. He could do with her as he pleased. Besides, we both know how much Rikard liked younger women. If he and Deirdre were ever lovers, it was a long time ago."

"Rikard might have had his own reasons for wanting to keep his relationship with Deirdre a secret. It is one thing to enjoy women indiscriminately as a youth, but it is quite another as a man of sixty. Such interest is unseemly. And if she and Rikard were together last night, it would go some distance towards explaining why both ended up dead. A thief could have come upon them thinking the warehouse was empty and killed them when they discovered him stealing. I know what Ragnhild told you, but I'm still not convinced Sanne isn't involved in Rikard's death somehow."

"If she is, it isn't in this way or for this reason. She was happy every night he didn't ask for her, believe me."

Godfrid pressed his lips together, disconcerted by Cait's certainty—and bitterness. He knew enough of her by now to understand its source, and he inwardly cursed her father and uncle for giving her to Niall. They were all fortunate that her marriage hadn't worn her down so much that the light within her no longer shone. He could see now that Sanne's light was dimmer than it should be. Perhaps she too could find new purpose now that Rikard was dead.

"Besides," Cait added, "I can't really picture Sanne tying Deirdre to a chair and beating her, can you?

"No." Godfrid shook his head regretfully. "I suppose an accomplice is possible, but it all sounds needlessly complicated."

Cait tipped her head back and forth noncommittally. "Still, Deirdre didn't strangle herself. What I *can* easily believe is that Rikard telling us that we weren't supposed to go near the warehouse last night had the opposite effect on Deirdre than he intended."

"She would disobey him like that?"

Cait laughed. "Deirdre would do far worse for a bit of gossip."

Then someone cleared his throat behind them, and they both turned to see Conall in the doorway. It had started to rain, darkening the sky behind him, against which Godfrid could see water dripping off the eaves. They had been so involved in their conversation that they had noticed neither the rain nor the footsteps on the flagstone pathway.

Conall gestured to the bodies. "Cait—" The word came out somewhat despairing.

She put out a hand to him in a gesture meant both to appease and forestall him. "I wasn't going to be here. I swear it. But then we found Deirdre—" To speak her friend's name caused Cait to choke up again, and she made her way to her brother, who wrapped his arms around her. He softened towards his sister, but he looked daggers at Godfrid over the top of Cait's head.

Godfrid let out a breath, knowing he needed to explain, but somehow unable to muster up a proper excuse. "We have been beset here."

"Then it's probably a good thing I brought more help." Conall waved a hand, motioning someone forward, and another familiar shape darkened the doorway.

"Abbot Rhys!" Godfrid bounded towards the door. If the moment of intimacy with Cait had to be broken, it couldn't have been at the behest of a better man. "I am so glad to see you!" He spoke in Welsh.

Abbot Rhys answered in Danish, a language he had apparently acquired in a matter of weeks. "I arrived in the city just now and was astounded to hear of these deaths and that you were charged with discovering the murderer. Of course I had to come find you. Well met both of you." He looked from Conall to Godfrid. "I'm beginning to think it is more than mere coincidence that I returned to Dublin on this day of all days. God has guided my steps, as He always does. I think I can help you."

16

Day One

Conall

"**D**on't lecture me, Conall," Cait said. "I'd rather not fight just now."

Conall eyed her for a moment, and then he nodded. "It has been a long day. While we wait for Godfrid and the abbot, tell me what you've been up to. Have you discovered yet how Rikard died?"

"Sadly, no."

By the time Cait was done with her narrative, Godfrid and the unexpected Abbot Rhys had finished the examination of the bodies, and the four of them walked through the darkened and nearly empty streets to Conall's home.

After their very public fight earlier in the day, he and Godfrid hadn't been seen together, and it wouldn't do for them to appear too friendly now. Conall half-wished he hadn't stopped by his house before seeking them out in order to change his garb from Fergus to Conall. He'd been stuck, however, in that he didn't want anyone to know about Fergus, which meant he couldn't show up at the church dressed like a sailor and ask for Godfrid.

With Cait and Abbot Rhys accompanying them, Conall hoped they could brazen out any questions from people who looked too closely. The time when their animosity towards one another was useful was coming to a close anyway.

His house was located a short distance from the palace and was very much a single man's home, plain in its furnishings but far too large for one person. Conall had only three servants, a husband and wife couple and their daughter, because he didn't like the fuss of anything more complicated. The house's former owner had died last year with no heirs, and Conall had been on hand to take over the house (with Ottar's permission). For a few days, the daughter, Bláthin, could act as a lady's maid, but if Cait stayed with him for much longer, he would need to add to his staff.

When Conall had entered the laying out room, Godfrid had looked more weary than he'd ever seen him. But now, with the arrival of Abbot Rhys, though the weariness remained, Godfrid had a renewed spark in his eyes. Abbot Rhys had arrived in Ireland a month ago to participate in a conference with abbots from all over Ireland and Wales. Until that time, Conall hadn't realized that Godfrid and Rhys hadn't actually ever met. Conall had remedied that lack immediately, at the time using Gregory's church as a safe place for them to confer. Rhys had brought word from Gareth and Gwen, particularly regarding the arrival of their son, Taran, along with the broader news of the world beyond the Irish Sea.

Tonight, the four of them settled around the large table in the center of Conall's house. Bláthin was right there with a platter of bread, cheese, and meats, followed by a large flagon of mead, which Godfrid immediately picked up and drained. She refilled it, and his expression finally eased into something more Godfrid-like. He even took a piece of bread and buttered it.

"Examining the bodies was that bad?" Conall asked.

"There is a great difference between being on hand when Gareth investigates a victim of murder and being the one who takes the lead oneself."

Conall nodded, his eyes on his friend. Cait, who was sitting beside Godfrid, put a hand on the prince's arm. "I hope my presence didn't make it worse."

Godfrid shook his head, looking down at her. "I was grateful you were there." Then he turned back to Conall. "I'll have you know that Cait had originally declined to participate, in large part because she knew you would object."

"It was my place to be there. If it had been just Rikard, I wouldn't have, of course, but Deirdre needed me."

Conall pressed his lips together, his eyes flicking from his sister to his friend and back again, trying not to smile. They were two intelligent, stubborn, independent people, and yet they were sitting beside each other very companionably. He had never seen Cait so accommodating to any man before, not even—and maybe especially—her late husband. Certainly not to Conall himself. He had initially been highly amused by the thought of them together, but now he was going to have to take it seriously and decide how he felt about it—and then he laughed to himself because what he thought might shortly be entirely irrelevant.

Godfrid tipped his head. "What did my brother have to say?"

Conall launched into the details, and when he finished, Godfrid was looking grumpy again. "Ottar is so two-faced. The Bregans killed *my* father, and yet rather than ally with us to face them, or at the very least allow us to confront them alone, he seeks to ally with them against us. They will have no respect at all for him now."

"First, we solve the murder of Deirdre. Then you can think about rebellion." Though Cait's words were decisive, her tone was amused rather than repressive.

"I know; I know." Godfrid reached for her hand and squeezed.

Conall glanced towards Abbot Rhys, who was looking on with something of an amused expression himself. He was, in fact, more jovial in this moment than Conall had ever seen him. "Did I ever tell you how Gareth and I met?"

Conall raised his eyebrows. "He was investigating a murder, I presume."

"He was. The first time he appeared at my monastery, he was on his way to Chester, and my information allowed him to hunt down a young man who'd attempted to assassinate King Owain. I could tell within moments of meeting him that Gareth was a worthy fellow, but I had no notion I'd ever see him again. He returned at an inconvenient hour—after midnight," he shot a grin at the others, "as of course it would be. One of my brothers came to fetch me. It was my information that then allowed him to apprehend the traitor within King Owain's ranks, the one who'd actually arranged for that assassination."

"And you've been helping him ever since." Conall nodded. "In what way do you think you can help us now?"

Rhys tipped his head to Cait. "First, let me just say that I've come from the newly dedicated Bective Abbey, where I have been participating in a conclave of abbots from all over Ireland."

Cait bobbed her head. "I didn't know, but thank you for clarifying."

Rhys nodded too: "We have discussed at length the state of affairs in the secular world and the extent to which none of us can ignore what is happening beyond our respective walls."

Both Conall and Godfrid straightened. "And?"

"Brodar is right that Brega is unsettled." Rhys's eyes narrowed as he looked from one to the other. "I am glad I haven't caught you entirely off guard, but it's worse than you know. I have reason to believe that the high king himself is behind the unrest. Or rather, one of his sons is." He grimaced. "And he has set his sights on Leinster."

"Let me guess," Conall said. "You speak of Donnell."

Turlough O'Connor, High King of Ireland, had ruled for forty years. He'd overthrown his own brother to take the throne and had held doggedly onto the reins ever since. Fifteen years ago, Turlough had opposed King Diarmait's ascension to the throne of Leinster after the unexpected death of Diarmait's older brother and had sent his son Rory on a campaign of death and destruction across Leinster. It was only when the rest of the clans of Leinster had risen up to oppose Rory that Diarmait had managed to retake the throne.

Since then, Turlough and Diarmait had maintained an uneasy peace, to the point of occasionally becoming allies, a necessary accommodation to hold off Connaught's more hated rivals, the O'Briens of Thomond. But Turlough had more than twenty sons, and the infighting among them had surpassed any sibling machinations in the history of brotherly rivalry, up to and including Cain and Abel.

While the Danes held to a tradition of having only one wife and (usually) allowing only legitimate sons to inherit, Irish kings could have multiple wives. Though far more fair to the child in question, it often resulted in situations exactly like what the O'Connor clan was currently experiencing: all the sons of a high king's many simultaneous wives vied for the throne, which could only seat one man at a time. Donnell was older than Rory, and his father had chosen him as his heir, but that didn't stop Rory from thinking he had a chance, even though he was the son of his father's third wife.

The Welsh had a similar problem, except they'd gone so far as to not bother with having the king marry every woman who produced a child for him. All children were legitimate if the father acknowledged them. Conall supposed the advantage of that was it made the king's household quieter and less full of women vying for their lord's attention. Though, according to Hywel, that hadn't stopped Cristina from plotting to raise the status of her own sons.

Cait had been her husband's only wife. While Diarmait had wanted her to marry Niall, this was only after she'd turned down the offers of several men for whom she would have been their second or third wife, all still living. Maybe some women could make that work, but having grown up in a household in which her mother's second marriage (the first being to Conall's father), meant that she shared a house with two other wives, Cait knew it wasn't for her, and her uncle had accepted her right to make that decision.

"No need to guess," Rhys said. "It's a certainty. Donnell was named his father's heir, but after last year's aborted raid against the O'Briens, he is finding that he has lost much favor. His brother Rory is on fire to be named in his place, and his star has been on the rise. Leinster has no fond memories of that one, I'd guess."

"We do not," Conall said. "What is he planning?"

"Of late, it has been impossible for Connaught to make headway against the O'Briens, so Donnell has been seeking a way to solidify his position through other means."

Godfrid's jaw dropped as his understanding finally caught up. "He is getting at Leinster by turning his attention to us?"

Rhys nodded. "He has allied with the Bregans, who need only a single spark to ignite into a conflagration. What could be a better path to the throne than ridding Ireland of the hated Danes forever while at the same time depriving Leinster of a significant source of wealth?"

Cait wet her lips. "Our uncle is not going to be happy to hear any of this. He has been assiduously courting Donnell, even to the point of suggesting an alliance with me." Here, she interjected a snort. "Not that it will ever happen."

Conall gave her a small smile. "Indeed. But if Donnell thinks he can take Dublin from Leinster—or remove Godfrid's people from the table entirely—he is going to have to fight us for the right."

To Conall's surprise, Godfrid laughed. "You and I will no longer be unique! What a sight that would be to see Irishmen and Danes fighting together."

"It would hardly be the first time," Rhys said. "In the Battle of Contarf, the King of Leinster fought alongside the King of Dublin against the High King."

Conall tsked through his teeth. "And lost, as I recall. If this comes to pass, we'd be wise to take steps to ensure their fate is not ours."

"I hear you, friend." Godfrid looked at Rhys. "I cannot thank you enough for bringing us this news. Is it common knowledge among the clans?"

"I wouldn't say so. This comes from the Abbot of Killaloe himself."

Conall laughed, and Godfrid's head swung around to look at him. "Am I right that Killaloe is in Thomond?"

It was Cait who answered. "The O'Briens seek to make mischief, dare I say, as usual."

"But in this case, we appreciate it." Godfrid looked again to Rhys. "He knew you would tell me, yes?"

"Oh yes. The O'Briens have no wish to see Dublin fall to anyone from Connaught. They don't like King Diarmait, but they like the O'Connors even less."

"Do we tell Ottar?" Cait asked.

Godfrid and Conall studied each other. "We may have to," Godfrid said finally.

"It depends on how quickly Donnell and his Bregan allies are moving," Conall said.

"What of the investigation?" Cait said. "Where do these deaths fit into any of this?"

"I can tell you what I observed," Godfrid said. "Rikard doesn't have any bruising around the mouth or on his face. He wasn't suffocated or stabbed. He had some vomit in his mouth, but he has no other wounds."

"Could he have been poisoned?" Cait said. "Is that why he vomited?"

Conall's eyes widened. "Wine could have been poured onto the floor not to cover up blood but to prevent anyone else from drinking it." Then he frowned. "I'm not sure that makes sense either, since the wine was poured after Rikard was in the vault. And if it was tainted, better to dump it on the ground outside."

Godfrid shook his head. "I find myself totally out of my depth with this investigation."

"I don't see that," Rhys said. "You are doing just what Gareth and Gwen would have done: asking questions, poking your nose into everyone's business, and waiting for something to happen. Rikard died only this morning. It's early days yet."

"Perhaps it would help to talk about what we know rather than what we don't know." Cait raised one finger, reminding Conall enormously of Gwen. "Rikard was found dead in his vault. He had arranged to be left alone last night at the warehouse, ostensibly for a business meeting. Deirdre *was* murdered sometime last night, presumably in the vicinity of the warehouse— or at least she was dumped there. Strangled, right?" She looked at Godfrid.

"She was beaten first and then strangled, and her body was rolled in hemp sacking and left in an alley. I would have thought the river would have been a better choice, but perhaps the murderer knew he couldn't get the body through the gate and decided simply to leave it in a convenient spot."

"We have at least one murderer, then, one who may or may not have had something to do with Rikard's death," Cait said.

"Rikard's warehouse was ransacked," Conall added, "and someone poured wine on the floor after Rikard was already in his vault."

Godfrid spoke again. "Furthermore, Rikard was trading in secrets as well as goods. It is through him that we know about Ottar's negotiations with Knut of Denmark and the call for Brodar's head, neither of which are currently public knowledge."

"It would not be a misguided assumption to think that the impetus behind all of this is what Rikard knew," Conall said, "but he was also a rich man."

"Greed is the oldest motive, that and its close cousin, jealousy." Rhys had been listening closely throughout their narrative.

Cait made a rueful face. "I have to say that the thief was remarkably inept at his work if he ransacked the warehouse but didn't steal Rikard's gold medallion."

"He didn't ransack the vault either," Conall said. "Why?"

"I have no idea!" Godfrid said.

When they looked at him, Rhys also shrugged. "I am only a student like you."

Godfrid picked up his cup, but before he took another long drink, he grumbled under his breath, something Conall was sure was along the lines of: *Where is Gareth when we need him?*

17

Day Two

Conall

"Where are you going?" Still in her borrowed nightdress, Cait looked down at Conall as he stood on the floor of the main hall. He had breakfasted already, bathed and dressed, and was preparing to leave the house.

It had been late evening by the time they'd finished their meeting with Rhys, too late to accomplish anything further on what had turned into a brutally long day. Rhys had retired to the quarters provided for him by Bishop Gregory in the enclave of the cathedral. The pull of home was growing stronger, and Rhys had confessed that he was worried about how his prior had managed his brothers while he was gone. But he agreed to stay for a few days more, if only to learn how things turned out in Dublin.

Both Godfrid and Conall had given him a message of congratulations to Gareth and Gwen, and Godfrid had returned to his home to spend the rest of the evening composing a letter to

Hywel for Rhys to deliver. He had promised to let Conall add his own message once he was finished.

Conall looked up at his sister. "What do we do when we are looking for answers in an investigation?"

Cait frowned. "Is that Gareth the Welshman speaking again?"

"Close enough. Prince Hywel, in this instance." Conall continued: "We ask questions and listen to the answers, which then lead us to more questions until we find the one answer that will give us our killer. My aim this morning is to ask more questions."

Cait looked a bit disgruntled. "I want to come too."

"Not to the docks."

"I see you're not going as Fergus the Sailor. Why not?"

"The disguise is growing thin, I think, especially there, since my ship sailed away two days ago. I may have to retire him permanently." Conall put up a hand. "Bathe, eat, rest a while. I will return, and then we will decide where to go from here. I won't do anything else without you or without at least telling you I'm doing it. I promise."

Cait looked slightly mollified, but even if she hadn't, Conall wouldn't have brought her to the wharf. He meant what he said. While she'd spent the last three weeks in slave quarters in the warehouse district of Dublin, the docks were no place for a woman, much less the lady she had become.

A quarter of an hour later, he knocked on the door of Thorfin's warehouse and was admitted by a harried foreman, who merely gestured to the back of the building to where Thorfin sat at a table, his head in his hands, staring down at papers in front of him. The rear door was open, letting in the bright morning light. Even so, Thorfin was flanked left and right by candelabra, which appeared to be giving him enough light to read by.

If Conall hadn't wanted another look in the vault yesterday, he might have barged in while Thorfin had been meeting with Finn and asked questions of them both. In retrospect, he was glad he hadn't. He'd learned a great deal more since then, the better to beard Thorfin in his den, so to speak.

"Finn came to me to explain what happened." Although there'd been tension in Thorfin's posture as he'd gazed down at the documents before him, at Conall's approach, Thorfin ranged back in his chair and affected a casual pose, waving a hand to indicate that Conall was welcome to sit in the chair opposite. "He related where he'd been all this time, to head off any objections or obstacles to his inheritance. He actually apologized for living."

Conall took the merchant up on his offer of a seat, desiring in this moment to stay unconfrontational. "What did you say to that?"

"I laughed." Thorfin was a large, well-built, handsome man, near in size to Godfrid, though twenty years older, with a big laugh that reverberated around this section of the warehouse. He had an open manner about him, which made questioning him easy. Conall distrusted it, of course. "With his resurrection, Finn knew I would be disappointed. Since Sanne is my daughter, upon Rikard's death, I would have assumed responsibility for her business interests. I told Finn that my disappointment was short-lived, since I hadn't realized Rikard was dead until he told me."

"But with the loss of his sons, for the last two years you must have been assuming you would take over when he died. Rikard wasn't going to live forever. He was sixty, wasn't he?"

"And me a decade younger? I did hope to outlive him and, with any luck, blend his business into my own to pass on to my sons. I wanted that, it's true." Then he gestured expansively to his domain and gave Conall a sardonic smile. "Somehow, I will find the strength to carry on."

"And Arno?"

Thorfin's brow furrowed. "What about Arno?"

Conall thought Thorfin was being deliberately obtuse, and it irked him. The man was smart and intuitive and should have no need to play games with Conall. "What would Arno's role have been in your business with Rikard dead? Would you have dissolved the partnership or continued with him?"

"Oh, continued, certainly. Arno is a gifted negotiator."

"But?"

Thorfin waggled his head. "But he is no good at the part of a business that actually includes running it. That was Rikard's gift. He knew men, and he had an intuitive understanding of what people wanted. It was he who told Arno where to go and what to buy from one place and sell in another."

"Arno spoke yesterday when we talked to him of a new source of wine he was pleased to open up for trading."

"In France? I know about that. I confess I was jealous of that contract." Thorfin paused thoughtfully. "Arno is going to need assistance with the running of the company. Perhaps I will speak to him."

"He has Finn."

Thorfin made a dismissive gesture, though, until he spoke, Conall wasn't sure if he meant to dismiss Finn or the comment. "Finn may have found purpose in his years away, but he lacks experience. He is going to need advice and assistance."

Conall leaned back in his chair. "Which you can provide." It wasn't a question.

"I am his step-grandfather. Family." He nodded. "I see prosperity in Dublin's future."

Conall managed to swallow down a snort at the self-satisfied pose Thorfin was maintaining. It was a little too casual, in fact, and he longed to disturb his overt complacency. "I heard you lost three ships this spring and accused Rikard of sending his men to sink them. I heard you were in debt."

Thorfin had been reaching for the sideboard where two cups and a flagon rested, but he stopped in mid-motion. "Who told you that?"

Conall shrugged in a manner he knew had to be irritating.

Thorfin pointed a finger. "It was that witch Ragnhild?" Conall didn't think he'd given himself away, but Thorfin laughed anyway and poured Conall a cup of wine. "It was, wasn't it?"

"I can't comment on an ongoing investigation."

"But you can come here and ask me anything you like?" The question was combative, but then Thorfin's hand waved again, back to his affable attitude. "It is a temporary shortfall, that is all. Nothing to worry about. What did Finn say about his visit to me?"

"Again, I can't comment."

Thorfin smiled before taking a sip of his drink. "Do you actually think Finn had something to do with his father's death?"

Conall made another noncommittal motion with his head.

"So you suspect me. On what grounds?"

"You had something to gain, more than most."

Suddenly Thorfin was on his feet. "It's time to go. We are due at the church shortly."

Conall stood with Thorfin but without understanding. "We are?"

"Hadn't you heard? The mass for Rikard is this morning." He put up one finger, pointing to the ceiling, telling Conall to listen.

Sure enough, in the distance, bells tolled. If he knew Danish funerals, afterwards he would be expected to feast at the palace.

"Half of Dublin is invited, though nobody will be turned away today. I would have thought someone would have told you."

Conall tried to keep his face expressionless. "An oversight, I'm sure. And I've been up for hours. Perhaps the messenger tried to find me and couldn't."

"Of course. That must be it."

But as Conall walked beside Thorfin out of the warehouse, he picked up the pace. He'd been home all evening and this morning until an hour ago. The only reasonable conclusion he could draw was that it had been an intentional lapse.

18

Day Two

Godfrid

“I shouldn't be sitting here,” Conall said as he settled himself on the bench next to Godfrid and Cait. “But it's so crowded hopefully we can get away with it. When did you learn the funeral mass was today?”

All of them could have found seats closer to Ottar in the front row, where he was sitting with his chief supporters. Introducing Cait to Ottar was Conall's role, and Godfrid was just as happy to pray in peace and not have to speak to Ottar just yet. He hadn't managed to damp down his irritation at the king, and he needed to remain in control of himself. Ottar's downfall was so close Godfrid could practically taste it. He wasn't going to do anything to jeopardize something for which they'd worked so hard.

“I learned far too late to do anything about it,” Godfrid said, keeping his voice well below the hum of the crowd. “They're burying both Deirdre and Rikard this morning whether I want them to or not.”

Cait picked up the story. "Apparently, last night Holm reported everything he'd discovered so far and that Godfrid was examining the bodies. King Ottar consulted with Bishop Gregory after we left, and they decided that the burial should be now." She was sitting between Godfrid and Conall to bolster the illusion that Conall was with them only because he didn't want to leave her alone with Godfrid. She was wearing a different dress from the red one Ragnhild had given her, though not her slave garments. It was a dark gray and didn't suit her, and Godfrid guessed Conall's cook had come up with it.

To bury a man the day after he died was customary, particularly in late spring. Bodies begin to smell very quickly after death, and Godfrid could understand why Gregory wanted Rikard and Deirdre in the ground.

Godfrid nodded. "That isn't what's bothering me."

"It's the fact that nobody bothered to tell us." Conall finished his thought for him. "Is it an oversight or a deliberate desire to embarrass us?"

"To my mind, it's because Ottar wanted the bodies in the ground," Godfrid said, "and not because of the smell."

"Was there more to learn from them?" Conall asked.

Godfrid shrugged. "I can't help but think that if I had more experience in these matters, I would have learned everything I needed to the first time around. At the same time, Ottar doesn't respect me and might not have listened to me anyway."

Conall grimaced. "You are a prince with less authority than Gareth."

"Admittedly, his authority is well-earned." Godfrid shook his head. "I didn't even have a chance to consult with an herbalist about the possibility that Rikard was poisoned. I should not have assumed that I could leave it until morning."

"We had a long day yesterday," Cait said. "The mind needs food and rest to remain sharp."

Godfrid patted her hand as it lay on her lap. "Unfortunately, today may be an even longer day and much worse because of what I didn't do."

"I didn't go out again either," Conall said. "This isn't all on you."

"Our great-grandfather was poisoned," Cait said in a casual tone. "Even knowing that, when my mother tried to teach me about herbs and healing, I wasn't interested."

"Gwen knows her herbs," Conall said.

Cait wrinkled her nose at her brother. "I must meet this woman. I'm feeling quite intimidated."

"She can sing too," Godfrid said, intending to tease, but at Cait's continued sour expression, he added, "Sadly, you may never meet her. Only an event of great importance would get her in a ship. The voyage across the Irish Sea is not even two full days, but she gets terribly seasick."

Cait snorted. "I have that on her, anyway."

Godfrid made to put his hand on hers again, but he drew it back before he touched her. Though he'd patted her hand earlier, he was uncertain if he had the right. "There's no competition here. Nobody is perfect. She was a spy for Hywel, as you were for

Diarmait, but she could never have lived as you've done these last weeks."

Cait looked slightly mollified, and then her expression cleared. As usual, her temper was short lived. "More experience would be welcome, I do admit. And I wouldn't mind some insight into the minds of the women here. Very often two heads are better than one."

"Almost always, I've found," Godfrid said.

Then the chanting in Latin that marked the start of the funeral mass began at the back of the church, and the three of them stopped talking. Godfrid was interested to see Abbot Rhys near the front of the row of priests in the choir, and he thought he could make out his baritone, rising above the rest. Bishop Gregory had been wise to include a Welshman in his service. Godfrid hadn't yet met one who couldn't sing.

Godfrid was very aware of how close he was sitting to Cait—or maybe how close she was sitting to him—but he had no place to go that would put more room between them, and he didn't want to anyway. Cait herself seemed content, though halfway through the mass, her hair brushed against his arm, and then her head leaned against his shoulder. She was asleep.

Even though Godfrid himself had been exhausted last night, he had lain awake for hours—and not an insignificant amount of his ruminating had been about her. But he didn't inquire what Conall thought about the interest Godfrid was taking in his sister. Nor what their uncle might think. For now, any such worry was somewhere down the road.

Conall, meanwhile, said in a whisper, "These last weeks have been harder on her than she will admit." Then he straightened and said a little louder. "Don't think I'm not keeping an eye on you, faithless prince."

Godfrid kept his face expressionless, and said out of the side of his mouth, just loud enough for the good people in front of him to hear. "Your tongue bites like a horsefly, my lord."

Godfrid was quiet for some time, allowing the words of the mass to wash over him. Then as the people around him shuffled and rose to their feet, he stayed sitting, since he didn't want to wake Cait, and said softly to Conall, who stayed sitting too, "I don't know if I could have done what she did. It's one thing to pretend to be something other than what you are, but it is quite another to cede control of yourself in the process. She was a *slave*."

"I hope you can forgive me someday for letting her do it." Conall's tone was light, but his expression, when Godfrid looked at him, was very serious.

Godfrid pressed his lips together, trying to find the right words to say. He hadn't realized until Conall spoke—perceptive as usual—how much it bothered him. "I accept that the choice was not yours, and I'm glad to know that you remained close by in a disguise of your own."

Then he closed his eyes for a moment as he took in a deep breath and let it out, attempting to ease the tension in his back. Still leaning against him, Cait stirred, but remained asleep. Meanwhile, the mass went on.

Conall nodded. "You and I both know that to do otherwise would have been unforgivable."

Godfrid waited through a pause in the singing, smelling the incense wafting towards him from the thurible. "I would like to ask you of her husband. She implied that it was not a happy marriage."

Conall looked sharply at him. "He is dead, Godfrid."

Godfrid looked down at his hands, understanding that Conall was telling him to look forward, not back.

But then Conall shrugged. "He had no children, so she inherited everything he had. She owns extensive estates in Leinster." He smiled ruefully. "It turns out Cait has a fine head for business. She needs a steward only because she chooses to be away. Not content with doing the same thing every day is our Cait."

Godfrid smiled as he glanced down at the top of Cait's head. Her breathing remained soft and even, and he was loath to wake her, but the final invocation had begun. Giving in to impulse, as he had when they'd discovered Deirdre's body, he kissed the top of her head. "It's time to wake up."

Cait straightened and blinked, and then she looked slightly askance at Godfrid, realizing that she'd been leaning against him for almost the entire mass. "I'm sorry. I-I—"

He grasped her hand. "Conall and I were just discussing the fact that you've had a hard time of it. I was happy to serve as your pillar."

Still with her hand in his, he rose to his feet and lifted her as well. They stood to watch the priest and his acolytes progress back down the aisle, followed by Ottar and his men. As the king passed by, Godfrid bent his head, deliberately avoiding Ottar's gaze. Unfortunately, he didn't wait long enough to look up again and found the king's attention fixed on Cait. Ottar's steps slowed, and his followers bunched up behind him.

For a moment, it was as if everything in Godfrid's immediate vicinity slowed down too. The colors brightened, the lilac scent of Cait's hair filled his nostrils, and to his dismay, he met the eyes of the king full on. He endeavored as always to maintain as bland an expression on his face as possible, but Ottar's eyes widened. Godfrid didn't know if he was merely surprised to see him with such a beautiful woman—and one he didn't know—or if he was reading something in Godfrid's face that alarmed him.

Hatred, maybe.

Then the world speeded up again, Godfrid deliberately allowed the crush of people to shift Cait and him around, and he found himself facing away from the king.

Perceptive as always, Conall made a humming sound at the back of his throat. "I should have introduced Cait to Ottar last night. An oversight."

Now that the king was past them, Cait began edging towards the main aisle. As Godfrid went to follow, Conall caught his arm, and she got a few paces ahead. It allowed Conall to say in an undertone. "I didn't tell you the rest of my conversation with Brodar, but I feel I must now. He has plans for you to woo and ultimately marry Sanne."

Godfrid had been only half-listening, since his eyes were on Cait's back, but at Conall's words, he gaped down at him. "What?"

"He said you would be pleased to do your duty. I didn't disabuse him of the idea, but I see now that I should have."

Godfrid felt a flash of anger at his brother, an anger he allowed to show on his face, since onlookers would assume it was directed at Conall. He had been nothing but loyal, doing everything in his power to restore their family so Brodar could become king, keeping nothing tangible for himself except the right to make his own choice in matters of the heart. Then he took another breath and unclenched his fists. Sanne, like Cait, was a widow, and within Danish law, could now make her own choices. It was the only time a woman had more say over her life than Godfrid did over his own.

Calmer, he nodded at Conall. "Thank you for telling me."

"It seemed necessary." Conall's eyes flicked from Godfrid to Cait, who'd found a spot by the door to wait, openly telling Godfrid that he was aware of whatever might be transpiring between them. "Is there something you need to say to me?"

Godfrid took in a breath. "Yes, but—" he shook his head, "—not yet. I don't know what's in her mind."

Conall studied him a moment, long enough for them to suddenly be all but alone in the church. The look was also long enough for Godfrid to feel uncomfortable—even worried—about what Conall was thinking. But then his friend said, "I wish you both happiness, whatever God has in store for you."

Godfrid eased out a breath. "Thank you. That's certainly all I wish for her."

* * * * *

As at mass, the three of them chose to sit at a table near the front of Ottar's hall, but not with Ottar on the dais. For Godfrid and Conall to be seen together was again in defiance of their public hatred of each other, but they hoped their proximity would be viewed as a convenience rather than choice. Both certainly could have found room at the high table, but neither dined so often at the palace that they were an accustomed sight at that table—and neither wanted to sit within conversational distance of Ottar anyway.

Godfrid had spoken honestly when he'd told Conall that he had no idea if what he felt growing between him and Cait had lasting power or might result in a true meeting of the minds, but he counted himself lucky that Cait sat next to him again almost as a matter of course.

They had just settled themselves when Sturla approached and bent stiffly at the waist in Conall's direction. "King Ottar requests that you approach the high table."

"Of course." Conall stood immediately and held out his hand to Cait. "I have been negligent in not introducing him to my sister."

Cait's eyes widened, but she took her brother's hand. Godfrid found it amusing that she could disguise herself as a slave for three weeks, but the thought of standing in front of a full hall and being introduced to the leading men of Dublin had her in a panic.

Conall had spent a lifetime in royal courts, however, and knew just how to behave and what to say. "King Ottar, Queen Helga, may I present to you my sister, Caitriona, newly arrived from Leinster."

Ottar's usual expression was something of a glare, but at Cait's approach, he produced a wide smile. "Welcome to Dublin, my dear. Your beauty is a true adornment to my hall."

Helga smiled too and said in a voice nearly as deep as her husband's, "So pleased to have you with us." It was clear a moment later, however, that her smile was a mask, because she directed a look at Cait that, had it been made of metal, would have pierced her heart.

Cait pretended not to see it and curtseyed deeply. "My lord. My lady."

Ottar's expression had turned grossly covetous, and Godfrid had to resist his urge to leap to his feet. Fortunately, the short meeting was all that was required, and the pair returned to their seats.

As she resettled herself beside Godfrid, Cait said, "Maybe I should find my headscarf again."

"You absolutely should not," Conall said. "We don't want anyone connecting you to Rikard's slave."

"Only Finn and Sanne know, and they aren't going to tell anyone." Though at Conall's arched eyebrow, she didn't argue further.

Still, in a moment of clarity, Godfrid realized that Cait was actually made uncomfortable by the attention. Many women would have preened and paraded before the open stares, but she was hunched over the table, for all intents and purposes hiding from the prying eyes behind Godfrid's bulk.

He leaned closer to her and whispered, "You can look up now. Nobody is staring."

Then Ottar bellowed his name from the high table, as if Godfrid was an old drinking friend instead of a rival prince and was sitting a hundred feet away instead of ten. "Godfrid! Get up here!"

Holm had arrived and stood before the king, his hands clasped behind his back, looking more than a little awkward. Unlike Cait, he was one who, before Rikard's murder, might have lapped up the attention. What a difference a day made.

"My turn." Ignoring Cait's subversive eyeroll, Godfrid rose to his feet and strode three paces to reach the high table.

"You should have come to me last night, Godfrid," Ottar said, almost petulantly. "Holm, here, has been telling me about the great progress you've been making."

As Godfrid hadn't accomplished anything so far today, and it was already past noon, this was surely a gross overstatement. But Godfrid didn't deny Ottar's words and merely said, "I'd be pleased to know what Holm has told you."

At a nod from Ottar, Holm cleared his throat. "I have given the king a full summary of what we discovered yesterday. It is clear now that Rikard was murdered by thieves who came to his warehouse seeking to enrich themselves. Deirdre happened upon the thieves, and rather than run away, they killed her. I spoke with all of the merchants and citizens within hailing distance of the warehouse, along with all of the guards at the three city gates. Nobody suspicious went in or out, and all these events occurred without witnesses."

Godfrid had wanted to speak to the guards at the gates himself, but he had left the task to Holm because to do otherwise would usurp his role. He couldn't really believe nobody had seen anything, but now wasn't the time to say so. He also found it interesting that Holm had decided they were looking for multiple culprits, something for which, as far as Godfrid knew, they had no evidence.

"Do you have anything further to add, Prince Godfrid?" Ottar said.

"I examined both bodies, my lord. Rikard's cause of death is unclear at this time. It is possible he was poisoned, though with the body in the ground, that can no longer be determined." He thought he managed to keep most of the bitterness out of his voice. "In turn, Deirdre was strangled. Given that her body was dumped in an alley, we believe the murderer realized he couldn't get her out of the city to dispose of her in a more hidden spot like the river."

"In the aftermath of Rikard's death, I ordered the guards to stop anyone leaving the city," Holm added. "Strangers were to be detained until they were identified."

Godfrid looked at the sheriff. "Has anyone been detained?"

"No." Holm frowned.

Ottar gazed from Godfrid to Holm. "Are you saying the man who murdered Rikard and Deirdre is still in Dublin?"

"He may well be." Godfrid spoke lightly, striving still not to undermine Holm. Godfrid had spent the last five years hiding his true thoughts as a matter of course, so it wasn't hard. "If the guards at the gates saw nothing suspicious, that means either the culprit is from Dublin or, if he was foreign, he is still here."

"It seems to me that you are looking at this entirely wrong," Ottar said, in something of a haughty manner. "Rikard must have had a traitor in his midst, one who until now has not been identified. Isn't it true that most murders are committed by someone known to the victim?"

"Y-yes. I have heard that." Out of the corner of his eye, Godfrid glanced at Holm, who wore a stunned expression. "But we have no evidence that would point to one of his slaves, my lord. Only Deirdre was unaccounted for. The rest were locked in their barracks for the night."

"So they say." Ottar shifted in his chair, excited by his idea. "Rather than a house-to-house search, which likely would result in nothing but offended housewives, you must round up all of Rikard's male slaves for questioning." He directed a beady eye at Holm. "This crime was committed by a man, yes?"

"Almost certainly, my lord," Holm said. "No woman would have been strong enough to move a body."

Ottar smiled with satisfaction. "With enough pressure, one of them is sure to talk."

"I've already questioned all of them, my lord. They could tell me nothing."

"Then you didn't apply enough pressure, did you?"

Holm blinked and then bowed. "A failure I will remedy, my lord."

Now Ottar glared at Godfrid. "You and Holm will work together on this. I see you have already mended your relationship with Ambassador Conall as I instructed."

"Yes, my lord." Godfrid didn't see how he could argue with the king in the middle of Rikard's funeral feast. This new direction for the investigation could be an attempt to calm Dublin's citizens. Far better to think the murderer was a slave than a worthy citizen of Dublin. But Godfrid couldn't help thinking that his first instinct was correct and Ottar wanted to deflect them from the notion that the culprit or culprits had come from outside the city. "Have you confirmed Rikard's son, Finn, in his inheritance?"

"I have. It isn't every day a son of Dublin returns from the grave. It is just too bad that it happened on the day of his father's death."

Sturla then stepped forward, his hand out, and Holm and Godfrid understood they were dismissed.

"I will see that the slaves are brought to the west gatehouse," Holm said to Godfrid in an undertone. "You will come?"

"Of course," Godfrid said, deciding suddenly that this course might actually be a good thing. Cait had been installed in Rikard's house to discover a traitor, and intentionally or not, Ottar had latched upon the same idea. Just because Ottar came to his conclusion for the wrong reasons didn't mean it was a bad idea to question all of Rikard's servants again. At a minimum, it could lull the true killer into a false sense of security. "Don't forget to inform Finn. As they are his property, he has the right to be present when they are questioned."

Holm grunted his assent and set off towards the door, while Godfrid returned to the table where Cait and Conall waited.

Conall's first thought was the same as Godfrid's had been. "He's trying to deflect you."

"I have no doubt of that," Godfrid said. "Unfortunately, it means I can't pursue other inquiries today. He gave me a direct order."

"I fear the longer we delay, the more likely the murderer will get away with it," Conall said. "The trail goes cold, as Gareth says."

"And yet, if the murderer is still in Dublin, he will be feeling safe," Cait said. "Maybe that's a good thing."

Conall shook his head. "All he has to do is wait. The citizens will grow impatient with the increased security and will start to complain. The gates will be open tomorrow, mark my words."

"Godfrid, you aren't going to get anything from Rikard's servants, you know. No slave will betray another, no matter how serious the crime." Cait canted her head. "Perhaps I could discover more if I could be a slave again."

"No!" Both men were adamant in their refusal. Then Conall added, "You can't go back."

"You did. You were Fergus yesterday."

"But not at the dock. And maybe not ever again in Dublin."

Cait had her chin in her hand. "Whatever the outward reason—lust, greed, jealousy, revenge—a man kills because he wants something. What we need to do is figure out who has the most to gain from Rikard's death."

"Thorfin," Conall said.

"Ottar," Godfrid said.

"Sanne," Cait added.

They laughed.

Conall smirked. "Should I say it or do you want to?"

"Say what?" Godfrid said.

"I wish Gareth and Gwen were here."

* * * * *

Eight hours later, Godfrid wearily returned to his house. Looking back, he blamed his inattention on how wasted the day had been. As Cait had said, the slaves and servants were never going to tell him anything.

Because he'd been gone all day, he'd given his steward and servants the afternoon and evening off, and thus he didn't think anything of not being greeted at the door. He did notice that his hearth fire had gone out. Even with an afternoon to herself, the housekeeper would have made certain that didn't happen.

He was staring at the fire, only just beginning to worry that something was wrong, when he felt, more than saw, a shadow move behind him. It gave him enough of a warning for him to shift his feet, such that the heavy object swinging towards him hit his shoulder first instead of his head, which took only a glancing blow. It was still enough of a wallop to drop him to the floor, but he remained conscious. Meanwhile, his attacker escaped through the open front door into the darkness of the street.

19

Day Two

Caitriona

Cait fell to her knees beside Godfrid, who was sitting on the floor of his house with his back against the wall and his knees up. "Are you all right?"

"I will be," he said, though he groaned as he spoke.

Conall stood with his arms folded across this chest, looking just about as severe as Cait had ever seen him. "Can you tell us what happened?"

"Somebody hit me." Godfrid looked up at Conall. "That is entirely what I know about my situation. Honestly, I'm more embarrassed than hurt."

Cait reached for his hand. "Jon says that you gave everyone the evening off because you wouldn't be in."

"I did." Godfrid's expression was more than a little bleary. "Is that how you're here? Jon went to find you?"

"He's patrolling the house now—too little too late." Cait was trying not to be irate on Godfrid's behalf. "Why wasn't he with you?"

"This isn't his fault. He walked me to my doorstep, and I told him to go home. I foolishly assumed I would be safe on my own threshold."

"Rikard wasn't," Conall said softly. He bent over to examine the four-foot-long piece of wood Godfrid's assailant had dropped. It was a good two inches thick too. Cait's own head hurt just thinking about being hit with it.

Godfrid put a hand on Cait's shoulder while at the same time reaching for Conall's hand. "Help me up."

Cait didn't think protesting would do any good, so she allowed Godfrid to use her as a crutch to get to his feet. She pursed her lips as she studied the side of his head. "The skin isn't broken."

Godfrid rolled his shoulders. "It hurts, but I'm starting to feel better already. I didn't lose consciousness. He surprised me more than anything."

"Who was he?" Cait said, "And what was he doing in your house?"

"That's the question of the hour, isn't it?" Godfrid paced forward, somewhat more slowly than usual, towards the central hearth. "The fire is out." He crouched down and ran his fingers through the ashes. "I think someone put out the fire to look under the brazier."

"Why would anyone do that?" Cait asked.

Conall answered for Godfrid. "It's an old Viking trick to hide valuables in an iron chest underneath the hearth. It is literally the last place anyone would look—or so it was once thought."

"Only a fool would hide anything there now." Godfrid straightened again, and Cait moved to his side to help him with an arm around his waist. He put his arm across her shoulders, swaying a bit, before he steadied. "The air moves as if a stranger has been here." It was a very Irish thing to say.

"Can you tell if anything else has been moved or taken?" she asked.

"I'll know in a moment." He moved with her the full length of the room and back. At one point, she glanced up and saw his eyes flicking continually up and down and from side to side, taking in the entire space. "He touched everything." Godfrid actually shivered, again very much like an Irishman. "I feel unclean."

"Someone was looking for something," Conall said. "The question remains—did he find it?"

Godfrid and Cait returned to where Conall remained standing, and the three of them exchanged a long look.

"We're all thinking the same thing, of course," Cait said. "This is King Ottar's doing. He fears we found something in Rikard's warehouse ... like Brodar's death warrant?"

Godfrid pursed his lips as he thought. "It was my hope that he wouldn't yet know it hadn't reached its intended recipient."

"That's what Sturla was doing," Conall said heavily.

Cait nodded. "I highly doubt that he came to the warehouse because he wanted to discuss a contract with Finn. While he didn't appear to know about the vault, we know for certain that he knew about the warrant, because he wrote it."

"I've thought from the beginning that Sturla knows more about Rikard's death than he's telling. He was just a little too commanding yesterday morning in the warehouse." Godfrid grimaced as he studied the assailant's weapon, prompting Cait to reach up and gently touch the spot behind his ear where a lump had formed.

"You realize that you cannot tell anyone about what happened," she said.

"I know." Godfrid's head had been bowed, but now he looked up at Conall. "Why search my house and not yours?"

"He could have tried there first, but my servants didn't get the day off." Conall shrugged. "Besides, Ottar considers me an ally, remember? And he believes you and I hate each other. He might even think that if I'd found the warrant, I wouldn't have objected and might even have helped."

Cait's eyes widened slightly as she looked into Godfrid's face. "And since the two of you hate each other, the only logical place to hide the death warrant—or whatever else you might have discovered that you might not choose to share with Ottar—would be in your house. He would have no notion that he really should be looking in Conall's."

Conall's tone when he spoke next was all satisfaction. "Godfrid, my friend, I believe our little deception has finally paid off."

20

Day Three

Godfrid

"Prince Godfrid! Prince Godfrid!" A pounding on the door of his house roused Godfrid out of a deep sleep.

Fortunately, his steward was there to answer it. Last night Godfrid had left the shutters near his bed half-closed, and he could see the gray pre-dawn light peeking through the opening. It was very early in the morning. And certainly, after yesterday, it was far earlier than he'd hoped to rise. He swung his legs over the side of the bed and rubbed at his face to wake himself. To say his head and shoulder hurt was to woefully understate the case, but he could see well enough—and hear well enough too—so he could be grateful for small blessings.

The steward was continuing to speak to the man at the door, so Godfrid heaved himself to his feet and went to the railing overlooking the main room of his house. "What is it?"

His steward looked up at him, but before he could answer, the man at the door, who turned out to be Alf, Holm's second-in-command, spoke, "Sheriff Holm asks that you come immediately, my lord. Two more bodies have been found, murdered."

"Have they been identified?"

"No, my lord. Nobody recognizes them."

Even in a city of nearly four thousand people, everybody knew everyone else, so that meant they'd come from outside Dublin. "Where?"

Alf visibly swallowed. "In Holm's own yard, my lord. He is afraid that King Ottar will think he murdered them. Please come!"

Godfrid pressed his lips together tightly, implying a worried or concerned demeanor—when really the idea that Holm would not only murder two strangers but leave their bodies in his own yard was laughable. Then again, after the debacle of yesterday, if Holm's intent was to conduct a house-to-house search this morning, hiding the bodies in his own yard would have been a good way to prevent them from being discovered.

"Who found them?" Godfrid reached for his pants and then his boots and pulled them on.

"They were buried under a mound of hay in his barn." Alf spun his hat nervously in his hand. "One of his pigs discovered them."

Godfrid started moving a little more quickly. "How long was the pig at the bodies before he was stopped?" It was a known fact that pigs would eat anything, and if you wanted to get rid of a murder victim, leaving the body where a pig could eat it wasn't a bad way to do it. Horrifying, but almost smart.

"A bit, my lord, but they'd been in their pen all night. One sneaked through the rails this morning. We've since hauled the bodies into the yard. Their faces are intact. That's how we know we don't know them." He shuddered. "They do smell."

"I imagine." Godfrid grimaced. "Did you send someone to Lord Conall's house to tell him of this?"

"No, my lord." Alf blinked in genuine surprise. "Should I have?"

The implication was that Conall would be the last person Godfrid wanted to see, and Godfrid was happy to let Alf continue to think so. "No. You did the right thing coming to me. Let's see what's what first, shall we?"

"Yes, my lord."

On the whole, Godfrid wouldn't have been sorry to have Conall at his side. He certainly hadn't balked at the idea for the reason Alf thought, but now that Conall had Cait with him, he had to consider what she might do as well. If she knew something was afoot, she would refuse to be left behind. Godfrid could understand, sympathize, and admire her fortitude. That didn't mean he wanted her to see pig-gnawed bodies.

Alf was tall and lean—taller than Godfrid actually—and their long strides took them to Holm's house within a quarter of an hour.

A white-faced Holm was there to greet him. "Thank you for coming." His words were fervent, and Godfrid marveled that, in only two days' time, he had gone from the object of Holm's derision to his savior.

"What can you tell me?" They came to a halt five feet from the bodies, which Godfrid had no interest in touching as of yet.

Holm went through what he knew, with the further explanation that the bodies had been dumped face-down. They'd only been settled onto their backs when they'd been moved from the barn into the yard. As Holm finished his explanation, Godfrid could hear Gareth commenting in his ear, *The murderer laid them face-down because he didn't want to see their faces in death. Likely this murder was not planned.*

He had to agree with Gareth's spirit on the latter point at least. He bent to the closest man, lifting an arm to discover that the hand was cold and the arm moved easily. "How is it that it took until today to discover them?"

Holm waved his hand in front of him. "I haven't entered the barn recently. The smell of the animals covered the stench of the decaying bodies."

"Rikard was found two days ago, and these men appear to have died about the same time." Godfrid shook his head. "That's four deaths within a very short span."

Holm folded his arms across his chest. "We don't know for certain that these deaths are connected to Rikard's and Deirdre's."

"Don't we?"

"Even if true, that observation won't exonerate me."

The moment Godfrid had spoken, he'd put Holm on the defensive, which hadn't been his intent. "You would have to be a true idiot to dump the bodies of the men you killed in your own barn. And you are not an idiot."

The tension in Holm's shoulders eased slightly, though his expression remained pinched.

Godfrid put a hand on his shoulder. "Act as if you are innocent, as if the very idea that you were involved in these men's murders is absurd, and everyone around you will find themselves willing to believe it too. Nobody thinks you killed Rikard and Deirdre. So therefore you didn't kill these men either. It is in your best interest to see these deaths as connected."

Holm's expression brightened, and he nodded vigorously. "I was asleep with my wife and children two nights ago. Everyone will attest to it."

"Exactly." Godfrid returned to the first body. The man had dark, curly hair and bad teeth. He was wearing a cloak over a coat, indicating the air had been chilly when he'd died. His companion was taller, with straight auburn hair that he'd cut short. Godfrid didn't recognize either man.

"Do you want me to move them to the church for you to examine?" Holm asked.

"No. Bishop Gregory wouldn't thank me for that." The men smelled of death and pigpen, which was a terrible combination. "I will examine them here."

Godfrid had already noted the heavy bruising on the neck of the curly-haired man, indicating that he was strangled by a man's fingers. In turn, his auburn-haired companion had been stabbed through the heart, as evidenced by the slit in the cloth of the man's shirt and the blood stain. Though, at this point, it was hard to tell what was blood and what was mud. The manner of death for both men indicated that they'd allowed their attacker to get close enough to kill in a very personal way.

Godfrid began patting down first one man and then the other. The curly-haired man had a purse, which contained real wealth in ten silver coins and a ring with a signet Godfrid didn't immediately recognize. He held it up to Holm, who shook his head.

But then Conall's voice spoke from behind him. "Brega."

"Are you sure?" Godfrid handed the ring to Holm. Rather than examining it, the sheriff looked from Godfrid to Conall as if he feared they would at any moment come to blows.

"Of course I'm sure," Conall said. "The Bregans killed your father. I would have thought you'd recognize it too."

Holm clenched the ring in his fist. "Give me a moment, I have … something to see to."

Conall watched him go. "He does that every time, doesn't he?"

"It's convenient, if nothing else." Godfrid crouched to the body again. "I'd say welcome, but I don't want to be here any more than you do. Where's Cait?"

"Asleep still."

"We can thank the Lord for small blessings." Godfrid put out a hand to his friend. "Not that I wouldn't be pleased to see her again, but—"

"But not here."

"No."

"I almost hate to ask," Conall said, "but how are you?"

"Well enough."

Conall chuckled. "I always knew you had a hard head. Now we have proof."

Godfrid snorted under his breath, still moving between the bodies of the dead men. "I'm glad I amuse you." A moment later, he found the second man's purse, which contained only coins. Then his coat pocket produced a length of silken rope, expensive and smooth to the touch, and when Godfrid held it up, the light of day revealed it to be stained red along the middle of its length. "Blood?"

Conall took it to examine it more closely. "Could we have just found Deirdre's killer?"

Godfrid straightened. "I can't tell exactly without comparing side by side, but I'd say it's the same type of rope used to tie Deirdre to that chair at the warehouse. It's a finer weave, meant for a household rather than a sailor's use."

Holm, who'd been standing by the stables, couldn't help but notice that they were huddled over something, and he approached, albeit warily. "Did you find something, my lords?"

Conall showed him the rope.

Holm was jubilant. "I must tell the king that we've solved the mystery! It will make up for yesterday's failures." He took the rope from Conall and immediately set off for the street at a brisk pace.

"Wait—" Godfrid made to call after him.

But Holm wasn't waiting. He turned to walk backwards, sketching a wave. "I'll leave Alf with you. When you're done, he'll find men to move the bodies to the graveyard to await burial." Then he was gone.

"Fool." Conall shook his head. "If these two killed Rikard and Deirdre, the mystery isn't solved. Ottar is still going to want to know who killed these two."

Godfrid's eyes remained on the entrance to the yard by which Holm had left, but the sheriff didn't return. "He woke me because he was afraid of being blamed for their murders, seeing as how they were found in his barn."

"He could still be blamed," Conall said. "Doesn't he see that?"

"I wouldn't be sorry if King Ottar loses faith in Holm, though I find myself starting to like the man." Godfrid tipped his head. "At the same time, to kill a killer is practically self-defense, and Ottar may see it that way. He might even be happy to assume Holm killed these men because it will put the entire investigation to bed."

"I can't decide if that's to our benefit or not." Conall tapped a finger to his lips. "You do realize that if anyone else knew what we know, the most obvious person to have murdered these two men is you. Or your brother."

Godfrid's head came up. "Are you really suggesting—"

Conall made a slicing motion with his hand. "I wouldn't blame you if you had. Given who and what Ottar is, *nobody* would blame you for taking matters into your own hands. But I would appreciate the courtesy of the truth. Did you have anything to do with these deaths?"

Godfrid fixed his eyes on Conall's. He wasn't offended by the question, so much as wanting to make sure Conall heard the plain truth in his voice. He and Conall had come to an understanding months ago, but that didn't mean they knew everything about one another. On the outside, they couldn't be more different, but Godfrid recognized a cold practicality in Conall now. He wanted to know the truth, because until he had it, he couldn't know how to proceed.

"I did not kill anyone. My entire role in this endeavor began the moment I walked into Rikard's warehouse two days ago."

Conall had been wearing a very serious expression, but now he grinned. "I almost wish it had been you. We could have amused ourselves covering it up." He sighed. "As it is, we can speculate all we like, but there's still too much we don't know."

Both men turned back to the bodies, and together they rolled them onto their fronts so Godfrid could strip off their cloaks and coats.

Conall yanked off their boots, and then held up a knife in a sheath that had been hidden in the stabbed man's boot. "It was good planning, not that it did him any good."

"I would guess that he was taken out first," Godfrid said. "It would be good to find the knife that killed him, if it is here to be found."

While Conall summoned Alf and had him start the search in and around the barn and pigpen for the murder weapon, Godfrid noted that the curly-haired man's breeches had a slight bulge at the small of his back. He lifted up the shirt to reveal a rolled document. He glanced around the yard, trying not to look furtive but not wanting to be observed either. Fortunately, Alf and Holm's other men were occupied with their new task.

Godfrid tugged out the piece of parchment and slipped it inside his own coat. Then he rose to his feet and waved at Alf. "We're done here. Send word if you find anything."

Conall spoke out of the side of his mouth. "I am a bad influence, I see."

"We will retire to your house," Godfrid said. "This we can share with Cait."

21

Day Three

Caitriona

Cait had been annoyed when she'd woken to find Conall gone—and to learn from his steward the reason he'd left—but she hadn't set off after him. Though she'd often chafed at the restrictions placed upon her as the king's niece and had been jealous of Conall's freedom, she did believe that she had gifts. A woman didn't have to behave the same as a man. She didn't have to examine pig-eaten bodies to contribute.

And as it turned out, she had just sat down to breakfast when both men returned, in good humor and their eyes alight in a way she'd come to recognize as resulting from a session of public, over-the-top bickering. In fact, she wasn't sure she had ever seen such an excited look on Conall's face before.

"We found this hidden among the garments of one of the dead men." Before she could ask how he was doing, Godfrid spread a document in front of her.

At first, her heart warmed to think that he had come to the house specifically to include her, and then the blood started pumping a little faster when she realized what she had in front of her. Unlike Brodar's death warrant, which had been written on paper, this was parchment, implying that it was official, since only the most important documents were given such permanency.

It was written in Latin again, not Danish, and Conall began reading:

Sed est contra usus pactum aeternum hoc sanctae foedus inter Otharus quidam, Ebbonis rex Dublin, et Donnell Mortem Festinamus Mideach Ua Conchobair, princeps est ad herede regni Hiberniae ... This treaty represents an agreement between Ottar, King of Dublin, and Donnell O'Connor, heir to the high kingship of Ireland ...

Godfrid let him get that far before he cut him off, impatient with the Latin. "It's an agreement between Donnell O'Connor and Ottar in which Donnell agrees to kill my brother Brodar in exchange for Ottar arranging for the death of Donnell's brother, Rory." He explained also about the finding of the rope and the signet ring. "This document has to be associated with the contract we found for Brodar's death."

Cait wasn't one to dramatize, but her hand had gone to her mouth in her shock and surprise. "So these men were at the warehouse with Rikard? They killed him and Deirdre?"

"That is what we are thinking." Conall then looked at Godfrid. "What would be the response of the leading men of Dublin if we told them of this treaty Ottar has made with Donnell?"

"I'm more interested in what King Diarmait might think. Or better yet, the high king himself." Godfrid met his friend's gaze. "That said, for the men of Dublin to learn that Ottar was plotting against one of their own—a man who to all appearances has been loyal these five years—and not only plotting against him but *with* the Irish? It would not sit well."

"I am interested to see how Ottar is taking the news of these men's deaths," Cait said. "We *know* now that he is involved. They were at Rikard's warehouse to acquire this treaty, and he has to know that they had the treaty on them when they died. And yet, all Holm has with him is the bloody rope and the ring indicating they were from Brega."

"He is going to be wondering if Holm has both this treaty and the death warrant for Brodar and isn't saying, or if we have it." Conall put his hands together. "Perhaps he already knew that these men never made it out of Dublin and sent that man to search your house, Godfrid! He will be in real fear of discovery now."

Cait looked down at the parchment. "So ... who killed these two? And why leave the treaty behind?"

"It was well hidden," Conall said, "and we don't know the circumstances of their deaths."

She wrinkled her nose. "Last night, we talked about looking closer at Ottar, Thorfin, and Sanne for Deirdre's murderer, but I find the idea laughable that Sanne could have killed these two men, or that any one of them murdered four people on the same night."

"Ottar could have," Godfrid said.

"We have no evidence that places him at that warehouse, and he, of all people, would have no reason to murder the two Bregans," Conall said. "Nor, quite frankly, would Thorfin or Sanne."

Cait bit her lip. "Brodar may have an ally we don't know about. We *could* be looking at two villains, as Conall suggested in the warehouse."

"Holm was appalled at the thought, but according to Gareth and Gwen, it wouldn't be the first time," Conall said.

Godfrid grimaced. "I admit that the risk to Ottar if he was seen wandering the streets in the middle of the night would be very great. More likely, if he is behind their deaths—all these deaths—he sent someone else to do his dirty work."

"Like at your house," Cait said. "Sturla."

Godfrid nodded. "That is my conclusion as well."

"How might we find out?" Cait said. "It isn't as if one of us can walk up to him and ask him."

Both Conall and Godfrid looked at her, and suddenly she felt very wary. "You want me to ask him?"

"Not him," Godfrid said. "Helga."

Cait relaxed slightly. Helga had glared at her last night, but Cait was no threat to her or her marriage. She didn't think it would be too hard to convince the queen of that fact. "You want me to go to Helga and get her to admit ... what? That Ottar was not in bed beside her two nights ago?"

"Ideally, yes," Conall said.

Cait snorted. "You make it sound so easy." But even as she spoke, her mind began working over the problem.

"If you think you can't do it ..." Conall let his voice trail off.

"Oh, don't even start. Of course I can do it," Cait said, which was how, an hour later, she found herself being admitted to Helga's private chambers in the palace. While the main hall was the province of her husband, just like Sanne in her house or Arno's wife, Ragnhild, in hers, Helga ruled supreme in the back, in this case, in her own small hall connected to the main building by a covered, stone pathway.

"Queen Helga." Cait curtseyed.

The queen was in her middle forties, with blonde hair going gray and the thick waist of a woman who'd borne her husband many children. While she was well-groomed overall, she defied convention by wearing no rings or other jewelry, and her dress wasn't adorned with elaborate embroidery. She had a contentment about her that implied she had nothing to prove to anyone anymore.

At the sight of Cait in the doorway, Helga's eyes initially narrowed, but then she gestured Cait into the room and said in her near baritone, "Welcome."

"Thank you." Though it was a warm day, and Cait wasn't cold, she took the seat next to the fire that Helga offered. Cait's plan was going to succeed only if she could convince Helga that she was friendly and sincere. She was glad that she'd again put on the dress Ragnhild had given her. Her brother's cook had conjured a different dress for her to wear yesterday, but it had been ill-fitting and less pretty. "I apologize for not coming to see you sooner, but my brother has been so busy ..."

Helga put on her regal face. "My dear. I was sorry to speak to you only in passing yesterday at Rikard's funeral feast. How terrible for you that you arrived in Dublin for the first time under such difficult circumstances."

Cait found herself admiring the woman. Anyone who could remain married to Ottar all this time deserved the benefit of the doubt. Cait had assumed she would dislike her, and in the process of planning her approach to the queen had considered and rejected a half-dozen openings. Now, since Helga had begun the conversation with a reference, however oblique, to the murders, she decided to throw out all of her previous ideas, take the topic, and run with it.

"Isn't it awful! My brother was showing me the town when we heard that Rikard was missing. One thing led to another, and I found myself standing over the body of not only one of your citizens, but two!"

Helga's eyes widened. "You were there when they found Rikard *and* the slave?"

"I was." Cait pretended to hesitate. "Did the king not speak of the details to you?"

Helga's lips pinched. "No."

Cait smiled in what she hoped was both a sympathetic and conspiratorial way. "Men like to protect us from trouble, don't they? But that's how false rumors get started. Just this morning, I heard someone say that King Ottar himself was out and about in the wee hours of the morning Rikard died."

"How absurd! He was in bed beside me the entire night." Then she frowned. "To speak frankly, his attention surprised me, since it's unusual these days. There's always a young thing floating about the palace." She paused and the look she directed at Cait was akin to the spear she'd thrown at her the previous day.

It wasn't a topic Cait would ever have thought Helga would address directly, but since she had, Cait felt an obligation to do the same. "I would never ever—"

Helga put up a hand. "No need to say more. I realize that now. You have your eye on our Prince Godfrid ... and he on you."

"Do you think—" Cait blinked and started over. "We only just met."

Helga wagged her finger at her. "Don't tell me I'm wrong. I can see it. I don't care when you met."

Cait pressed her lips together, endeavoring not to smile. "I don't think I should say anything more about it."

"Of course not." Helga reached out and patted her hand. "Forget I said anything. I was speaking of my husband." She paused. "Come to think on it, the night was unusual for more than one reason. Sturla knocked on the door to wake us not long after dawn. If anyone was about in the night, it was he."

Reaching this point had been almost too easy, and Cait wanted to make sure she didn't give away her pleasure, since Helga, a longtime veteran of a royal court, would recognize triumph when she saw it. Still, as Cait made her eyes go wide and innocent, she wondered if Helga had guessed the reason for Cait's appearance today and, for whatever reason, decided to hang Sturla out on the line to dry.

"What did Sturla want with the king?"

Helga turned up her nose—not at Cait so much as at the event. "This business with Rikard, of course. They whispered to each other in the corridor for a good quarter of an hour before Ottar returned to bed. Of course I asked him what it was about. He told me that Rikard the Merchant was missing, but not to trouble myself over it. It was ridiculous, of course, for him to think that I could sleep after that, but it is always better to know than to not know."

Cait couldn't agree more, and they were getting along so well, she decided to take one more chance. "You don't like Sturla?"

"You never heard me say so."

That was a Danish way of saying, *yes, I hate him!* Cait licked her lips. "Would you tell me what troubles you the most about him?"

Helga clasped her hands together in her lap, her eyes moving up and down over Cait. "Where did you get that dress, my dear? It's lovely, though I must say, of a slightly older style."

The criticism was well-placed, and Cait took it for exactly what Helga intended: that her questions were enough, and she wasn't to pry any further, so she repeated the lie she'd told Ragnhild. "You are right that it is older. All of my things were lost in a river crossing on the way here. I had only my traveling clothes when I arrived, and Ragnhild, wife of Arno, Rikard's business partner, took pity on me and gave me this dress. She'd saved it for many years for a daughter who would never wear it again."

Helga smiled. "I apologize. My words were meant to wound and belittle. It was unkind of me. I had no idea you had no proper clothing, and I will send you several of my dresses before the end of the day, along with my seamstress to fit them to you. You are staying at your brother's house?"

"Yes, my lady."

Helga gave Cait's hand another pat, which was meant as a dismissal, and Cait stood. "My lady, I can't express my thanks to you enough."

Helga waved dismissively. "It will be enjoyable to dress you. I expect to see you in one at the evening meal tonight."

Cait curtseyed. "I am looking forward to it." She left, closing the door behind her and breathing a sigh of relief. She couldn't help but think she'd escaped by the skin of her teeth.

But she'd gone only a few steps before Sturla appeared in the walkway leading to the main palace building. She pulled up short because he entirely blocked her way.

"Lady Caitriona." He bowed in that ingratiating way of his.

"Lord Sturla." Cait wasn't exactly sure of his station, but it was best to err on the side of caution.

"What brings you to the palace on this troubled day?"

"My brother told me about the two bodies found in Holm's yard. Terrible."

"Yes, it is." His eyes moved up and down her body, making her intensely uncomfortable. She had a feeling he was doing it deliberately, and she took in a deep breath to clear her head. "One wonders what these new deaths have to do with Rikard's and Deirdre's. That's four people murdered on the same day. It can't be a coincidence."

He stopped looking at her body and focused on her face, which wasn't necessarily better. "What do you know about it?"

She widened her eyes as she had with Helga. "What could I know about it?"

Sturla took a step forward. "Who does your brother suspect?"

She smiled as sweetly as she could, even as her heart began to race. "My brother doesn't discuss such things with me. You will have to ask him." Then she let her mouth fall open in feigned shock. "You don't fear that he suspects you, do you?"

Sturla snorted. "Why would he?"

"I don't know. I believe he mentioned something about you being seen in the warehouse district that night."

"That's ridiculous! Who said that?" Sturla's right hand clenched into a fist.

Cait waved a hand. "Oh, I couldn't tell you that. It was just something I heard. If you'll excuse me." She started forward, aiming for the right side of the pathway, determined not to slow or stop, even if Sturla touched her.

Fortunately, he moved aside at the last moment. Happy to escape, Cait didn't look back and hastened around the main hall to where she had left her brother loitering near the stables. Godfrid was at the palace too, but the two men had thought they shouldn't be seen together.

"Anything?" Conall asked in an undertone.

"King Ottar was in bed all night." And then she told him about Sturla.

Conall made a humming sound deep in his throat. "I hadn't intended to attend the dinner at the palace tonight, but since your presence has been all but commanded, I will be happy to escort you." The humming turned into a rumble. "We are getting close to the truth. I can feel it."

22

Day Three
Godfrid

While Cait had been meeting with Helga, Godfrid had been cooling his heels on the porch of the hall, having learned that Holm had been admitted some time ago, and by now had imparted his momentous news.

King Ottar had then spent a full hour in close consultation with his counselors and the leading men of Dublin. This was more normal than not since it was his responsibility to manage his kingdom. Almost daily, the king heard issues, complaints, and disputes from the various settlements of Danes throughout Ireland. Ships sailed in and out of Dublin every day, bringing goods and news from every corner of the world, and that too was digested and assessed over a lengthy morning meal.

Godfrid thought it just as well that he hadn't been a participant in that initial conversation, since that meant they could now meet with Ottar with more information, thanks to Cait. The treaty had been left in Conall's house with a guard standing over it, too precious a document to risk bringing into Ottar's palace. The knowledge of it was dangerous enough, and Godfrid felt the weight of his secret as it settled next to all the other secrets he'd kept from Ottar over the years, chief among them being his own disloyalty.

Because Cait would not be welcomed in a conference with Ottar, Conall had taken her home (she was not pleased), and then returned. He now lounged in the porch alongside Godfrid, his shoulder propped against a side wall and his arms folded across his chest. No matter how he tried, Godfrid could never quite look as casual and nonchalant as Conall.

Fortunately, they didn't have to wait long. Soon Sturla himself poked his head out the door of the hall. "The king will see you now."

Godfrid, who'd been sitting on a bench near the door, pushed to his feet, but when he approached the entrance, Sturla put a hand on his arm. It was unlike Sturla to actually touch Godfrid, and Godfrid could almost feel the evil oozing out of the man's fingers onto his skin. "I should warn you that the king is in no mood to hear more bad news, but if you have any, best to say it without delay and not pretty it up with fine words."

"You know me, Sturla," Godfrid said. "I do not have a silver tongue."

Sturla scoffed. "You speak the truth." Then he looked at Conall. "King Ottar will be particularly concerned about the response of Leinster to the news that Brega sent assassins to Dublin to murder our citizens."

"Is that what they were?" Conall asked mildly, but then headed inside before Sturla could make an answer.

Godfrid wasn't displeased at Conall's rudeness, feigned or (as he suspected in this case) genuine. For his part, it was all he could do to remain polite. Perhaps overcompensating, he gestured magnanimously that Sturla should precede him, but as he strode down the length of the hall behind the steward, he could feel the battle lines being drawn. Godfrid didn't take kindly to how easily Ottar plotted to murder his brother.

Unusually for the palace—and as evidence of the seriousness of the proceedings—the only occupied table was Ottar's. Various lesser lords and notable merchants surrounded it, including Finn, Thorfin, and Arno, all three of whom seemed to be getting along better than Godfrid would have expected, given the private conversations he and Conall had conducted with each.

Bishop Gregory was there too, along with Abbot Rhys, which was something of a surprise, and Godfrid felt a little of his tension ease to see them both. Though he knew Rhys less well, he had trust in both churchmen, who strived always not to take sides in political disputes. Though Gregory was unmistakably loyal to the Church, he would no longer be bishop if Denmark or one of the Irish clans overcame Dublin. Which meant, to Godfrid's mind, that he would be on Godfrid's side once he knew the whole truth.

Not that either Conall or Godfrid intended to openly acknowledge in this hour that there *were* sides.

"So it seems we have our murderers." Ottar leaned back in his chair and gestured expansively. "God is good."

For a heartbeat, Godfrid hesitated, fearing that Ottar had somehow decided that he and Conall were the murderers, but then his breath eased as he realized Ottar was referring to the two dead men.

Holm rocked back and forth on the balls of his feet, looking satisfied. "It is a good day for Dublin." He had begun the day fearing that he would be accused of their murders, and now he was basking in the glory of solving the case.

"You all have done fine work, I must say." Ottar clapped his hands together. "With the funeral done, I think we can put these deaths behind us." He looked at Finn. "Do you feel that justice has been done for your father?"

"Yes, my lord." Finn bent his head. "You will find no argument from me or from my partners." He indicated Arno and Thorfin, both of whom nodded.

Godfrid glanced at Conall, who'd just met with Thorfin yesterday when things weren't nearly as congenial. His focus was on King Ottar, however, and Godfrid waited a moment, thinking his friend was going to say something. He didn't, so Godfrid let out a sigh, knowing he couldn't in good conscience leave the matter alone. "Are we not at all concerned as to the reason two men from Brega would kill a leading merchant of Dublin?"

Finn held up his hand. "With the help of my partners, I am in the process of thoroughly searching my father's records, looking for any transaction that could account for their presence. We will scrutinize everything and report our findings to the king."

"Sturla has agreed to help in the search as well. I have sent word to the King of Brega that further forays into Dublin by his men will not be tolerated." Ottar looked hard at Conall. "I expect you will send a full report to King Diarmait?"

"Of course." Conall paused. "My lord, I don't want to deflect from pressing issues, but what of the murderer who remains free?"

Ottar's smile became stilted. "What murderer would that be?"

"The one who killed the men from Brega?"

Ottar affected an innocent look. "It seems obvious to me and to Sheriff Holm that they had a falling out. One man was strangling the other when his victim stabbed him. No more needs to be said about it than that."

Conall coughed politely. "Someone dragged them into Holm's stables and buried them under a mound of hay."

Everyone at the table frowned, but Ottar still gestured dismissively. "Holm has made enemies in the time he has been sheriff. One of them stumbled upon the bodies and took advantage of their proximity to his house."

Sturla nodded with satisfaction. "The King of Brega sent two murderers into Dublin. He can hardly object when they lost their lives in the process. Killing them was a righteous act, one my lord would reward most generously if he knew who'd done it." He put up a finger. "Surely King Diarmait will see that the matter has been resolved internally. I can't imagine there will be any more trouble from that quarter."

It was only then—with some shock—that Godfrid realized everyone at the table really did think that Holm had killed the two men. Their smiles and nods and dismissal of the investigation were their way of praising him for it without open acknowledgement that he'd done it.

Godfrid couldn't believe it, but he could find no words that would penetrate their mutual complacency. He found that his feet were frozen to the floor, but Conall simply bent his head politely and turned on his heel. When Godfrid didn't immediately follow, he subtly tugged on his elbow and got him moving. Side-by-side they strode down the length of the hall, Godfrid's temper rising with every step.

He held it in until they were actually through the palace gateway, at which point he stopped and turned on Conall. "Can you believe—"

"Not here, Godfrid." Conall's voice was sharp and commanding. "We will regroup again at my house."

23

Day Three

Conall

"You can see why he made the decision he did," Cait said a quarter of an hour later as the three friends sat down to a small meal. They would have to return to the palace for the evening meal nearer to sunset, but that was still many hours away. Conall found that he needed to eat less in his old age, but Godfrid was still in his early thirties. Conall had heard his stomach growling during the walk from the palace.

"Of course I can see it!" Godfrid said.

"But you don't like it." Cait reached out to put her hand on top of Godfrid's, before quickly moving it back.

Godfrid had greeted Cait with a kiss on her cheek when they'd arrived, and she'd accepted it as her due.

Conall pretended he hadn't noticed their exchange. "Just because Ottar is finished with the investigation, doesn't mean we have to be."

Godfrid eased back from the table, his eyes curious and somewhat appeased. "I am convinced that Sturla was in that warehouse at some point the night Rikard died. It is his hand that wrote the document. Ottar could not have met directly with the men from Brega, so he would have sent Sturla. But what happened next?" He gestured to Conall. "We didn't mention it. Holm clearly hasn't thought of it. But since Ottar found neither the death warrant nor the contract in my house, he is asking himself about—and hoping for—a third man who got away with both."

"But we know the truth." Cait grinned. "This time keeping secrets is fun."

Conall was amused too. "King Ottar's refusal to continue the investigation is exactly what I assumed would happen, so I was prepared for it. Short-term thinking is far more common than the ability to see past one's nose."

Cait's chin was in her hand as she picked at her mutton. "Exactly whose nose are we seeing past?"

"Ottar's, apparently," Godfrid said, finally relaxing enough to laugh. "What do you mean by that?"

"Ottar is thinking of his immediate problems and has so far given no thought to what is going to happen in Dublin if he *doesn't* look into these second murders. He can credit Holm all he wants, but eventually that ruse is going to crack, because Holm didn't kill them, and his men know it, and then where will we be?"

Godfrid snorted. "As I told him, with another murderer on the loose."

Conall nodded. "Right now, Ottar is happy to put aside the investigation because nothing has gone as he planned, and I'm certain he feared we were getting too close. He shouldn't have brought either of us into it in the first place."

"I'm wondering again at his motive for doing so," Godfrid said.

"He did it because he knew that at one time Rikard had been your friend, and he didn't want you looking into Rikard's death on your own without Holm at your side. He thought he could control you better with you serving him than with you wandering Dublin unattended."

Cait eyed Godfrid. "He fears you."

"As well he should." Now Conall grinned. "Ottar doesn't command my loyalty. I will carry on with the questioning alone." Then he put up a hand to stop their sputtered protests before they turned into real arguments. "Now that Cait has been introduced at the palace, you should take her on another walk about the town, introduce her officially to the worthy people of Dublin."

Godfrid eyed Conall warily. While he'd escorted Cait from the warehouse after Rikard's murder, causing quite a bit of gossip at the time, this would be the third day that they would be seen together. Godfrid knew as well as Conall what such an act would mean. "It would be my pleasure, but—why?"

"Just as when I rode to Brodar's manor, while everyone is looking at the two of you, nobody will be wondering what I am up to."

Cait shook her head. "You're heading back into the shadows, just the way you like it." But rather than critical, her tone was admiring.

"You have to admit, I'm good at it."

"Will you dress again as Fergus?" Cait asked.

"I don't dare."

Godfrid made a shooing motion. "Fine. Go."

Conall went with hardly a backward glance, knowing that his presence was surplus to requirements anyway and wanting to leave before either of them questioned his ulterior motive. Godfrid and Cait were very aware of each other's presence, but neither might yet realize how well-suited they were to one another. After a circuit of the city, either they and all of Dublin would know, or, alternatively, the pair would spend the day at each other's throats and learn that they could only ever be friends. To Conall's mind, it was best to learn these things sooner rather than later, before a physical connection or emotions progressed past the point of no return.

He whistled tunelessly to himself as he strolled towards the dockside one more time. The guards at the gate were different from yesterday, but they knew him, and he raised a hand as he passed through the open doors.

Though Cait wasn't wrong that he liked the shadows, today it was more that he was hiding in plain sight. In fact, he felt something like a ghost because he knew many of the men he passed—but they no longer knew him, and most ducked their heads and looked at the ground rather than into his face. He was the ambassador from the Kingdom of Leinster now, not Fergus the sailor. With his thick Ulster accent and crude sense of humor, Fergus had been amusing, and he wondered if his friends and acquaintances outside of the crew of his boat would be angry at him to learn that he'd deceived them for three weeks. Conall had been living this way for years, and he'd learned it was usually better if they never found out.

Finn's boat was docked towards the far end of the dozen or so boats moored along the Dublin dockside. These were seafaring vessels, much larger than the river going boats that sailed the Liffey or stuck to the coastlines of Ireland and could easily be drawn up on a muddy bank. The Dublin Danes had modified the war boats, by which they'd terrorized the coasts of every kingdom with a shoreline for nearly four centuries. Though still sleek with a relatively shallow draft, the vessels built now were more suited to holding cargo than fighting men.

As before, instead of approaching one of Finn's crew directly, he sauntered over to an adjacent boat and spoke to a seaman loading packages of foodstuffs into the hull. He also noted that the Welsh ship from two days ago was gone. "What is your name, and whom do you serve?"

The man glanced at him, and then did a double-take as he realized he was talking to a nobleman. He stopped what he was doing and gave Conall his full attention. "I am Ivar, my lord. I serve Harald Magnusson. We sail for Waterford with the tide and from there on to Galway."

Conall didn't actually care what the man's name was, but he'd learned that men were more forthcoming when one addressed them personally. "Ivar, how long have you been docked here?"

"Three days. We would have left earlier, but Harald wanted to attend Merchant Rikard's funeral."

"So you were here when Finn Rikardson's boat docked?"

The man's lip curled at the mention of Finn's name, but he answered civilly enough. "Yes, my lord."

"You don't like him?"

Ivar waggled his head in the Danish way of qualifying a statement. "He was a spoiled man-child last I saw him. I hear he's grown up. A close encounter with death has a way of doing that to a man."

"I hear the same." Conall paused. "When was this exactly?"

"Two mornings ago."

Conall deflated slightly. It was the same story he'd heard three times now. It was silly of him to keep going over the same ground, because of all the things that could be verified, when the boat docked was the easiest.

After thanking the man, Conall moved to resume his stroll down the dockside, but he hadn't gone more than two steps away from the boat when Ivar called him back. "Finn wasn't on the boat when it docked, my lord, if that was your underlying question."

Conall swung back, startled at the man's perception. "Wasn't he? How do you know?"

Ivar smiled to have Conall gazing at him intently. "Because, my lord, as the boat docked, he came out of the shadows and boarded it. It was the dark before the dawn, which comes early enough this time of year."

"How did you come to see this?"

"I was on watch."

Conall was impressed that Ivar's captain had kept a man on watch even when docked in port with no cargo. "I would appreciate it if you said nothing about this to anyone."

The corner of the man's mouth quirked. "Perhaps our Finn hasn't changed as much as all that?"

"We'll see." Conall put a finger to his lips to emphasize his point.

Ivar grinned. "As you wish, my lord."

Conall turned back to the dockside gate, his heart beating a little faster in anticipation of what needed to happen next. Finn had lied. Not pressing him on his alibi had seemed a kindness at the time, seeing as how he'd just lost his father. But it was a shameful oversight. His only consolation was that, just like Gareth had taught him, he had continued to ask questions even when he thought he knew the answers.

24

Day Three

Caitriona

If anything, this walk on Godfrid's arm today sparked more astonished looks and curiosity than the one they'd taken to Arno's house after Rikard's death. It was well into afternoon by now, and, for many of Dublin's women in particular, their daily chores were over. They'd fed their families their afternoon meal, and now they had a few moments to lounge on their front stoops and gossip. She and Godfrid were going to be the primary topics of conversation, exactly as her brother had predicted. She didn't know whether she should be impressed or irked by his insight.

"They are admiring your beauty," Godfrid said.

Cait pulled a sour face.

Godfrid looked down at her. "I noticed yesterday in Ottar's hall that you don't like to be thought beautiful, or—" he paused for a moment, real surprise crossing his face, "could it be that you actually don't think of yourself as beautiful?"

Cait found herself grimacing even more. "When I was married to Niall, my whole day, every day, revolved around what I looked like. He expected me to devote many hours a day to my appearance. I realize that isn't so unusual for a noblewoman, but it never suited me."

Godfrid laughed. "Fate seems to have held a different view."

Cait wrinkled her nose yet again. She knew herself to be beautiful, and had been young enough at the time of her marriage to appreciate admiring looks, but that experience had made her distrustful of appearances. "Beauty was a mask I put on every day and behind which I hid my unhappiness."

Godfrid's expression turned thoughtful. "Is that the real reason you sought out service to King Diarmait as a slave?"

Cait blinked, startled, though by now she should be used to his perceptiveness. "It's true that I didn't hate my time as a slave as much as many women would have." And then she decided to confess further, "Especially at the beginning, I treated it as a lark, to see how fully I could envelop myself in my new identity."

"Perhaps that was necessary to maintain the deception," Godfrid said, again speaking thoughtfully. "I imagine for much of your brother's career he has felt the same way—up until he was beaten, imprisoned, and almost died."

Cait tsked through her teeth. "Up until." She shook her head. "He spent the last three weeks as Fergus to ensure what happened to him was not going to happen to me."

"I should hope not."

Deirdre had been the one, if anyone, who'd made some headway penetrating Cait's mask. The thought had Cait steering Godfrid back across the city towards Rikard's warehouse.

"Where are we going?"

"I must see my friends. Explain what happened to me."

"That isn't what Conall had in mind." Godfrid protested. "He would say it is unwise. If Sanne was shocked that a noblewoman could become a slave, how will those who are slaves feel?"

"What if nobody explained my absence? They will be worried. It isn't fair to just leave and tell them nothing."

Even though it had been her choice, she still approached the barracks with some trepidation, prompting Godfrid to whisper in her ear, "You don't have to do this."

"I do. I really do."

"I could speak to them or—" he paused as he thought, "—you could become a slave again just long enough to assuage their fears."

"No."

Godfrid nodded his understanding. She had known he would appreciate what she needed to do, which was something to marvel at in and of itself, and that was the reason she hadn't fobbed him off with a different excuse. "Then be assured that I will rescue you within the hour. If the meeting is too painful, there's a time limit on how long it will last."

"Thank you." She squeezed his hand and stepped across the threshold to find four of Rikard's female slaves in the kitchen.

Lena, the cook looked up as she entered, instantly abandoning the dough she'd been shaping and coming forward. Her expression was the careful one she plastered on in the presence of nobility. Then she looked harder, and her eyes widened. "Caitriona?"

The other women in the room stopped what they were doing, jaws dropping as they stared at her.

"Yes. It is I."

"I thought you'd taken advantage of Rikard's death to escape." Lena approached more closely, looking Cait up and down as she did so. "Others thought you were dead until Tilda said that she saw you at the other end of the alley when Prince Godfrid found Deirdre's body. I didn't believe her then, but I see I should have. What is going on?"

"I'm still Caitriona, but I was never really a slave." She cleared her throat, painfully nervous. These women had welcomed her from the very start, accepting her somewhat superior position as a weaver woman without question or jealousy, and she had repaid them with deception. It had been an oversight on her part that she'd never considered how they would react if they learned the truth. "I am sister to Lord Conall, the ambassador from Leinster."

Utter silence greeted this statement, and Cait knew she had to apologize. "I am sorry. It was never my intent—"

"To deceive us?" Lena said.

"That was not my—"

"Then what?" Tilda spoke from behind Lena. "Why did you come back?"

Cait bent her head. "I thought you would be worried."

It was exactly the wrong thing to say, and she knew it the moment the words were out.

"We were worried." Tilda continued to glare at her. "I guess we shouldn't have been."

Cait tried again. "Rikard knew who I was and why I was here. He agreed to my presence because he feared he had a traitor in his midst. King Diarmait and he hoped I could discover what was going on before it ... turned deadly." She finished with her eyes on her feet.

Total silence greeted this statement too. Cait could feel their continued hostility, though perhaps it was less pronounced than it had been a moment before.

Finally it was Lena, their leader, who spoke. "What is it you want with us, my lady?" She ruled her kitchen with an iron hand, but she wasn't an angry person by nature.

Caitriona had wanted their forgiveness. But as they weren't going to give her that—and she didn't deserve it anyway—she decided to come up with a reason for her presence that they would view as valid. So she asked a question. "The night before Deirdre died, did she go to bed as usual?"

Lena's brow furrowed as she considered the question, and she gave herself time to think by returning to her dough, kneading and shaping it as she talked. "The curtain was pulled when I went to bed. I didn't disturb her."

The others agreed that they'd seen the same, but nobody had checked to see if Deirdre was actually present.

"None of you saw her leave?"

"No," said Ana, a laundress.

"Do you know why she would be poking around the warehouse when Rikard told nobody to come?"

"You know the answer to that," Tilda said. "She hated not knowing everything that was going on."

"Some of the people we talked to speculated that she was with Rikard that night." Cait cleared her throat and added somewhat delicately. "In bed."

Lena guffawed. "Not likely. Not for a long time."

"But they were lovers once?"

"She had a child by him, but he died at birth," said Iona, one of the older women. She was Welsh, but had been a slave in Dublin almost as long as Deirdre. "As it turned out, shortly thereafter Rikard's first wife died giving birth to Finn, and Deirdre became his wet nurse. She lived in the big house for years. That's where she learned to weave so well."

Cait was stunned. "She never told me."

"She didn't like to talk about it, especially once Finn didn't return." Lena patted the dough into shape and set it in a bowl. The others had begun moving towards a rack near the door where cloaks and head coverings were hooked. Lena followed. "Now that you're here, you might as well come with us."

"Of course," Cait said. "Where are we going?"

"To visit Deirdre's grave. We weren't welcome at the funeral." Iona's tone was accusing, as it had every right to be.

But Lena put out a hand to her to shush her. "Lady Caitriona was there for us, weren't you?"

"I was. I'm sorry I didn't seek permission for you to attend. It wasn't that I didn't think of you. I didn't know that you couldn't be there, and I didn't even learn of the funeral until a quarter of an hour before it happened."

Tilda snorted. "We are slaves. Our men were rounded up afterwards and spent all day without food or drink at the hands of that sheriff."

Cait took in a breath. "I'm sorry. I will speak to Finn about what will become of you now that Rikard is gone—"

"Don't pretend you are troubled by our problems." Iona strode away towards the back door with Tilda and Ana following.

Lena, however, stayed behind. "Don't mind Iona. She and Deirdre were close."

"I understand that, and I can only say again how sorry I am for deceiving you. It was never my intent."

Lena nodded. "I know it wasn't. Perhaps next time you'll look before you leap."

Cait looked down at her toes. "One can hope."

Lena patted her forearm. "It isn't in your nature. I understand that too, and I understand why Deirdre took to you so well."

Cait looked up. "I really did like her very much. I wish I had thought to check for her before I went to sleep that night."

"It might not have mattered," Lena said. "If she wasn't in her bed, what would you have done? She knew her own mind, did Deirdre, and she did what she liked. Does your brother think she was prying at the warehouse and that is what got her killed?"

"It does seem the most likely scenario."

"She did have more privileges than the rest of us. Rikard always had a soft spot for her as, of course, did Finn and she for him."

"I meant what I said about speaking to Finn about your fate," Cait said. "Slavery is not condoned by the Church. I know Bishop Gregory would like to tell his superiors in Canterbury that there are no more slaves in Dublin. Perhaps Finn would be amenable to a different arrangement."

"You think he might pay us for our work?" Lena scoffed. "That will be the day."

"It will be. Someday." Cait had a sudden thought to speak to Bishop Gregory and ask him to personally intervene on the slaves' behalf with Finn. She was the sister of Leinster's ambassador. He might listen.

The cook looked at her sadly. "On my deathbed, my dear. It is something for which a slave can never hope, else it becomes impossible to find happiness anywhere. That is why Tilda and Iona continue to suffer."

Cait gave her a small smile. "I shouldn't come with you to Deirdre's grave, after all, should I?"

Lena patted her again. "Best not. Find your young prince and forget about us. Your life lies elsewhere now."

25

Day Three

Godfrid

Rather than loiter around the warehouse while Cait spoke with Rikard's slave women, Godfrid set off on an aimless circuit of the city. He wanted time to think, to take out each piece of the puzzle that was this investigation and examine them. Church bells tolled immediately after he left, and then again, marking the quarter hours. He'd been wending his way west and then, without conscious intent, he fetched up at the western gatehouse.

Holm claimed to have questioned the guards at all the gatehouses about the comings and goings during the night of Rikard's death. Godfrid believed he had done so. At the same time, he didn't necessarily trust that Holm had done as thorough a job as Godfrid himself would have. While Conall had spoken to guards at the dock gate, perhaps more could be done here, even at this late date.

As Godfrid approached the western gateway, the guard on duty straightened to full attention. "My lord."

"Hello, Markus." Godfrid had made it his business over the years to know the names of every guardsman in Dublin, but Markus was more than a simple guard or even a brief acquaintance, for that matter. He'd sailed to Anglesey during the debacle with Prince Cadwaladr five years ago. "How is it that you pulled this duty today?"

"Sheriff Holm has allowed us to leave the gates open so people can once again enter and leave freely, but he still wanted experienced men on duty, ones who know what to do if danger comes calling."

"That was good thinking." Godfrid put a hand on the man's shoulder. "Do you have an accounting yourself of who came in and out of this gate the night Rikard died?"

"I wasn't here, you understand? But after Merchant Rikard died, I took it upon myself to question my fellows. Nobody remembers anything unusual, I'm sorry to say. But then, a dozen people at least come in and out of this gate every hour, day and night."

"Surely not after midnight?" Godfrid said. "It wasn't so long ago that we were at war with Brega."

"You'd be surprised," Markus said. "People have short memories. I think they want to forget ... Anyway, several instances stood out in particular: a courting couple, caught out late by a rainstorm; Matthias the drunk, who'd slept the day away in a field; and before dawn, a young man with a lame horse, who said his name was Niklas. The guard didn't know him, but he was clearly wealthy and Danish. No Irishmen arrived after the gates were closed. They would know better. If strangers entered the city, it was earlier in the day or by a different gate."

Godfrid harrumphed, not pleased to hear it. Then he had a thought. "What about departing?"

Markus looked rueful. "Sheriff Holm came inquiring on that matter as well. He was told that an Irishman did leave just before dawn. But he was a servant, not a merchant or an ambassador from any kingdom in Ireland. Just a scrawny lad— though admittedly on a fine horse. He didn't stop to talk, and the gatekeeper had no reason to detain him. Dublin is a free city, as you know. People come and go as they please as long as there's no trouble." His expression turned rueful. "Do you think he was one of the killers?"

Godfrid shrugged. "I don't know. Thank you for your help."

With no more to ask, Godfrid left the gate and steered directly now towards Rikard's own house. It was another place Godfrid had not yet visited, in large part because he hadn't seen the point, since they'd already spoken to Arno, Sanne, and Finn. Now, Godfrid had something of a perverse desire to see how Finn was handling his transition from sailor, to prodigal son, to owner of his own business. He had certainly looked content yesterday in the company of Arno and Thorfin.

Godfrid thought he had just enough time, a quarter of an hour or so by the toll of the bells, before he needed to return to the warehouse to collect Cait. And really, if Finn mentioned to Ottar that Godfrid had come to see him, Godfrid could explain that he'd merely stopped by to see how the grieving son was doing.

Finn's yard was bustling with servants, indicating that Finn was well on his way to making his father's kingdom his own. Godfrid did not find his overt lack of grief endearing. Then again, when Godfrid's father had died, Godfrid had endeavored to keep as busy as possible so he wouldn't have time to think. Perhaps that's all Finn was doing.

Godfrid was a known friend of the household, so he was admitted into the yard without question by a harried stableman who was observing a boy walking a lame horse around the yard. It was a fine animal, as befitting one of the leading merchants of Dublin.

"What happened?" Godfrid said.

"He put a foot wrong. It happens," the stable man said. "His hock isn't broken. With rest, he should be better tomorrow."

Then a servant opened the door to the hall and stood on the threshold, waiting for Godfrid so he could greet him courteously. Once inside, Godfrid had expected to find Finn triumphant, or occupied making his father's house his own, or at the very least busy with paperwork. Instead, he found him sitting alone at the end of his long table in the main hall, having taken his father's chair, drinking wine from a carafe that was more than half empty.

At Godfrid's approach, Finn should have risen to his feet out of respect, but instead he waved a hand and made an attempt at bowing from a seated position. "Welcome, my lord." He articulated his words too carefully. "I have discovered that getting up would be unwise."

Godfrid gently moved the carafe another foot from Finn and then sat near the end of the table on a long bench. "You are very far gone for the sun being high in the sky. Perhaps I should take away your cup."

Finn gripped the cup in question more tightly, cradling it to his chest. "My father is dead." His tone was belligerent, and not undeserved, since Godfrid had no right to stop him drinking in his own house.

"I am aware, Finn." Godfrid reached out a long arm and placed his hand on Finn's shoulder. "Your father and I were very different in age, but I felt he was my friend. I am very sorry for your loss."

Finn took a long drink and set down the empty cup. He stretched forward for the carafe, but it was beyond his easy reach now, and Godfrid picked it up and moved it another few inches down the table, just to be safe. "You may have it, but only if you answer some questions for me first."

"What do you want to know?" Rather than protesting, Finn's voice sounded resigned, with a touch of gloom.

"Ask him when he really arrived in Dublin."

Godfrid had been so focused on Finn that he hadn't noticed the front door opening. Now Conall strode towards him, Cait on his heels. At the sight of her, Godfrid rose to his feet again and approached. "I didn't forget about you, I swear."

"I know you didn't." Cait put out a hand to him. "However, it was time to leave, and fortunately, as I stepped from the barracks door, Conall was passing by on his way here."

"How did you know where I was?" Godfrid asked.

"I wasn't looking for you." Conall lifted his chin to point to Finn. "I was looking for him."

Cait grinned. "But we knew where you were anyway because several people mentioned you'd passed by on the way from the warehouse to here."

Conall had come to a halt at the far end of the table. "Tell us the truth this time."

"Why?" Finn said without asking what truth he was supposed to tell. "What good will it do? My father isn't coming back."

"It might bring him justice."

Godfrid looked from Conall to Finn and back again. "Are you suggesting Finn killed his father?"

His hands on his hips, Conall was glaring at Finn.

Finn was drunk enough, however, that he could barely muster the appropriate amount of outrage. "I didn't kill him."

"I don't believe you," Conall said flatly. "I spoke to a sailor who saw you board your ship just as it docked. You didn't arrive in Dublin when you said you did."

Finn stared into his drink. When Godfrid had risen to speak to Cait, he'd reacquired the carafe and had poured himself another cup. While he wasn't drinking it yet, he seemed to find its presence comforting.

Cait sat on the bench where Godfrid had been sitting a moment earlier and leaned forward slightly, her hand placed gently on Finn's arm. "Maybe you didn't kill your father, but you do know more than you're telling. The truth won't bring your father back, but you will feel better if someone else knows what really happened."

Finn responded to her as he hadn't to anyone else. He put down the cup, leaned back in his chair, and closed his eyes. "You are both wrong and right. My father's death was my fault, though I never intended him to die."

Conall didn't object to Cait taking lead, and he even tempered his animosity enough to take a seat on the other side of the table. Godfrid moved to occupy the space on the bench next to Cait. Gareth would have recognized the importance of a moment when the truth was coming out, and all they had to do was not get in its way. This was one of those times.

Finn was too absorbed in his own misery to care where anyone sat. "Stupid of me to think nobody noticed. Yes, the man speaks the truth. I arrived earlier, though not by much. I told you the truth when I said that we went first to Wexford. The next day, however, the winds weren't in our favor, and I knew it would take longer to sail to Dublin than to ride. I took a horse from the stables." He laughed mockingly. "It should have been quicker. As it was, the horse pulled up lame, and I ended up walking most of the way. I arrived in Dublin well after midnight."

Godfrid harrumphed under his breath. "The horse I saw in the yard. That's the one you rode?"

Finn nodded.

Godfrid looked at Cait and Conall. "A guard at the western gate remembered a young man entering in the wee hours of the morning with a lame horse, though he said his name was Niklas." He turned back to Finn. "That was you?"

Finn nodded again. "I didn't give my real name, since I wanted my arrival to be a surprise for my father."

"Then what happened?" Cait asked. "Naturally, the first thing you did was come here to wake the household and proclaim your resurrection."

"Of course. I left the horse in the care of the stableman, but the steward told me that the women were at a coming-of-age celebration at Arno's house, and my father had gone to his warehouse. So I went there." Finn chose to direct his next comment at Godfrid. "I found my father standing in the middle of his warehouse, alive, but Deirdre dead at his feet."

Conall, Cait, and Godfrid gasped in unison.

"*Rikard* killed Deirdre?" Cait found her voice first.

Finn snorted. "Of course he didn't! Though I admit I initially thought the same, and I accused him of it. I'd spent two years anticipating our reunion, and I was on fire." He eyed Godfrid again. "As you may know, we hadn't parted on the best of terms."

Godfrid had known Finn his whole life, though he hadn't been aware of him as a person until he came of age. Rikard had favored his eldest son, as most fathers did, and this younger son had resented that fact, as most sons did. "Then what happened?"

"My father was weeping and barely looked at me. It was like he didn't even realize who I was. He kept saying, *They killed her.*"

"Are we speaking of the men from Brega?" Conall asked. "Just like everyone thinks? You do accuse them after all?"

Finn nodded, bleary from the drink and reliving the scene in his head. Then he blinked several times as if suddenly realizing to whom he was speaking. "Oh! You don't know!"

"What don't we know?" Godfrid understood Finn's grief and drunkenness, but the storytelling was more disjointed than he would have liked.

Finn straightened in his seat and cleared his throat. "In recent months, my father has been the go-between for King Ottar and various potential allies. Sometimes they used the warehouse as a meeting place."

Godfrid and Conall had both known that, of course, but neither wanted to interrupt now that Finn appeared to putting his thoughts in order.

"That night, one of Ottar's men met with the men from Brega, the ones found dead by Holm's pig. My father was supposed to leave them alone for their meeting, but he hid in his vault instead in order to overhear what they said to one another. Before they started talking, he didn't know anything about who they were."

"Did the king ask him directly for this favor?" Godfrid asked.

Finn gave a vigorous shake of his head which almost unbalanced him. "It was Sturla."

That was no surprise, but it was gratifying to hear his hunch confirmed anyway.

"What did they talk about?"

"A treaty between King Ottar and Prince Donnell O'Connor." Then Finn pierced Godfrid with his gaze, belying his drunken state. "My father intended to report the results of the meeting to you."

Godfrid bowed his head. "He was a true friend."

Finn grimaced. "Unfortunately, Deirdre, who'd always been too curious for her own good, came prowling around the outside of the warehouse. Maybe one of the men heard her, or perhaps he'd gone outside to relieve himself and saw her. My father couldn't say. Either way, she was brought inside. The Irishmen assumed she'd been sent to spy on them. They wanted to know for whom she was working. After they hit her, she told them she was one of Rikard's slaves and that she had seen him enter the warehouse earlier in the evening and not come out."

"Your father overheard all this?" Cait's hand was to her mouth. "Sturla stood by and watched?"

"Though my father had arranged with Sturla for the meeting, he couldn't say that it was he who'd come to meet with the Bregans. It was hard to hear down in the vault."

Godfrid frowned, remembering the conversation they'd overheard between Sturla and Jon, both of whom had been standing above them. Godfrid had heard them just fine, but perhaps Rikard's hearing had no longer been what it once was.

Then Finn began to weep. "When they began hurting Deirdre, my father wanted to come out of the vault, but he knew that if he did, likely they would hurt him too."

"Were they all speaking Danish?" Cait asked.

Finn nodded. "Ottar's man was furious at being spied upon, but instead of shouting, his voice grew quieter and deeper. He ordered the Bregans to search the warehouse from top to bottom to discover where my father had hidden himself. When they couldn't find him, they killed Deirdre to prevent her from telling anyone what she'd seen." He shuddered. "Ottar's man had a voice like ice, and as Deirdre died, he said, *Nöd kommer gammel Kierling til at trave.*" *Sometimes events compel a person to do what he'd rather not.*

At the last, Finn's voice trembled, and he looked down at his hands. "All this my father told me in tears as he cradled Deirdre in his arms. He wanted to call the watch, but I talked him out of it. I had a better idea."

Godfrid let out a breath, finally understanding where this was going. "You went after the men from Brega? *You* killed them?"

"They killed my mother!" Finn threw the words at him, and only afterwards did he appear to realize what he'd said.

Nobody said anything for a moment, and then Godfrid said, "How long have you known Deirdre was your mother?"

Finn looked into his cup. "Part of me always knew, but my father told me the truth when I was fifteen. He swore me to secrecy, of course. I couldn't inherit anything from him if I was a bastard, and since I *was* his son, he saw no reason for anyone to know the truth."

"This, of course, is why you've kept silent about what really happened," Conall said, speaking for the first time since Finn had started talking.

"In part. I'm determined to revenge myself on whoever King Ottar sent too, but without knowing his name, he is out of reach."

"Did you take anything from the men you killed?" Godfrid asked.

Finn focused on Godfrid's face. "One of them had a warrant for the death of your brother, my lord. I took that back to my father, but I couldn't find the treaty they talked about. I searched their bodies as best I could, but it was dark, and I was in a hurry. Maybe it was in a boot. Maybe they had a third man with them who got away with it." He frowned. "I have looked in the vault for the death warrant in order to give it to you, my lord, but I don't know what my father did with it after I left him."

Cait reached for Finn's arm again. "How did Deirdre end up in that alley?"

"After I returned, we rolled her in sacking and left her there, thinking she would be found quickly."

"And your father? How did he die?"

"When I left, he was heading down the stairs to hide the death warrant. At his request, I closed the trapdoor so nobody could come upon him unawares while he was looking for a hiding place."

"And the wine poured on the floor?"

Finn scoffed. "A full carafe had been left on the table for the visitors to enjoy while they talked. Before I left, I poured myself a cup. But as I turned, I knocked over the carafe with my elbow, and the wine spilled everywhere. I called down to my father to tell him what I'd done, but he told me not to worry about it and to get to my ship."

"Oh, son." Godfrid had his fingers to his temples.

"I don't understand why you went to such lengths to confuse things," Cait said.

"I do." Conall sighed and looked at her. "Finn couldn't accuse Ottar of orchestrating Deirdre's murder without exposing his father's alliance with Godfrid." Finn had buried his face in his hands and didn't appear to be listening, so Conall gripped his shoulder to get his attention. "Am I right?"

Finn looked up and, suddenly animated, threw out a hand to Godfrid. "Finally your brother had real leverage against the king! My father couldn't wait to tell you about it. He intended to go straight to you when he was done in the vault."

Cait looked near to weeping. "Why didn't he tell *me* what he was doing that night? That's what I was there for!"

Finn shook his head. "He knew how important the meeting was, but he didn't want to put you in danger. He thought he could handle it. From inside the vault, nobody would ever know he had overheard." His eyes grew sad. "He had grown fond of you, you see."

His words also explained why Finn had showed so little concern about Cait's transformation from slave to noblewoman. He'd known in advance that she existed.

Finn continued, "I timed my arrival at the wharf perfectly, since the ship was just docking. My father had gone down in the vault for only a moment, long enough to hide the paper. But somehow, in that brief time, his heart gave out, and he died down there all alone."

26

Day Three

Conall

Godfrid's impulse was, of course, to tell the truth immediately. It was hardly surprising, but Conall was steadfast. "We can't," he said flatly.

"Why not?" Godfrid was on his feet, waving his hands.

"That's a mare's nest, and you know it." Conall leaned forward. "Think about it, Godfrid. Ottar's treaty with Donnell should be discussed privately, in the dark, on a quest for an outcome that doesn't rip a hole in Dublin society. Surely you can't want to see Dublin disgraced before all of Ireland?"

Godfrid took in a breath, seeming to settle himself, and then came back to the table. Cait patted the seat beside her, and he resumed his place. "Instruct me, because I can't see it."

"First, there's Finn." Conall gestured in the young man's direction. Maybe they shouldn't have been discussing this with him present, but as he'd already acted in their interests, killing two men, he wasn't worried about him betraying them to Ottar. "It turns out he's a bastard. Do you want to ruin his life? Nobody but Ottar and Donnell are sorry Deirdre's murderers are dead, and while Finn might not be punished for their deaths, he would lose everything else."

"It's more than that, though," Cait said. "As Rikard realized, you finally have leverage—real leverage—against Ottar. If you reveal the treaty in open hall, Ottar could potentially bluster his way out of it. His supporters will claim it's falsified and accuse you of treason."

Conall nodded. "But if you show it to him in private, he can't appeal to anyone else for relief."

Cait smirked. "Even while blackmailing him, you keep the moral high ground."

Godfrid shook his head. "You really are brother and sister, aren't you?" But then he let out a puff of air. "Maybe you're not wrong, but it goes against my instincts. While keeping secrets these last five years has become a habit, it has also worn away at me."

"I am new to this as well," Cait said, "but believe me, I realize secrets do that. Still, this is Ottar we're talking about."

Finn, meanwhile, was acting as if they weren't there. He'd finished all the wine in his cup and poured himself more before Conall noticed, emptying the carafe. At this juncture, Conall didn't see a reason to take the cup away from him. If he was honest about it, he wanted Finn malleable for the next few hours while they decided what to do with him.

Conall stood. "Let's get him to my house."

Neither Cait nor Godfrid asked why Conall thought moving him was necessary. Finn, however, protested blearily when Conall forced him to stand and, after three steps, started to retch. Cait, a veteran of many feasts and well versed in drunken men, grabbed a bowl from a sideboard and shoved it under his face. Finn sank with it to his knees, his head hanging.

Godfrid patted Finn's hair. "Get it all out. It's better that way."

Conall knew enough of guilt and grief to understand that Finn was vomiting up both along with the wine.

One of the household servants, this one not a slave, appeared out of the back of the hall. He hesitated ten feet away, and Conall motioned with one hand that he should see to his master.

While they waited for Finn to clean himself up—and sober up enough to walk—Conall folded his arms, half-perching on the table. "I don't think you should tell your brother about this just yet either."

"Unless he comes to Dublin, I don't feel as if I have any way to do so," Godfrid said. "I am under constant scrutiny. If I left by any gate, everyone would know it and want to know why."

"I am wary of showing Fergus the sailor again too," Conall said. "This is how I suggest we proceed—"

"My lords!" A breathless Alf burst through the door. At the sight of the three of them talking, he wavered for a moment on the threshold, and then continued, "Some men—" He bent over, gasping for air. "Some men from Brega have arrived, sent by the King of Brega himself!"

Conall didn't bother to ask how Alf had known that the three of them could be found at Finn's house. It was now self-evident that Godfrid was right about being watched continually.

Godfrid moved towards Alf. "We only discovered the bodies this morning. How could he possibly know of the deaths of his men?"

Alf shook his head, still catching his breath. "I couldn't say, my lord. I know only that they do, and that they are here to convey their displeasure. Holm asked that you come to the palace to hear them speak."

Godfrid made a shooing motion with his hand. "Tell Holm to consider us on our way."

"Yes, my lord!" And Alf was off again.

Conall came to stand beside Godfrid to watch Alf go. "Ottar all but ordained Holm the murderer. How is he going to explain these deaths away to Brega?"

Godfrid glanced back to Finn. His servant was dabbing at his cheeks with a wet washcloth. "Do we leave him here?"

"I think we have to. We don't want him anywhere near King Ottar or these emissaries from Brega. Not today, and he would present quite a spectacle, limping through Dublin on the way to my house."

Cait refused to be left behind either, so they brought her, hoping that everyone would be so unsettled by the arrival of these ambassadors that they wouldn't question her presence.

Sure enough, they arrived at the palace to find it in an uproar, more even than it had been on and off during the last three days. Alf's headlong run through Dublin was rewarded too, since they arrived in time to have missed only the initial greetings between Ottar and the four representatives of Brega's king, Gilla. Conall wondered if these four knew what the two dead representatives had been doing. By appearing in Dublin, they could be putting their lives on the line for Gilla. At the same time, there was definitely safety in numbers, as well as a public spectacle.

Conall was honestly surprised that Ottar hadn't cleared the hall to speak to these ambassadors in private and whispered as much to Holm, whom he stopped beside.

"They asked that everyone remain to hear what they had to say," Holm said in an undertone.

Conall frowned. Something was wrong here—more wrong, that is, than murder and intrigue had already produced.

A richly robed man took a step in front of his fellows, who stood in a line facing Ottar's high table. All four men wore clothing similar to what Conall himself wore today, as necessary when visiting a king. While the Danish men around them, in keeping with their warlike past, wore short tunics, breeches, high boots, and summer cloaks, these men wore more flowing garments, with longer tunics, floppier pants, and ankle-length boots.

Conall routinely chose his clothing with the idea of using it as a mask to hide behind, and what unfolded in the hall over the next quarter of an hour was in keeping with that principle. Ottar knew some truths, and Brega's emissaries knew others, but because they were in open hall, they could admit none of them. Cait and Godfrid might prefer not to keep secrets, but Conall himself was very much enjoying the fact that nobody but the three of them knew the whole story.

The ambassador spread his arms wide. "King Gilla of Brega seeks justice for the murder of his men and demands that you produce the one responsible!"

King Ottar didn't bother gaping at the man. Given the ambassadors' solemnity, the purpose for their visit couldn't have been a surprise. Instead, his eyes narrowed, and Conall could see him adding up his options and deciding that he had no choice but to pretend that the surface reason for this meeting was the only one. Ottar's impulse was always to be combative anyway. "Your men murdered a leading merchant of Dublin. They died as a result."

"Who says they murdered anyone? We demand proof!"

"I say. And we have all the proof we need."

The two men glared at each other, neither backing down.

Then Ottar waved regally in Conall's direction. "I asked the ambassador from Leinster, who has experience in these matters, to look into Merchant Rikard's death. He can tell you that our conclusions are valid."

Conall was surprised to be called upon—and suspicious of Ottar's motives—but he could hardly refuse to reply. "What King Ottar says is true. These men came to Rikard's warehouse for a meeting, a meeting that left Rikard dead and his servant strangled.

A bloody length of rope was found in the pocket of one of your men."

The leader of the ambassadors, a tall, spare man with red hair the color of Conall's, glared at him. "So you say."

They'd been speaking in Danish, which Conall had done deliberately, and Ottar pounced. "We do say. From whom did you hear a different version of these events?"

The ambassador turned magisterially back to the high table. "They had a third man with them, who stayed with their horses. He witnessed the murder, but could do nothing to stop it. Because he feared for his own life, he rode for home immediately afterwards."

Conall took three steps towards the ambassador and switched to Gaelic. "Did he get a good look at the attacker? Could he describe him?"

The ambassador transferred his glare to Conall. "No."

Conall subsided. "Pity."

The Bregan returned to Danish. "Your supposed proof does not satisfy me, nor will it satisfy my king. His wrath at these deaths is very great."

"You dare threaten me?" Ottar surged to his feet, forced to bluster through a difficult situation, one which Gilla couldn't help but misconstrue. Ottar had invited his men to Dublin as part of their new alliance, and they'd ended up dead. It looked as if Ottar had changed his mind and the so-called alliance had been intended as a ruse—to what end Gilla couldn't be sure.

"It is not I who threatens, my lord." The man bowed and held the pose. It was a good reminder that these men themselves had done nothing wrong, and Ottar slowly lowered himself back into his seat. "We take our leave. Bring the guilty man to the ford of the Liffey at Lucan tomorrow at sunset."

Ottar remained sitting with his elbow on the armrest of his chair and one finger tapping his lower lip. "Or what?"

"My king warns you not to test him. If we do not have the culprit in hand by tomorrow night, you will not like the consequences."

Ottar felt he was being bullied. Conall could see it in his face, but Ottar couldn't very well expose the ambassador and the King of Brega for what they were, lackeys for Prince Donnell, without exposing himself. Conall had started out in his role as ambassador with an open mind as to the character of both Ottar and Godfrid. Of course, Godfrid was Gareth's friend, so he was predisposed to like him, and today, the differences between the two men couldn't be more clear.

Today, Ottar's lack of a solid core could be the ruin of Dublin.

Then Helga appeared out of the shadows. He'd never seen her approach her husband in the company of men when they were consulting, but she did it today, to the point of resting a hand on his shoulder. All side conversations going on around the hall stopped, and Ottar appeared frozen to his chair.

Helga lifted her chin. "We will not be delivering any citizen of Dublin to your king." Her deep voice resonated throughout the hall. "You may as well return to him right now and tell him so. If he decides to come at us with an army tomorrow at the Liffey, he will find us there to meet him."

Dead silence greeted this announcement. The ambassadors had no idea what to make of her. The chief ambassador appeared to be stuttering. Helga was calling his bluff.

Some Danish farmers had ventured to settle north of the river as it ran west to east and flowed into the Irish Sea, but the vast majority of Danish settlements outside of Dublin, including Brodar's steading, were to the south and southwest. The Liffey was a major river and formed the border between Meath, of which Brega was a client kingdom, and Leinster. If King Gilla crossed the Liffey with an army at the village of Lucan, he would be taking a great risk. King Diarmait would see it as an act of war against Leinster.

For Ottar's part, he reached up to place his hand on his wife's where it still lay on his shoulder. "You heard her. My men will be pleased to escort you to the gates of the city."

There was some scuffling as people backed away from the men from Brega while Holm and Alf moved to their side with an alacrity that was almost comical. In short order, the entire party had left the hall. Ottar, meanwhile, was whispering with Helga, who'd pulled out the chair next to him so she could sit.

Once the door closed behind Holm and the others, Ottar turned to face his audience and swept out an arm. "Leave us."

There was some grumbling among his advisers at their summary dismissal, especially since Helga's intervention had possibly committed them to war. Godfrid exchanged a look with Conall, tipping his head towards the door, but before either could take a step, Ottar barked, "Not you two."

It was Conall's preference to stay anyway, so he turned back. The detached part of him that had nothing invested in the outcome was highly amused by the entire situation. Godfrid, for his part, was emotionally and personally invested. Even so, he managed to keep his expression blank, and together they approached the high table.

Out of the corner of his eye, Conall saw Cait move towards a side wall, behaving as if there was nothing out of the ordinary in her staying. She had learned these last weeks to blend into the background, and Conall had no intention of calling attention to her.

Within a few moments, the only people left in the hall were Ottar, Helga, Sturla, Godfrid, and Conall, with Cait leaning against the wall by a post.

"Will Leinster help us?" Ottar said without preamble.

"Are you making a formal request?"

"Yes."

"It depends on your intent."

"We will march, of course," Helga said. "We have no choice now."

"It would probably be important for King Diarmait to know that Connaught as well as Brega is involved," Godfrid said, his tone casual, as if the statement was a mere by-the-way.

Ottar's jaw clenched and bulged. "Why would Connaught be involved?"

"Because you made a treaty with Prince Donnell, the heir to the throne of Connaught *and* the High Kingship." Godfrid's expression was severe. "You conspired with him to murder his brother and my brother. As part of the exchange, you agreed that when Dublin falls to Brega tomorrow, authority for Dublin would transfer from Leinster to Connaught." The second half of that statement was only a guess, but Conall thought it was a good one.

Ottar's expression turned fiercer, but it was Conall who spoke, "I see you don't deny your conspiracy."

"Where is the document?" Ottar spat out the words.

"Safe," Conall said.

"I can send men at any time to rip your house apart," Ottar said. "Then you will have no proof of anything."

"The way they tore apart Rikard's warehouse and murdered the merchant and his servant?" Godfrid was rocking back and forth on the balls of his feet. His ire was up, and he was focused. "The way they tore apart mine?"

Sturla scoffed. "We had nothing to do with any of that."

"Nothing? Why are you lying?" Godfrid canted his head. "Tell me the truth. I have the treaty and the warrant for my brother's death. I know Sturla was at Rikard's warehouse that night, meeting with the men of Brega. Just admit it." He glared at the steward. "Did you kill Deirdre yourself, or did you let the Bregans do it for you?"

"Don't answer that, Sturla." Ottar's eyes were like ice. "Why does it matter?"

"Because I want to know the truth."

This time it was Helga who scoffed. "The truth is for children."

But Sturla was too intent on his own survival. "What do you intend to do with the document?" It was, of course, the only question that mattered.

Ottar sighed. "He intends to expose me in open council."

"He can't," Sturla said.

"He can, Sturla," Helga said. "You know he can, and he will be believed."

"What I do, I do for Dublin." Ottar leaned forward, his attention focused on Godfrid, who was standing directly opposite from where the king sat at his table.

"What you do, you do for you. As usual," Godfrid shot back.

"As usual, you misunderstand. By the end of the day, Dublin won't be bowing to Connaught." Ottar snorted. "We will be free."

Conall released a puff of air as he comprehended the intricacy of the plot, which it appeared Ottar had come up with on very short notice once he understood that the treaty with Brega was dead. "You intend to put Leinster and Connaught at each other's throats. We will bloody ourselves, while you sit by and watch."

Helga whispered something in Ottar's ear, and though he shook his head, he was listening to her.

Cait came forward from her place against the wall, emboldened, perhaps, by the presence of another woman in the room to whom the men were listening. "Why did you tell the ambassadors that Dublin wouldn't give up the killer? Give them Holm, if that's who you think killed the Bregans, and be done with it."

Conall answered for Ottar. "It would show an unacceptable weakness, Cait. King Gilla believes Ottar to have ordered the deaths, so he asked for the culprit precisely because he knew Ottar couldn't give him up, no matter who was guilty of the crime. It would be too great an offense to Dublin's sovereignty."

Cait scoffed. "So much for your new allies."

But Godfrid gave a low whistle, as he finally understood what was really happening here. "All of you *want* war, but for different reasons, and each of you thought you could trick the other into it."

Cait shook her head. "So that means King Diarmait *shouldn't* come because then he will be at war with Connaught."

"No, Cait," Godfrid said. "That would play into Donnell's hands as well, because he sees it as an even better way to gain the upper hand over his brother. He seeks—"

"—to conquer Dublin for himself." Ottar's voice was heavy. "Again I ask, will King Diarmait support us with an army?"

Conall could feel no sympathy for the man. "Not if you lead it."

27

Catriona

Cait pulled her brother towards the side wall, well away from the high table, and spoke to him in Gaelic in an undertone. She thought Godfrid and Ottar could keep themselves occupied for a few moments by glaring at each other. "King Diarmait has to let Ottar lead the army. If your men ride for Leinster now, they can be in Kildare by midnight."

"I will send them, Cait. Of course, I will, if only as a warning to Uncle Diarmait of what is happening. He should know something of it already because of the rider Brodar sent the day Rikard died. But how can I ask him for an army? The king will have every right to be angry about Ottar's treaty with Prince Donnell. He will not let Ottar keep the throne, and he won't send support if Ottar leads whatever army the Danes do marshal."

"He must, and if you explain to him why he must, he will understand."

"I can't explain if *I* don't understand!"

"If Diarmait doesn't support Dublin now, and Ottar as the King of Dublin, there's a good chance he will lose all Danish holdings to Connaught," Cait said flatly.

Conall was silent a moment, and then he said, "The simplest solution would be to have Brodar lead the men of Dublin, since it is he who will become king when we bring down Ottar."

"We can't do that right now, though. If you take the throne from Ottar before any battle, the people will need an explanation. They will learn what he has done, which is exactly what you argued an hour ago Godfrid must not tell them. And you were right. While having everyone know the truth might be satisfying for us, it will create unrest, disbelief, and distrust. Such a move would shame not only Ottar but his supporters too, and for all that they are Danes, they will have no strength in them to fight." She paused. "And we need them to fight."

Conall looked away, towards the door, though she thought he was really seeing the fields between Dublin and the ford of the Liffey. He was the smartest man she knew, and she believed that he, like their uncle, would understand her reasoning if she explained it properly.

She lowered her voice even further. "Not everyone will believe what is written on that paper. People have a staggering capacity to lie to themselves, even when presented with what might seem to be irrefutable evidence. When the truth goes against what they want, it leaves room for doubt. While Prince Brodar might become king, it would be without the support of his people that he needs to be successful." She paused to look meaningfully at Conall. "And Ottar would still be alive."

Conall rubbed his chin as he studied Cait, and then he turned abruptly on his heel to return to the dais. "I will send men riding to King Diarmait within the hour," he said, back to speaking Danish. "I wish you hadn't already told the ambassadors from Brega that you wouldn't be meeting King Gilla's terms. We could have used a little more time."

Helga shook her head. "It is better this way. Men are better fighters when the threat is imminent. We will marshal the men of Dublin and the surrounding area and march them at dawn to a ground of our choosing above the ford at Lucan. We will burn the bridge across the Liffey before we leave, so the only possible approach to the city is from the west."

Her point about the Liffey was well taken, and Helga spoke with as much authority as her husband might have, as if she'd been giving military orders for years. While the men of the court conspired and fought, Helga had sat silently by, but Cait was thinking now that Helga had always been the mind behind Ottar's throne. Her brother and Godfrid had assumed it was Sturla.

It was too bad she'd been born a woman, because Cait would have liked to see what kind of king Ottar's queen would have made.

As they left the palace shortly thereafter, Cait said to Godfrid, "I don't suppose you had a thought to send for Prince

Hywel a few weeks ago?" She was walking beside him, her hand tucked into his elbow. It was in the back of her mind that they were starting to look a familiar sight to the gossips of Dublin.

Godfrid was rueful. "What I wouldn't give to have the men of Gwynedd fighting at my side tomorrow. But no. I didn't know it was time."

Conall grunted. "We shall just have to make do without him and Gareth."

Godfrid glanced down at her. "How did it go at Finn's warehouse with your friends, by the way? I never had a chance to ask."

"Not well." She shot him a rueful smile, quickly gone. "It's my own fault."

"In time, they will come to understand that deceiving them was never your intent. What you did was for good reason and never directed at them."

"You may well be right, but I am angry with myself—and ashamed, truth be told. All the while I was with them, I treated my disguise as a game. I didn't think about it as lying."

"I tried to warn you," Conall said mildly.

"You would know." Cait kicked a stray rock in the road out of her way. "Like a child, I'm angry at you for being right. It's easier to be angry at you than to acknowledge how badly I myself behaved."

"Here's the real question you need to ask yourself—" Though he appeared to hesitate at first, after a moment, Godfrid put an arm around her shoulders and squeezed. Then he let go and made sure to return to a position about a foot away. "Knowing what you know now, would you have come anyway?"

"I would have." The words came immediately and with a little more force. "I was of use. I think I would still be now if all this hadn't happened."

"Then don't be too sorry. Look how far we've come in a very short amount of time, much of it due to your efforts and insight."

She couldn't stop a smile from quirking the corners of her mouth. "We did a credible job uncovering a murderer or three, didn't we?"

Godfrid grinned. "We did."

"I look forward to telling Gareth of it," Conall said.

"And Gwen." Cait found herself clenching Godfrid's arm too tightly, and she tried to ease her grip.

Godfrid noticed and patted her hand. "Your brother and I will be fine."

"So you say. It is the worst feeling in the world to have to wait for the men to return from battle, not knowing if they will return."

"We will," Conall said. "You saw to that."

"I did?" She turned her head to look at her brother.

"Ottar won't want Brodar or Godfrid anywhere near him," Conall said. "Thus, they will be posted far enough from the front lines that they can't stab him in the back."

"Would you, if you had the opportunity?" She looked up at Godfrid. "Stab him, I mean?"

It was a genuine question, and Godfrid took it seriously. "Murder is not to my taste, and while I can't speak for my brother, fate does not smile upon a man who takes the throne over the murdered body of his predecessor."

Conall tsked through his teeth, clearly impatient with Godfrid's reasoning. "We are hoping that the men of Brega will kill Ottar for us."

28

Day Four

Godfrid

G odfrid's ancestors had lived for battle, though they had preferred to practice a very one-sided kind of warfare where they attacked unsuspecting and undefended steadings and villages. His family's wealth had been initially won that way. The enormously tall tower at Kells to the northwest of Dublin had been built precisely to warn the citizens of Ireland of the approach of marauding Danes and give the villagers time to flee. They could never take all their possessions with them, however, so the end result had been better from a Danish perspective. An easy victory was still a victory.

Conall and Cait's ancestors had lived for war too, but of a different kind. The Danes, for the most part, presented a united front, even back in Denmark. One lord might go to war against another for ultimate power, as was happening now for the throne of Denmark, but they didn't have the constant warfare among clans that appeared endemic to Ireland. It was one of the reasons the Danes had been able to gain a foothold in the country in the first place. All they had to do was pit one clan against another and stake their claim to the leftovers. The Irish were warlike enough to rule the world if they could ever leave off fighting among themselves.

Which meant that, as Godfrid prepared himself for battle the next morning, he had no illusions about what he faced. It could be a bloodbath, on either side—or both, even if King Diarmait marched an army to support them.

Just after dawn, Godfrid led his horse to Conall's house to find Conall awake and dressed in full armor. Until the arrival of the Danes, the Irish had been lightly armored—another reason Godfrid's ancestors had achieved so much here—but in time they'd adapted to their new enemy. Conall wore a chainmail vest with padding underneath and a leather tunic over the top of that. He had heavy leather bands around his upper arms and bracers on his forearms. His leather boots went up to his knees, and while his thick leather pants wouldn't stop a direct slash of a sword, they would slow it some without compromising his ability to move.

Godfrid was dressed similarly, with the addition of metal armbands, as his ancestors of old had worn, and a metal helmet that he carried under his arm. He wasn't going to wear it until he had to. He didn't want to wear it at all, really, but having just been hit on the head, he was reminded of how terrible it felt, and how much he didn't want it to happen again. It seemed all Conall was going to wear on his head was a leather hat with a wide brim and a big feather. It might not do much to protect his head in battle, but he was going to be better off when it started to rain.

Cait came a step or two behind, and when their eyes met, Godfrid felt a pull behind his navel. Conall looked from one to the other and said, "I'm going to see about my horse."

It was wholly unnecessary, since both horses were being held in the yard by stable lads, but Godfrid let him go, leaving him and Cait alone in the entrance to Conall's hall.

Cait approached and put her hands to Godfrid's chest, smoothing the fabric of his tunic that he wore over his mail. "I'm angry at you for going to war."

"I know. You have every right to be."

"I'm not a Danish shield maiden from the sagas, who picks up sword and shield when her man falls and fights in his place. I can't think anything but evil thoughts about what has led you here."

Godfrid put his hands on her upper arms and leaned forward until his forehead touched hers. "I will do everything in my power to protect your brother."

"And he you. I know." She gave a little laugh. "How odd to have reached this point where a Dane and an Irishman are best of friends."

"Or a Dane and an Irish woman?" Godfrid held his breath.

"That too," she said softly.

Godfrid felt the tension in his stomach ease, having been far more afraid of her response to his question than of fighting the coming battle. "You would give up your freedom for me?"

"Is that what I'll be doing?"

"By your law and mine."

"I'm not afraid of change."

They looked at each other for a moment, and then he bent his head to briefly touch his lips to hers.

"I will come back. I promise."

"You'd better."

Conall eyed him as he mounted his horse, but the bustle of leaving meant they were a quarter of a mile from the city before he spit out his complaint. "I see you and my sister have come to an understanding."

Godfrid cleared his throat, his eyes skating left and right as the men around them gave them a little more space. "I apologize for not speaking to you of her earlier. Do you object to the match?"

Conall scoffed. "I would have told you sooner if I did."

"I have been so focused on Cait, I realize I neglected the traditionally important opinion of her brother."

"I am quite certain Cait will do what she wants, when she wants, regardless of my approval."

Godfrid drew in a breath, while at the same time putting out a hand to Conall in a way that he knew was going to seem very different to everyone watching. He hadn't yet discussed with Conall the point at which their external animosity needed to end, but to his mind, it was time. "I not only want it, I need it."

Conall didn't smile all that often, but his bright eyes and the twitching of his lips told Godfrid that he recognized the moment too. Since he was riding to Godfrid's right, he twisted in the saddle and leaned across the space between them to grip Godfrid's forearm. "In truth, I could not ask for a better man for her, Irish or Dane."

Godfrid grinned back, touched and humbled. "Thank you."

Then Conall's expression darkened, looking more like his usual self. "We'll see what your brother has to say about it."

"He may not realize it, but it isn't his place to meddle."

"It is if he's your king." Conall released him and straightened in the saddle to look ahead. His tone was light, however. "And then there's my king."

Godfrid's chin firmed. "I won't borrow trouble." But inside, he wondered what Cait would do if her uncle forbade the union. And would he forgo Cait for Brodar and marry Sanne as was his brother's wish?

Godfrid frowned. *No.*

"Brodar is not your father," Conall said softly.

"I have come to the same conclusion." Godfrid shifted in his seat, cheerful again and basking in the memory of Cait's arms around him and her lips on his. "A glorious day awaits."

Conall snorted. "We are not your pagan ancestors."

"Nor yours." Godfrid said innocently. "Every day is a gift from God, is it not?"

"It is, my friend." Conall barked a laugh. "It truly is."

Then riding side-by-side, revealing a familiarity and contentment in each other's presence that had to be astonishing to everyone around them, they continued at the head of their marching men, following the southern side of the Liffey, which they would take all the way to Lucan. There, Ottar intended to occupy a ridge of higher ground overlooking the ford, the perfect spot to begin their defense, since it was a good hundred feet above the level of the river.

They'd ridden only a mile when Brodar appeared around a curve in the road at the head of an army of a hundred men, ten of whom were mounted. At the sight of them, a cheer went up from the fifteen hundred that marched from the city.

All Danes, of whatever profession, were warriors, and the men in their army ranged in age from fifteen-year-old boys to sixty-year-old men. Their enthusiasm was heartening, but the inexperience of many meant Godfrid didn't have a great deal of confidence in their ability to fight a pitched battle. While they had a strong core of warriors, many of whom had participated in the battle against the men of Brega in which Godfrid's father died, or in other raids, Ottar hoped that the Irish they faced would be intimidated by their numbers more than their experience. Thus, Brodar's seasoned warriors were very welcome.

After greeting Godfrid and Conall, Brodar sent his men to join the marching soldiers and urged his own horse towards the head of the army where Ottar rode among his personal guard and his captains, Sturla among them. Godfrid and Conall followed.

"I have some bad news. The Bregans have already crossed the River Liffey," Brodar said to Ottar by way of a greeting. "My scouts report that they've taken the heights above the river, facing Dublin."

Godfrid ground his teeth. "Those are the same heights we intended to take."

"Smart of them," Conall added.

"My scouts have not returned." Ottar's shoulders hunched slightly, but then he straightened in the saddle. He was conniving and dishonest, but nobody had ever said he wasn't brave.

"Likely they won't," Brodar said.

Godfrid had sent word to Brodar yesterday of what they faced, which was why he was here now, but he'd included very few details. Brodar knew about Ottar's warrant for his death, of course, but not about the treaty with Prince Donnell, something which Godfrid hadn't felt he could commit to writing. Still, Ottar might assume that Brodar knew all and had to be wondering not only what Brodar was going to do, but how much of the truth he'd told his men.

The front ranks were close enough to have heard Brodar's news, and the knowledge of the Bregans' move spread quickly among the rest of the army. Knowing he had to counter their fears, Ottar found a place to halt, and while his men took a moment to rest, he urged his horse to a patch of higher ground. Sturla, who rode beside him as his adviser and confidant, clenched his fist above his head, and everyone stopped to listen.

Ottar stood in his stirrups. "My fellow Danes! I speak to you now of the grave news our brother Brodar has brought us. The Bregans have crossed the ford of the Liffey, in defiance of us and King Diarmait of Leinster. What I haven't told you is who leads them ... We fight not only King Gilla of Brega but Prince Donnell of Connaught!" He threw his voice at his men, and the prince's name echoed over their heads.

The response was an immediate roar of outrage. Godfrid was reminded again why Ottar had not only managed to wrest the kingship from his father but keep it.

Sturla waved both hands above his head, asking for silence so the king could speak again. When it was quieter, Ottar went on: "We know Donnell fights his own brother for the right to rule as high king upon their father's death. He intends to push us into the sea, to wipe Dublin from Ireland like a cloth across a table in order to prove to his father that he is the man to rule after him. But he has not taken our fortitude into account. He has forgotten our courage and our resolve. He thinks he has the upper hand, but WE WILL NOT YIELD!"

The last words came quickly, shouted such that Godfrid, who thought he was resistant to Ottar's charms, felt the power of them buffet him.

Ottar got the reply he wanted. The men threw their fists into the air, pounded on their breasts, and cheered.

Brodar shifted in the saddle and leaned in to speak to Godfrid. "He always could give a good speech."

"He called you *brother*, the duplicitous snake."

Brodar scoffed. "Ottar does what is expedient. Always has."

Godfrid turned to look at his brother. "I apologize for not coming myself to tell you of what has transpired. I couldn't leave the city last night."

"You knew about Prince Donnell?"

"And more." Godfrid glanced at Conall, who nodded, having agreed to speak only of what Brodar needed to know to get through the day. "Suffice to say, Ottar's speech aside, his downfall is imminent, whatever the outcome of this battle. Be prepared to be crowned King of Dublin after we defeat the Bregans."

Brodar's mouth opened, but no sound came out, and then he transferred his gaze to Conall. "I have Leinster's support?"

"More has happened than we dare speak of here," Conall said. "I have not heard that King Diarmait sends his army in support, but you should know that if it comes, it is for you my kinsmen ride, not Ottar."

Brodar seemed to grow several inches taller, and though Godfrid hadn't meant to do anything more than tell his brother a bit of the truth, he realized now that, in this hour, there nothing he could have said that would have been better. They had both been beaten down by years of deception and being second best. It was as if Brodar was a butterfly, shaking off the casing that had previously contained a caterpillar.

"What of Ottar?"

Godfrid shrugged. "He is probably still hoping he can salvage his crown. Know that he can't." This wasn't the time to tell him that the sudden escalation of the conflict with Brega was

Helga's idea, and that Godfrid was quite sure she saw more clearly than her husband.

Ottar's choices were poor at best. If Leinster came, and they defeated Prince Donnell's forces, he was still a traitor to Leinster. If Dublin lost, they would be subsumed into Connaught, or worse, pushed into the sea. Then Ottar would be ruler of nothing. Of a fallen people.

It was a conundrum not unlike the one Godfrid's father had faced: die with honor or live a little longer but in shame.

29

Day Four

Caitriona

Nobody who knew Cait well would be surprised to learn that she hated waiting. The year her brother had been away in Wales had been excruciating for her. It had been one of the reasons she'd fought so hard for the chance to come to Dublin. It was a woman's fate to wait at home, but Cait much preferred to act rather than react.

But here she was, safe behind Dublin's walls while the men she loved risked their lives for hers. Against all expectation, Queen Helga appeared to view her as something of a peer, and she had invited Cait to the palace to wait.

Cait could hardly refuse an invitation from the queen, so she climbed the staircase to the wall-walk in order to stare out at the landscape. There was nothing to see. And there wouldn't be, possibly for many hours.

Cait didn't care. She could be no other place but here.

"My lady." The guard nodded. "Prince Godfrid is a mighty man. If anyone will survive today, it will be he."

She smiled sweetly, thanking him and grateful there didn't seem to be any resentment of her burgeoning relationship with Godfrid. She was Irish, even if from Leinster, so there could have been. The guard didn't even looked askance at her when she perched herself on the top of the rampart and pulled out her needlework. She would wait, and she would think, because she could do nothing else, but she could also keep her hands busy.

Hours passed with no result, until Cait's fingers ached from the constant in and out of the needle. Then she heard the scrape of a shoe on the steps, and Helga appeared at the top of the tower. "Wouldn't it be better to occupy yourself elsewhere?"

Cait turned her head just enough to look at the queen's face, and then looked back to the horizon. Storm clouds were gathering on hills in the distance. It would rain before this evening, though since this was Ireland, that was no prescient prediction.

"If they are dying out there, I can't be whiling away my time in my brother's house or yours. What would I do?"

"Weave? It is what our ancestors did when our men went into battle. How else to spare one's man from the Valkyries?"

Cait glanced sharply at her. Helga had moved to stand in the center of the square tower, her hands folded in front of her and a complacent smile on her lips. The guard took one look at her, bowed, and beat a hasty retreat, down one level to the wall-walk below.

"I am an accomplished weaver," Cait said, reluctant to admit anything she didn't have to, "but that is not my tradition."

"Come now." Helga advanced towards her. "We both know that you have found favor in Prince Godfrid's eyes. Soon enough, you will be a Dane. Though you didn't know it, that was the choice you made when you came to Rikard."

Cait allowed herself a breath in and out. They were within an inch of each other in height, neither tall nor short for women, and Cait was able to look the queen in the eyes. "How did you know about that?"

"Do you think it strange that a queen should be friends with a slave? Rikard loaned her to me when I first arrived in Dublin. I lost a friend too when she died."

"I am very sorry." Cait swallowed. "She was dear to me and didn't deserve her fate."

"Who does?" Now Helga moved to look out over the landscape to the west, her head high and her hands clasped at breast height. "Nöd kommer gammel Kierling til at trave."

Cait gaped at her, stunned. Helga's expression remained serene, still looking away towards the horizon, while Cait had a rock in the pit of her stomach. "It was you in the warehouse that night, wasn't it? Why?"

Helga didn't bother to quibble or deny. "Because Dublin needs to survive, and this was the best way I saw to ensure it."

"Did your husband know?"

There was a pause. "He signed the treaty, of course, but he learned of the events of that night only afterwards. He knew it was best to leave these things to me."

"But Deirdre—"

Helga's answer was immediate. "I did what I had to."

The justification made Cait instantly furious, but she felt paralyzed as to what to do with her anger. With Godfrid and Conall with the army, she had nobody to summon to help her, and what guard would believe that it had been Helga in that warehouse all along?

Then Helga looked down at her hands, showing her first indication of regret. "It wasn't by my hand, but it might as well have been. I gave the order."

"The other day, you implied that Sturla was responsible."

Helga barked a laugh. "The idea of his guilt appealed to your biases and was what you expected. It seemed prudent to keep you looking in that direction."

Her arrogance was both disconcerting and infuriating. "And Rikard? What of him?"

Helga shook her head. "If you think I would have ordered his death too, had I found him, you would be right. But I did not. I do not know how or why he died."

Cait wanted to rail at the queen, but Helga's attention had been drawn by something on the horizon. Cait looked too, and her heart caught in her throat as one or two at a time, and then by the dozen, men began streaming down the western road towards the city. Cait gripped the top of the palisade wall so tightly she gave herself a splinter.

When the man in the lead reached the gate, the guard at first refused to let him in, under orders to keep the gate closed and terrified that the Irish were following hard on the soldiers' heels. Cait glanced around for Helga, but the queen had disappeared.

So it was left to Cait to lean over the rampart to look at the desperate soldier. "What is happening?"

He looked up at her. "The Irish had already crossed the Liffey when we arrived! It is a rout!"

"What of the king?"

"He fell from his horse. That is all I know."

"Let them in!" She almost picked up her skirts then and there and ran away from the tower and the gate, as it seemed Helga had done.

But she didn't.

In her previous life, meaning earlier that morning, she might have given in to her fears, but she had spent the last five hours in the tower, and the waiting had slowly sanded off her sharper edges. She needed to know that Conall and Godfrid were alive. She would wait in the tower until she saw them coming, either of their own volition or on a bier.

30

Day Four

Godfrid

Somewhere along the way Godfrid had lost his helmet. He couldn't remember when or where he'd thrown it off, only that it had been preventing him from seeing what was going on around him. He'd lost his horse too and had picked up another, Irish or Danish he didn't know. His sword dripped blood, and he had only faint memory of the series of events that had carried him from one side of the battlefield to the other.

Godfrid's new horse shifted restlessly. Neither Danes nor Irishmen fought on horseback as a rule because their horses weren't built for charging. Nor did they have enough cavalrymen to have a real effect on the outcome of a battle. But Godfrid had seen enough of the world to have learned how Normans fought and to know also that he and the men who'd conquered England shared ancestry. He could see why staying on his horse was a good idea.

The ground they'd ultimately chosen had been bad. They'd known it from the start, even as they'd been forced to set up the shield wall with the river anchoring the right and blocked to the left by rising ground and a thick wood.

He had seen Ottar go down near the first wave of fighting and Sturla with him. Posted as Godfrid was with the other horsemen to protect the Danish left flank, he hadn't been able to tell how it had happened. The front ranks were still holding their own, but the moment Ottar's red feather disappeared, a shiver had gone through the Danish force. They might be good Christians these days, but a longing for Valhalla was in their bones, and Godfrid felt that Ottar was making his way there even now.

Brodar had started out as a leader of the right flank, anchored at the river so the Bregan army couldn't get past them to attack Dublin directly. With Ottar's fall, however, Brodar had left his captain in command and taken charge of the entire Danish force. It was his right, and it was really the only reason the Danes hadn't yet conceded defeat.

Unfortunately, once Ottar fell, a good two hundred soldiers in the rear of the force had broken off and fled back to Dublin. Half of him thought good riddance, while the other half wished he'd known in advance which men were most likely to flee and put them in the front of the lines from the start. But warriors and the foolish were chosen for the shield wall, his brother now among them. Brodar's white plume bobbed in the midst of the most seasoned soldiers.

For the first time, Godfrid cursed the loss of his helmet, because it would have allowed his own men to see him better. He peered over the heads of the men fighting nearby. But then, as the battle ebbed and flowed around him, he found himself on the edge of the fray.

Then Conall bobbed up beside him, still wearing his hat. His friend had declared himself too old for the shield wall.

Godfrid glanced at him. "You Irish know how to fight, I'll give you that."

"We can think too. I have an idea."

"I'm listening."

"We need to retreat to that high ground." Conall pointed to a barely discernible ridge two hundred yards to the west. The land around Dublin was for the most part flat, but here and there a ridge like the one Conall indicated or a hill poked up a hundred feet at most above the rest of the landscape. "We need to reform the line there and hold our ground until Leinster comes."

"If it comes." Godfrid spoke absently, without accusation, his eyes on the ridge. Although Conall had sent riders to King Diarmait, for the king to commit to open war against Prince Donnell, the heir to the high king, or, even if he chose to march, that he could get men here in time, had always been an open question.

But the first rule of warfare was always to seek higher ground, and the only tradition Godfrid cared about was the one that said Danes didn't ever lose. If they took the ridge, and his countrymen couldn't hold the wall, his cavalrymen could charge down the slope as a last hurrah before death took them.

Godfrid eyed the field before him. "How many of the men from Brega will speak Danish? If I give my men an order, will any Irish understand?"

"Unlikely," Conall said. "Danish is an impossible language."

"Only if your first language is Gaelic." Godfrid was jesting, not out of a macabre certainty of defeat, but with rising hope.

After a short conference with the closest of his men, who understood as quickly as Godfrid the necessity of Conall's plan, Godfrid urged his horse back into the main body of the army, which, despite the valor of Brodar and his men, had been retreating step by step back towards Dublin. The Irish would believe the rout was on because they wanted to—and all evidence told them it was inevitable.

Before he could shout his commands, Holm appeared in front of him, his sword drawn and his hairline bloody. His teeth were clenched, and he spoke around them. "What are you doing?"

"Turning the battle in our favor."

"You haven't the authority!"

"King Ottar is dead, Holm. You know that." Godfrid didn't have time for this, but the anger and pain in Holm's demeanor demanded a response.

"You lied! You've been lying all this time." He threw out a hand to Conall, who was some ways behind Godfrid. "You've been working with Leinster since the beginning? Against the king?"

As in the church, for a moment all sound around Godfrid was muffled, and the world slowed. "Yes." It was as if a bucket of cold water had been dumped over Godfrid's head. The relief at being able to speak the truth, at long last, was near-to-dizzying.

Holm gaped at him and appeared himself near to sputtering.

Godfrid shook off his own wonder and fixed his gaze on Dublin's sheriff. "After today, my brother will be king, and you will have to decide where your allegiance lies, with the past or with the future."

Holm spat out his next words. "As always, I am loyal to Dublin."

"Then we shouldn't have a problem, should we?"

Holm still wanted to glare, but then he met Godfrid's eyes, and he eased back in his saddle. "I guess we shouldn't."

Godfrid gave Holm a comradely nod, and then, as Ottar had done before the battle, he stood in his stirrups. In this instance, with no herald of his own, he swung his sword above his head to gain the attention of anyone within hailing distance and then pointed with it. "We will retreat to that ridge and reform the line!"

It took a moment for his words to penetrate above the shouting and grunting of the men on the ground. Then Holm cupped his hands around his mouth and reiterated the order. Those at the back were the first to understand, and they started calling to their fellows towards the front. Godfrid again pointed west with his sword, hoping that the gesture would confirm the idea to the Irish on the other side of the shield wall that their opponents were in full retreat—and then he spoke in a Danish simple enough for some of them to understand. "Run! Run! Run now!"

The initial retreat was orderly, but as the pressure on the front lines by those in the rear of the battle was relieved, the retreat got going in earnest. The shield wall collapsed as the men in the front line—Brodar included—threw down their shields and ran.

Even to Godfrid's eyes, it looked as if the Danish forces were routed, and Godfrid prayed that, once his men reached the ridge, they would actually stop and not run headlong all the way back to Dublin. Men, once set in motion, could be very difficult to stop.

Fortunately, the cavalry had taken the lead, easily outpacing the men running on the ground. The intent was that they wouldn't stop until they were over the ridge. Once they were below the curve of the hill, they would turn and demarcate the ultimate line of defense.

His chest nearly bursting with fear and anticipation, Godfrid scooped up a running boy, who couldn't have been older than sixteen and who'd dropped both his shield and his axe.

A moment later, the boy, who'd managed to seat himself behind Godfrid, pointed ahead. "Look there!"

Godfrid had been so focused on the men running around him that he hadn't looked up to the ridge again. Now he saw dozens of banners—Irish not Danish—waving over the heads of hundreds of men lining the ridge before them.

It took a moment for the symbols to register, by which time Conall was whooping and caterwauling, showing more emotion than Godfrid had ever seen from him. "Diarmait has come! Diarmait has come!" He actually threw his hat into the air.

In an instant, the whole tenor of the battlefield changed. What had been triumphant roars from the men of Brega, who'd started gleefully forward at the collapse of the Danish shield wall, turned into shouted commands as the leaders attempted to curtail the headlong rush of their men after the falsely retreating Danes. Those Danes at the back, some of whom had pelted through their fellows at a startlingly impossible pace, almost keeping up with Godfrid's riders, turned to look. And jeer.

It was an old trick, skillfully played. A Norman might protest that the deception had been dishonorable, but these were Danes, and they knew that the only thing that mattered was winning.

In short order, the Danish line reformed along the ridge amidst the fresh men of Leinster. Except for a few scattered fools who'd led their fellows too far east, the Bregan line had halted and was being held back a hundred yards away by their commanders. The Bregans weren't blind. They could see that the odds might no longer be in their favor.

The Bible said, "Put up again thy sword into its place: for all that take the sword shall perish with the sword." The Irish had been Christians longer than the Danes, but that didn't stop them from turning the proverb on its head, believing that a man should never unsheathe his sword unless he intended to use it. The men of Leinster had unsheathed their swords and axes, and if they'd been horses, they would have been champing at the bit, ready to fight even if their very appearance may have already won the battle.

Conall was right that King Diarmait himself had come, and by the time Godfrid trotted up to the ridge, the king was in deep consultation with Brodar, with Conall translating as needed.

All of a sudden, Godfrid was exhausted to the bone, to the point that he hardly cared to join the conversation. He let the boy he'd rescued slide to the ground, dismounted himself, and tossed his reins to Holm's man Alf, who appeared out of nowhere, missing his helmet and with a slash to his cheek, but otherwise unharmed.

Diarmait's captains were forming the new shield wall, and Godfrid found himself moved back—politely for the most part— away from the front line, and fetched up beside Holm again.

The sheriff's eyes were alight, and he slapped his thigh. "It is done, my lord. Look! Our enemy retreats."

Sure enough, the men of Brega were backing away from the field. Their few cavalry held a line at the closest edge, prepared to engage again if the men from Leinster offered battle, but meanwhile allowing their foot soldiers to escape in an orderly fashion, ultimately to recross the Liffey and return to Brega.

The army from Leinster continued to jeer and call, but no amount of ridicule was sufficient to entice their opponents to turn and engage. In the end, the Bregans had achieved nothing of what they came for. Prince Donnell would have to retreat to Connaught with his tail between his legs, his only accomplishment the death of Ottar, who'd been his ally and co-conspirator.

Dublin was saved for Danes, and it remained to be seen if anything was left of King Diarmait's alliance with High King O'Connor, or if it had also been left for dead on the field.

31

Day Four

Caitriona

The great hall, in what had been Ottar's palace, had been given over to King Diarmait and his household troops. Helga had fled with her young son—to where Cait didn't know. The Isle of Man was her best guess. In victory, Brodar had been magnanimous and had chosen to let her go. With Ottar dead, she had no power, and he viewed her loss of the throne as suitable payment for her crimes. Besides, nobody wanted to see the former Queen of Dublin hanged for ordering the death of a slave.

"How well do you know this Brodar, Conall?" King Diarmait ranged back in his chair, replete with good wine and good food from Ottar's extensive stores. He'd asked that the hall be cleared of everyone but Cait and Conall. Brodar and Godfrid weren't present anyway, since they were celebrating the victory with their men at their camp outside the city walls, awaiting tomorrow's ceremony, which would include a grand procession into the city and Brodar's crowning on the top of the *thingmote*.

"Not as well as I know his brother, Godfrid."

"Whom you trust," Diarmait gestured with his goblet, "despite all evidence to the contrary."

Conall grinned. "Yes."

Diarmait canted his head. "No equivocation or caveat? Nothing to add?"

"No."

The king smoothed his beard with his thumb and forefinger as he studied Conall. Even though they weren't far off in age, Diarmait had always been the heir, the son of the previous king, while Conall had been his nephew, a sister's son, destined for a lower level of greatness. It had been a truth between them, but not a barrier. There might have been more tension had Conall been the elder. Any free man had a right to challenge for the throne, and Conall would have been a credible rival for it.

Then Diarmait transferred his gaze to Cait. "What about you?"

Cait swallowed. "What about me?" She was in attendance because Conall had brought her, and they were all family, but she hadn't expected her opinion to be asked, any more than it had been in Ottar's hall.

Diarmait sighed. "For all that I was skeptical of your foray into the heart of Dublin, I am not displeased with the result."

Cait laughed. "Ottar achieved a hero's death, and Brodar is on the throne, beholden to you for his position. All at very little cost to yourself."

Diarmait beamed at Cait but then returned his gaze to Conall. "It was a fine day when my father gave permission for your mother to remarry, for she produced a daughter who is both intelligent and beautiful."

Cait snorted, though only under her breath. Diarmait was behaving as if she was a prized heifer at market. The thought had her eyes narrowing. "Uncle Diarmait—"

The king clapped his hands together. "Don't be difficult, my dear. As went your mother, so will you go. We must make peace out of this moment."

Conall's eyes skated to Cait and then back to the king. "My lord, Cait is a widow, with the right to choose her next husband."

Diarmait's cheerful mood vanished in an instant, and he leaned forward in his seat, stabbing a finger first at Conall and then at Cait. "I shouldn't have to remind you that I am not speaking as your uncle but as your liege lord. Donnell O'Connor almost succeeded today! I cannot have Connaught thinking it can threaten Leinster. They have looked covetously at Dublin for years, and they will not have it!" He surged to his feet and began to pace.

His outburst caused Cait to shrink away from him. Diarmait had doted on her for the whole of her life, treating her with a benign affection and amusement. This was the first time his legendary temper had ever been directed at her, and she was unprepared for it.

She wet her lips. "I don't want to go against your wishes, Uncle, but please don't make me marry Prince Donnell."

Diarmait swung around, a look of astonishment on his face. "Is that what you think I want?" He began to laugh, so much so that he collapsed back into his seat. After a moment he seemed to recover, wiping the tears at the corners of his eyes. "I know I entertained the idea of giving you to Connaught, but after the events of today, it is impossible, even were Donnell to become High King." He shook his head, his shoulders still vibrating with laughter.

"Then who?" Conall glanced at Cait.

Her uncle shot her another grin, and with a gasp, genuine hope began rising in Cait's chest. "You don't mean—"

"Of course that's whom I mean. What do you say to an alliance with Prince Godfrid?"

Conall grinned openly, and he put an arm around her shoulders. "Well?"

Cait laughed, with relief and joy. "We say *yes!*"

The End

Historical Background

Before I learned of the Danish role in the assassination of Anarawd, King of Deheubarth, I had no idea that the Danes had ever conquered parts of Ireland.

The Danes, as a group, were part of a vast migration of men of the North to other regions of the world, initially for plunder and eventually for settlement. Coming from regions that now make up Norway, Sweden, Finland, and Denmark, these men went *a Viking*, and created widespread settlements: to the south, in Normandy and Sicily; to the east into Russia; and to the west in England, Ireland, Iceland, Greenland, and the coast of Newfoundland.

The Dublin Danes were part of that tradition, and Ottar and Brodar were real people as described in *The Viking Prince*, both ruling Dublin in the mid-twelfth century. Brodar and Godfrid were part of an extensive lineage of rulership of Dublin called the Mac Torcalls, whose hegemony was briefly usurped by Ottar, but then reestablished. Scholarship is confused about some of the specifics, but it is clear that members of their clan ruled Dublin until the arrival of the Normans under the leadership of Richard de Clare (Strongbow) and ultimately King Henry, who defeated the Danes and expelled them from Dublin for good in 1171 AD.

The ruling family of Gwynedd, as led for most of the twelfth century by Owain Gwynedd, had both Danish and Irish ancestry. Through Gruffydd ap Cynan, Owain's father, Prince Hywel is descended from both Sitric Silkbeard, King of Dublin; and Brian Boru, High King of Ireland.

About the Author

With two historian parents, Sarah couldn't help but develop an interest in the past. She went on to get more than enough education herself (in anthropology) and began writing fiction when the stories in her head overflowed and demanded she let them out. While her ancestry is Welsh, she only visited Wales for the first time while in college. She has been in love with the country, language, and people ever since. She even convinced her husband to give all four of their children Welsh names.

She makes her home in Oregon.

www.sarahwoodbury.com

Made in United States
North Haven, CT
03 August 2022